HIDDEN DESIRE

Book Six of The Hidden Saga

Amy Patrick

Oxford South Press/Sept 2016
Cover design by Cover Your Dreams
Formatting by Polgarus Studio

For my Hidden Honeys—the incredible readers who love my books and give me so much encouragement every day! You keep me going, page after page.

CONTENTS

Chapter One Little Red Riding Hood 1

Chapter Two Nowheresville 18

Chapter Three Sunset.. 30

Chapter Four Overnight Accommodations................... 46

Chapter Five Don't Mention It 58

Chapter Six Pop In... 62

Chapter Seven Stakeout... 73

Chapter Eight Adult Experiences................................. 88

Chapter Nine Look Inside... 104

Chapter Ten Morning Person 112

Chapter Eleven Angel of Death 118

Chapter Twelve Bucket List 129

Chapter Thirteen Neighbors 138

Chapter Fourteen Gala... 145

Chapter Fifteen Tribute and Tears 158

Chapter Sixteen Dance With Me 164

Chapter Seventeen Ugly Truth.................................... 180

Chapter Eighteen Generous Benefactor 187

Chapter Nineteen Assignment..................................... 202

Chapter Twenty Perfect Weapon 210

Chapter Twenty-one Game Plan 218

Chapter Twenty-two Shadow...................................... 228

Chapter Twenty-three Poetic Justice 244

Chapter Twenty-four Dual Identity 251

Chapter Twenty-five Reunion 257

Chapter Twenty-six Not Enough................................. 266
Chapter Twenty-seven Something to Live For 273
Chapter Twenty-eight His Past.................................... 283
Chapter Twenty-nine Wherever You Go 290
Epilogue 298

AFTERWORD.. 305
ABOUT THE AUTHOR... 307
ACKNOWLEDGMENTS.. 309

Chapter One
Little Red Riding Hood

What a hellhole.

This neighborhood is my least favorite district of L.A., and believe me, for a city with a reputation for beaches and sunshine and glittering movie premiers, it has *plenty* of areas you wouldn't want to be caught dead in. Actually—if you *were* caught in one of them and didn't belong there, you'd likely end up dead.

I walk past a seedy apartment building, a loud TV blaring from one of its screenless windows guarded by security bars. Behind a chain-link fence across the street a couple of pit bulls bark and snarl at me as if they'd love to have me for an afternoon snack and leave no leftovers.

I have no fears for my own security. For one thing, I don't give a shit. For another, they want *me* here. I bring the only thing the lowlifes in this part of town still care about. Whatever good people are left here are no doubt

1

cowering inside, hoping the "Scourge" will pass them by.

At least the streets don't reek as much as they used to— fewer drunks puking up their paychecks into the gutters. S has nearly taken the place of booze, cocaine, heroin, and every other recreational drug in this city—it's cheaper than any of them and far more addictive.

I arrive at the pre-determined street corner and check my phone—I'm early. Great. I lean against the side of an auto repair shop that's closed for the day and check my messages, scrolling through the list of texts, opening none of them. I already know what they want, and it's a guarantee *all* of them want something from me. Everyone does.

Something moves near my feet, startling me and making me jump to the side. At first I think it's a rat, then I realize it's a gray cat—a small one—a kitten actually. It's filthy and so bony it hardly resembles a domestic animal at all.

When it realizes I've noticed it, the scrawny thing mewls at me.

"Go away," I bark at it, and the pitiful thing skitters back, then it takes a few cautious steps toward my shoes again.

I lift one foot and kick the air. "Get! I've got nothing for you. Go find a mouse or something." It makes another noise, louder this time. "Listen here—you want some advice? Don't count on anyone to give you anything in this life—the sooner you learn that one, the better."

The kitten is apparently smarter than most human beings—it runs away from me. I snort a laugh at my own expense. Wouldn't Ava be so proud?

I can't stop myself from thinking of our last conversation four months ago. *You'll never be happy until you let your guard down and open your heart and let someone see the real you,* she said. What a laugh. The real me is right here, passing on cynical life lessons to a flea bitten stray. And I'll *never* be happy. That possibility died the minute she told me she was in love with that human farm boy.

As far as my heart—I'm not sure I even have one. I've never felt the kind of emotion she seems to have for that silly dimpled bloke, the kind of attachment the Light King Lad and his bride seem to have for each other. And I don't want to. They're all destined for disappointment—they're just too dumb to know it.

The afternoon sun is in my eyes, so I back into a doorway for shade. I'd really rather not think of Ava at all. With that glamour of hers, the least she could have done was erase her bothersome self from my memory—would have been the kind thing to do. But then "kindness" has never been my fate. Indifference and lack of interference is about the best I can hope for.

Down the street, the kitten shows itself again, making a beeline for its next panhandling target—the critter is persistent, I'll give it that. Seeing its determination, I develop a grudging sense of admiration for the scrappy little beggar. Clearly it's fending for itself on these mean streets—its mum was probably killed by a car, or maybe she abandoned it. I know the feeling.

Good luck, Dogbait.

The kitten cautiously approaches a girl on the sidewalk.

She's walking my way, dragging the fingertips of one hand along the side of the building next to her.

She's not the usual sort I see in this neighborhood. Quite the opposite actually. She's wearing a red sundress—and not one of those short, clingy kinds the girls wear to the clubs or for attracting *customers*. It's more of the go-on-a-picnic-to-the-park kind of dress. I can almost see her flying a kite in it or picking wildflowers or some nonsense like that.

She's got long, straight, sandy-brown hair—very clean looking—with a red headband holding it back from her face like freakin' Alice in Wonderland or something. She looks... proper. No, that's the wrong word. Innocent—that's it—almost like a primary schooler, but she's at least fifteen. Anyway, she stands out. Not a good thing around here.

I shrug. *It's your funeral, babe.*

I look down at my phone, but within a minute I find myself glancing up again. The girl has stopped walking. She's just standing there, turning in a slow circle with her head lifted. What the hell is she doing? And then it hits me. She's probably on S. That's what she's doing here—trying to score another hit. She's not the first dreamer from a small town to get off the bus in this city and get hooked on S right away.

The kitten reaches her and does a circle eight around her ankles. Immediately she stoops and picks it up, hugging it to her chest and smiling. I can't hear her, but she's obviously talking to the nasty little beast in her arms.

I shake my head and go back to my phone. *Stupid girl.* She and that mangy cat deserve one another. They can waste away together. She certainly won't be spending her money on cat food if she's hooked on S. There are suburban moms who don't feed their own children because they've blown the grocery money on the drug.

I blow out an aggravated breath. Five minutes until our meeting, and the guy hasn't shown yet. He'd better be here if he knows what's good for him. I'm not exactly thrilled about making a trip to this dump for no reason—especially since my "duties" usually take me to much more posh places, places where the drug addicts are much cleaner and more attractive. But I'm the least of this low level dealer's worries. My annoyance is nothing compared to Audun's wrath. He doesn't tolerate mistakes in his operation.

"Hey! Check this out."

I lift my head to see the owner of the very loud, very amused voice. It belongs to a heavyset, heavily tattooed man wearing a dirty white tank shirt and long, wide-legged shorts that expose all but the very bottom of his underwear. He's accompanied by two similarly dressed *gentlemen.* Unlike the foolish girl in the red dress, they definitely fit this neighborhood.

The three men are laughing, striding down the center of the street directly toward her. "Little Red Riding Hood came to bring us some goodies, I think," one of them says in a lewd tone.

The third one joins in. "Wonder what she's got in *that* basket?" The laughter grows louder and more raucous.

My pulse kicks up a notch as I watch them pass my location in the doorway and approach the girl. She doesn't seem to notice, still too wrapped up in that pitiful cat or her S high, or maybe both.

A text tone draws my attention back to my phone. It's from my father. Great.

-Meeting location has changed. New location two blocks south. A bar called Moco's. Your contact is there now.

Naturally. The one day I'm early for a delivery and my contact changes locations on me. I push forward out of the doorway and start down the street to where my car is parked. I'm ready to get this thing over with and get out of here before the locals decide to start helping themselves to some high end automotive parts. I've got more deliveries to make and in far more pleasant locales than this one.

"Hey, hey little girl. You lost or something?"

"Grandma's house is that way. Better watch out for the wolf."

Don't look. It doesn't matter. It's not your concern. Humans preying on other humans—happens all day every day all over the globe.

I will my eyes forward but they veer off to the left without my consent. The street thugs have reached Alice, as I've dubbed her. She's standing with her back to the wall now, the stupid cat cradled in her arms. The guys move in close to her, forming a human triangle around her. One of them tugs at her dress, and she spins to face him. She doesn't look particularly afraid, but she's not looking directly at any of them.

And you shouldn't be either, moron. You've got a job to do. Keep walking.

I stop walking.

Blowing out a long breath of resignation, I turn toward the scene on the sidewalk. As if possessed by a mind of their own, my feet move in that direction. My hands clench at my sides, tightening by increments the closer I get.

I'm not sure exactly what I plan to do when I get there. A couple of the guys are shorter than me, so I'd have the reach on them in a fistfight, but all three are considerably heavier. And in this neighborhood, probably armed. And did I mention there are *three* of them?

In spite of these very valid reasons to walk the other way, I don't. Instead, when I reach the sidewalk, I step right up to the group and through the stinking, tattooed human chain surrounding the girl.

She's older than I thought—maybe about eighteen. Prettier, too. Now that I get a good look at her, I can tell she's not high. She is frightened though. She's staring right at the sweat stain on the t-shirt of one of the guys, not making eye contact with any of them or with me. Her chest rises and falls with quick, shallow breaths. She's probably catatonic with fear by this point.

Reaching for the ugly gray kitten, I say, "There you are, naughty kitty. Thank you, love, for finding her. I've been looking for Cupcake everywhere."

"Who the hell are you?" the tallest of the guys demands.

"Well now I've just said that, haven't I? I'm the owner of Cupcake here."

"That cat's a *dude*, man. And he's running wild around here every day, begging for scraps."

"Even more reason I'm thrilled to have him back. Now I must be going. And I'll need the young lady to come with me. You see I filed a police report on my missing cat, and she'll need to come in and give a statement that she returned him to me and did not, in fact, steal Cupcake. Someone might have witnessed her holding him and reported her already."

One of the shorter guys laughs. "That's bullshit man. The cops around here don't care about no missing cats."

"Better safe than sorry," I say and slide an arm around the girl's back, steering her toward the street. She's trembling and so is the kitten. "We're going to my car," I mutter to the girl. "Just come along and I'll drop you somewhere safe."

Her feet stop moving. "I don't want to leave."

What? How stupid is this girl? Or are people really *that* naïve where she's from? "Don't argue," I urge under my breath. "Believe me—you *want* to leave—unless you particularly relish the prospect of gang rape and human trafficking."

"Oh," she says and starts moving again.

"Hey—English dude."

Great. "Keep walking toward the Ferrari," I say to the girl, tucking the cat under her arm again. I turn to face the delayed reaction of the neighborhood gang, who've finally realized I'm whisking their new toy away. "Yes?"

"We didn't say she could leave. We were just getting to know Little Red there."

"Yes well, I believe the young lady may be lost, and the last thing guys with your records need is a lost tourist disappearing on your turf—especially one who looks like this one. Now *there's* something the cops *will* care about. All of you ready to have your houses and cars thoroughly searched?"

The three men exchange glances. The answer visible on all of their faces is a definitive "No." My guess about their prison records was apparently spot on. Still, the leader of the group doesn't like that I've defied him in front of his underlings.

He sticks his barrel chest out and curls his lips into a nasty smile. "Wonder if they'd care about a smart-mouth English guy with his ass beat in?"

I release a weary breath. "I'm from Australia, actually, and this conversation is getting tedious." Eager to get the girl out of there and get to my meeting, I put a heavy dose of Sway into my next words. "Now you're gonna turn around, walk back over to your men, and order them to follow you. Then the three of you will walk to the farthest edge of your 'territory' and pick a fight with someone closer to your own size—preferably a member of a rival gang. This city could use a few less hoodlums. Have a nice day, *gentlemen.*"

The guy stares at me a second, then turns and shows me his back, gesturing to his men. "Come on. We outta here," he says.

Turning back toward the girl, I pick up my pace to catch up with her. Though I instructed her to keep walking, she's not far from where I left her. I grab her upper arm and move quickly, pulling her along by my side.

"Let's go before any of the Three Amigos' friends get a look at you and start coming out of the woodwork. The sun will be setting soon—and you think this place is bad during the daytime, you do *not* want to see it at night."

She nods and silently stumbles along beside me, clutching the kitten, clearly still in shock from her near miss. We reach my car, I pop the door locks, and open hers. She puts a hand on the door and lowers herself inside. I close the door and go around to the driver's side, sliding in and starting the car, not even waiting for the engine to warm before putting it in gear and driving straight past Moco's and out of the neighborhood. South L.A. can live without its S fix for one night.

When we make it to the 110 onramp and merge into traffic I finally breathe normally. And then I let her have it.

"*What* were you thinking going there? Are you stupid? Are you *blind*? Anyone can see that's no place for someone like you."

Her little chin juts out as she stares straight ahead through the windshield, holding the kitten to her chest where it's attempting to burrow into her. "I paid a lot of money for a taxi ride to take me there."

My jaw drops. Maybe I was wrong. Maybe she *was* there searching for a fix after all. But why go there? She could score S in almost any nightclub in the city. I glance over at her curled up in my passenger seat. She doesn't look like the typical S addict. Her skin is smooth and clear, her hair shines. She has all her teeth—white and strong. Her hands aren't shaking and her eyes, though still a bit dazed looking, aren't bloodshot or rimmed with dark shadows. In fact, they're a beautiful clear brown with spokes of greenish-gold.

She's not a junkie. Maybe she really *is* that naïve. "As you may have noticed from your encounter with the hood welcoming committee back there, that was *not* a good neighborhood. And when you saw those guys coming... you should have run."

The chin tilts higher. "If it's such a bad neighborhood, what were you doing there? Maybe *you're* a bad guy. Maybe I should have run from *you*."

Her sassy attitude is a surprise. I chuckle. "Without a doubt. I am a very bad guy indeed. But I'm also the guy who got your silly little arse out of danger, so I believe a thank you is in order."

"Thank you," she says. And that's all she says.

"Well, now that we've established your *undying* gratitude for my *saving your life*," I drawl, "tell me where you live—I'll take you home."

"You don't have to do that—you can drop me off anywhere. I'll catch a bus."

"Don't be daft. Look—I was sort of joking about that being a bad guy thing. Tell me where your apartment is. I promise not to stalk you. I won't even try to walk you to the door—I'll just slow down and you can jump out," I joke.

There's a long pause before she answers. "I don't have an apartment."

"Your hotel then, friend's house—whatever."

"I don't have one of those either. I was planning to look for a place near the clinic. That's why I went to South Los Angeles."

"Excuse me?"

I pull the car off at the next exit simply so I can get a look at her face and see if she's joking. Also, my hands have begun to shake. After steering the car into a convenience store lot and putting it in park, I turn in my seat to face her. The expression she wears is entirely serious. She's not kidding. Which means she's insane.

"You can't mean the S clinic. The one next door to the *drug den*. Why in God's name would you look for an apartment *there*? You're not using are you?"

"No." She laughs. "No, I'm going to work there—as a volunteer. I spoke to the director on the phone before coming out to Los Angeles. I don't drive, so I need a place that's nearby. I can't afford to keep taking taxis."

I don't know why, but this girl's insistence on putting her life at risk in that drug-infested neighborhood is driving me nuts. She's clearly unfamiliar with the area. What is she *doing* out here all alone? Doesn't anyone realize she's far too naïve to even be in the *good* parts of this city? Where are her parents? Where are her friends?

My fingertips dig into the back of her seat. "Look at me please."

At first she doesn't move, but then she slowly turns her face toward me.

"What is your name?" I ask.

"Laney."

"Laney what?"

She opens her mouth but hesitates. Finally she says, "Just Laney. What's yours?"

"Culley Rune. And where are you from, Just Laney?" *Because I'm going to make it my personal mission to send you back there—today if possible.*

She must be reading my mind because she gives me a vague answer. "The Midwest."

"Where exactly?"

"You ask a lot of questions."

"I'm a curious guy." I wait for a more specific answer until it's clear she's not going to give one. "Okay fine. I'm taking you to a hotel in a *safe* area for tonight. Tomorrow, you're going to get on a bus or a plane or a train or however the hell you got out here from *wherever* the hell you're from, and you're going back there where you belong before you get yourself hurt or worse."

I expect anger, defiance, or maybe resignation if I'm lucky. But there's none of that in her eyes. She gazes at me with the strangest expression.

Ah, I know what this is. I'm used to it by now. While some humans respond to my appearance with immediate lust or desire in their eyes, others are thrown off balance by all the sensory input. It's an effect of my glamour.

But then... this one is different somehow. I can't quite put my finger on it.

"No thank you," she says sweetly. "All the hotels out here are pretty expensive. You know what? Just drop me off at one of the beaches, and I'll sleep there tonight. I like the feel of the sand, and with the sound of the ocean it'll be like falling asleep to my sound machine in my room back home."

"That—is ridiculous." I don't understand why, but I can feel my blood pressure rising. The temperature inside the car has increased by at least fifteen degrees in the last minute. I lower the windows, letting in some air and the sounds of traffic from the nearby street.

"You can't sleep on the beach." I jam my hand into my back pocket and draw out my wallet, ripping a couple of hundreds from it and jabbing them at her. "I'll *pay* for the hotel." Delving back in again, I pull out more bills. "In fact, here—have a plane ticket on me."

Her fingers extend toward mine, passing over the money, seeking and finding my skin. She squeezes my hand briefly then lets it go.

"Thank you. Really. But I'm fine. I don't need your money or your pity. I can take care of myself." She pauses and smiles. "You know, I believe I will call a cab after all. You've been so kind, and I don't want to trouble you any further."

I'm being dismissed. She doesn't want my help. She doesn't want my money. Hell, she doesn't even want a ride from me. Who *is* this girl?

The sound of my phone's ringer startles me, making me realize I've been staring at her face. That's a first—I'm usually the recipient of human stares, not the other way around. I pick up my phone and check the screen. It's my father. *Damn it.*

"I have to answer this. Hold on." I hold up a finger to her to signal that our conversation is not over yet.

Ignoring the gesture, Laney puts one hand on the door handle, preparing to get out of the car. She turns back to me. "Thank you for what you did today." Then she leans close for a conspiratorial whisper. "You might not think you're one of the good guys, Culley Rune—but you're wrong."

Then she brushes my cheek with a soft kiss and opens the door, stepping out onto the sidewalk and taking the kitten with her. Blinking against a feeling of sudden disorientation, I answer the phone.

"Yes, Father?" My eyes follow Laney to the end of the block where she stops at the corner. I lift my hand and scratch the place her lips touched my face, attempting to erase the lingering sensation they left behind. It's a strange tingling, an annoying warm tickle like nothing I've ever felt before.

"You *missed* your drop." Audun's every word is imbued with a menace that would no doubt make the rest of his underlings tremble. Luckily, I've been inoculated with small doses my entire life, so it has a lesser effect on me.

"Yes Father."

"Well? What happened? Our associate waited as long as he was comfortable, and then he got nervous and left. That is *unacceptable*. What is your explanation?"

Through the windshield I watch Laney step up to the crossing sign pole and slide her hand down its side until she reaches the signal button, apparently intending to cross the street. To where? I thought she was calling a cab. Where is she going? Does she even know where she is?

"Culley?"

"I… got busy. I apologize. It won't happen again."

He snorts. "I should hope not. The last thing you need is *another* failure."

I roll my eyes at his reference to Ava and our bonding-that-never-happened. Naturally I can't let on that I lied about it without his realizing it. It's the one card I have in my pocket with him. It's better for me if he doesn't figure out I'm immune to his lie detecting glamour. So I told him Ava had used her glamour on me to make me *believe* we had bonded, when we actually had not. And then she had disappeared into thin air after our engagement ring commercial shoot.

He was infuriated by my "weakness" of course and ordered me to find her. I told him she must have removed most of my memories of her as well because I had no idea where to even begin looking.

"I'll make the delivery first thing tomorrow," I promise him.

The walk signal starts flashing in the pedestrian walkway sign, accompanied by a piercing beep for the visually impaired. Laney begins to step out into the crosswalk.

"Listen, I need to go. I'll speak with you tomorrow."

I hang up, already opening my car door and leaping out. Because I've figured out why Laney wasn't properly afraid of that godforsaken neighborhood, and why she never looked those thugs in the eye, and why when she looked at me, she wasn't glamoured like everyone else.

She couldn't see me.

She couldn't see any of it.

Laney is blind.

Chapter Two
Nowheresville

The crosswalk signal is flashing a warning and counting down three... two... one... by the time I reach it.

Darting across, I push through the other pedestrians to catch up with Laney. Before I reach her, she lifts her foot to step up on the lip of the curb, and it comes down wrong on the uneven surface, tripping her. As she falls forward, her legs splay behind her and into the street. The cat springs from her arms and lands—on its feet of course—on the sidewalk.

The next part happens in slow motion, as if I'm watching a movie. I take in the changing of the traffic light from red to green. The turning and gawking by the other street-crossers. The asshole driver behind the wheel of a bright yellow and black Lamborghini who's got his eyes on his phone instead of the road and his foot revving the massive engine impatiently.

And I know exactly how this is going to play out. He'll glance up, catch the green light from one corner of his distracted gaze, and hit the gas without ever seeing the girl who's fallen into his path.

Heart plummeting, I leap to close the distance between me and Laney, scooping one arm under her waist as she gets to her hands and knees, and haul her to the sidewalk, landing in a painful skid that removes nearly all the skin from one of my elbows.

The roar of the Lamborghini's engine drowns all other sound for several moments as it spins its tires and lunges into the intersection like a pouncing predator. I watch its yellow bumper and red taillights, fighting for breath and trying to calm my racing pulse.

"What... what happened?" Laney sounds as dazed as she looks.

"Oh my God—that guy almost ran her down! Anybody get that license plate?" someone calls.

I help her to sit up, and a woman in a vintage-style dress and pumps with cherry red-dyed hair rushes over, squatting down and brushing Laney's disheveled hair back from her face. "Are you okay honey? Do you need an ambulance?"

"No. I'm... fine. I'm not hurt," she answers, now turning her head as if looking around for clues as to what's just transpired. Or maybe she's searching for the cat. It's darted to the base of the light pole, away from the foot traffic.

The concerned woman nods and takes Laney at her word, moving away along with the rest of the busy

Angelenos. I get to my feet and slide my grip under Laney's arms, pulling her to a standing position then move my hands down to her waist to keep her steady.

The guy who was looking for the license plate number comes over and slaps my back. "Good job man. I thought your girlfriend was toast. You've got some moves."

Finally I say something, addressing the guy and waving off his praise. "Not really. Just lucky, I think."

Laney's body stiffens. "What are *you* doing here?" she says quietly. "I told you—I don't need your help."

If I thought it would have any effect on her, I might have rolled my eyes. Instead, I let the tone of my voice do the job. "I beg to differ. Your legs very nearly became a Lambowaffle. *Why*, pray tell, do you not use a sight dog—or a cane?"

She goes even more rigid. "I'm on the waiting list for a dog. And a cane would make me stand out. People already treat me like an invalid—I want to be treated like everyone else. Besides, I've never needed a cane before. I'm not completely blind... yet. I manage really well at home and in... my hometown." Her expression finally looks chastened. "Things are different here."

"Um, yeah. You could say that. And you can also come along and get back in my car—without arguing," I add as she opens her mouth to argue.

She huffs. "Where is my kitten?"

"*Your* kitten? So you really are trying to steal my pet, eh?"

She does roll her eyes. "You don't care about him and

we both know it. Here kitty. Here kitty kitty," she calls.

The kitten runs to her side, rubbing against her bare leg. Laney bends and lifts its skinny body with one hand, tucking it into the crook of her elbow.

Taking her free hand, I slide my other arm behind her back and start walking, causing her to stumble along beside me to keep up. "Where were you going?"

Her lips clamp together stubbornly, reminding me of a defiant little girl.

"You were headed for the beach, weren't you?" I demand.

"I asked someone where the nearest bus stop was, and they told me it was across the street and down a couple of blocks. I was headed there."

My hopes rise. "To go back home?"

"No. I'm not going home—not until I've finished what I came here to do."

"Which is what? Die in a crosswalk? Get raped under a pier? Acquire a raging case of fleas from that stray?"

Her jaw juts out. "Where are you taking me anyway?"

"Don't worry—you can trust me."

"I know that. I may not be able to see with my eyes, but I have a talent for seeing inside of people."

I huff a short laugh. If that were true, she'd run screaming the other direction instead of willingly going along with me. "We're going back to my condo complex. My neighbor Brenna usually has a spare room. You can stay there until you find an apartment *not* near the S clinic. She might even know of someone who's looking for a roommate."

As a dancer, Brenna is acquainted with plenty of starving artists. All of her roommates are Elven, like her, but she probably knows some humans from her work with area musicians and stage productions.

Laney stays quiet until we get into my car. Once inside, she turns to me. "I guess I should thank you… again."

She's so miserable about having to be grateful, I almost laugh. A feeling like summer sunshine warms me from the inside out. "You're welcome. Again. All right, seatbelt on. And hold onto Cupcake—I don't want him running loose in my car. He's filthy—and I wasn't kidding about those fleas."

She hugs the kitten tighter, and he begins to purr. "We can't call him Cupcake. He's a boy."

"What—you don't think guys enjoy cupcakes? I love them, especially vanilla—especially with a lot of frosting."

"What does he look like?"

"Oh, he's a real beaut. I think Cupcake fits him just right—unless you want to name him Mudpie."

"Fine—we'll call him Cupcake. But if he turns out to have gender confusion, don't blame me." She holds the kitten up to her cheek and snuggles him. "So, you were right about one thing—I don't really know where to look for a good place to live. Is your condo in a good neighborhood?"

"You could say that." I drive toward my place in Malibu, noticing for the first time in a long time the wide streets lined with tall palm trees, the expensive landscaping. Like mine, most of the cars we pass are new and high end. Many of the properties are walled off for privacy from tourists and less fortunate locals. My small complex has a gated entry with a twenty-four hour security guard. I nod to him as we drive through the gate, and I pull into the garage under my condo.

When we step out of the garage, Laney lifts her face to the sky and inhales. "You *did* bring me to the beach."

"In a manner of speaking, yes. My condo is on the water. Brenna's is right next door."

"Wow." Laney spins in a circle wearing an expression of joy. "The air feels amazing here. You are so lucky."

"Uh yeah. I guess so." I don't think I've ever once noticed how the air "feels" outside my building. It's owned by the Dark Court, and most of its residents are Elven. I live here because it was available and easy. I've lived near the ocean my whole life, so it doesn't seem all that special to me.

Laney's comment makes me wonder what the weather is like where she's from. Maybe if I ask a few questions, she'll let the location slip and I can arrange speedy transport for her back home.

"So, it's cold where you live then?"

"Oh no—right now it's boiling hot. And the air's so still you can hardly breathe. This sea breeze is incredible. I've been to the Gulf Coast before with my family, but the air there is warm, too. The Pacific is different, isn't it? Is the water cold?"

"I don't know. I guess so. I never really go in."

"You live at the beach, and you don't go in the ocean?" she asks incredulously.

"I'm busy. Come on, I'm going to take your arm and escort you up the walk to Brenna's door. Let's hope she's home."

Still smiling, Laney allows me to walk her to the door. I ring the bell and then knock, suddenly nervous about what I'm going to say to my neighbor. I know her only casually. Brenna's a friend and former roommate of Ava's. She's always been friendly, and from what Ava told me about her, she's not overly devoted to the Dark Council. She's got a live-and-let-live attitude toward the humans, working with them on a regular basis in the jobs she does here and in New York City. Hopefully she won't mind one small one underfoot for a day or two while I locate some suitable housing for Laney or figure out how to send her home.

The door opens, and Brenna's eyes pop wide at the sight of me. Like everyone else, she sees what she wants to see when she looks at me. I read attraction in her eyes, but it's my favorite kind—there's no intent behind it. I'm like a nice piece of scenery to her—pleasant to look at—but she's not interested in pursuing anything. One of the reasons I've always felt comfortable with her.

"Hello neighbor," she says. "What's up?" She slides her glance to Laney, then to the kitten, then a questioning one to me.

"Brenna, this is Laney. She's new to town and looking for a place to rent." *Don't worry*, I assure Brenna mind to mind, *I know you don't want a human roommate. Or another feline one.* "I was hoping you'd have a spare bed for a night or two until she finds one."

24

"Hi Laney." Brenna extends a hand toward Laney, who naturally does not see it.

Laney lifts her own hand in a tentative wave. "Hello. It's nice to meet you. It's very nice of you to take me in."

Brenna shoots me a concerned look. "Oh, well… about that. Listen, step inside for a minute and let me get you something to drink. Do you like tea, Laney?"

"Oh yes. Thank you. That would be nice. I am thirsty."

I hold Laney's elbow. "There's one step up."

"Thanks," she says, and we walk into the condo together, following Brenna toward the kitchen.

Immediately inside the doorway is a pile of suitcases. I'm starting to get a bad feeling. Brenna busies herself setting out glasses and getting a pitcher of tea from the refrigerator. She fills a bowl with water and puts it on the floor for the kitten, who squirms from Laney's grasp and goes right to it, drinking thirstily. Afterward, it helps itself to some dry food from a bowl belonging to Brenna's Persian cat, who's about five times Cupcake's size and thankfully the laziest animal I've ever seen.

"Where are you from, Laney?" Brenna asks. She directs a silent question at me as well.

She's blind? Where did you meet her?

Yes. We… ran into each other while I was working this evening.

I'm not sure if Brenna knows what I do for my father, but I think she suspects. I spend most of my nights out at clubs and travel a lot, and I've been vague about it when she's asked directly.

"From a small town… pretty far from here." Laney smiles. "Call it Nowheresville, U.S.A."

"What brings you to L.A.? Are you hoping to break into show business?"

"Oh no… I came to volunteer at a clinic. Of course I'll also need to find *some* kind of paying job in addition to an apartment. And… I'm looking for someone."

"Sounds like a lot of searching," Brenna says. "Who are you looking for?"

"Just… someone. I owe him something." Laney stops there and takes a deep drink from her glass. "Thank you—this really hits the spot."

"Well, okay then. Tell me what kind of place you're looking for, apartment-wise. I can check around and see if anyone I know needs another roommate. That is, unless you prefer to live alone."

"I wouldn't mind roommates at all. I need someplace cheap, though. I have some money saved up, but Los Angeles is a lot more expensive than I expected."

"I see. How cheap are we talking?"

"Well, I have six hundred dollars left after buying lunch today and paying for the cab ride."

Brenna flares her eyes at me, shaking her head in dismay. *This poor kid*, she adds silently.

Aloud she says, "I'm afraid that's not even going to cover first month's rent, much less last month's and a security deposit. You'll have to find a roommate, and one who'll let you move in without putting you on the lease. And one who doesn't mind pets. Unless you want to go to Chesterfield or

Watts or something," she jokes.

"That's where I *was* looking until Mr. Busybody came along and made me leave."

Now Brenna's mouth is hanging open in horrified shock. "I was kidding. Laney, Culley was right to make you leave. You can't live there—you shouldn't even *go* to those places."

The defiant expression returns to Laney's face. "Well, I *am* going back there—tomorrow. That's where the clinic is."

I give Brenna a weary look. *See what I'm dealing with?*

"Okay, well, we'll see. Now, about tonight… Culley, can I speak with you in the other room?"

Laney stands as if preparing to leave. "Oh no. Am I imposing? I can understand if you don't want a total stranger sleeping here. I told Culley I'd be fine."

"No. Not at all," Brenna says. "I've got some company, that's all. Actually lots of company. Don't worry—we'll work it out. Please, sit down and be comfortable. Culley and I will be right back."

Brenna draws me into the living room area. *I can see why you brought her here, but I don't have a single bed available for the next two weeks. Both my roommates are in town—and a bunch of my cast mates from New York arrived this morning. They're out to dinner right now, but they'll be back soon. I've got people sleeping on every available surface—couches, doubling up in the bedrooms. We only have two bathrooms. There's just no room for her. Plus, there are bound to be questions and inappropriate conversation, if you know what I mean.*

Shit. I run a hand through my hair. *What am I going to do? You've seen her. She's a disaster waiting to happen. I found her on the doorstep of a drug den about to be attacked by gang members. Then she nearly got herself run down in the street.*

Why can't she stay at your place?

An acute flutter in my chest makes me cough. *With me?*

Of course with you. Unless you'd like to come over and sleep in my bathtub and give her complete run of your place. And I have to say... I'm surprised you even care about what happens to this girl. You've never struck me as a human-hugger. Or a lover of small domestic animals.

I glare at her. *I'm not. But I'm not a heartless monster either—contrary to rumor. Someone's got to look after her. She clearly doesn't belong here. I'm trying to figure out where she came from so I can put her on a direct flight back to the blessed heartland.*

Well, until you do, it looks like you have a new roomie. Just don't let your father find out.

Chill bumps rise on my skin at the mention of my father, Audun. The thought of him in the same room with sweet, innocent Laney turns my stomach.

The text notification on Brenna's phone sounds. She checks it then types in a brief response. The look on her face is odd when she glances back up at me.

Speaking of your father... She holds the phone out to me. *Ava needs to talk to you. She says she can't call you directly because he's searching for her and your phone is probably bugged, but she says it's urgent she speaks to you. This is my private number. I use the phone I got through Alfred's agency only for work. Anything I don't want the Dark Council to know, I discuss on this line. It's safe. Here. Her number's up—press the button.*

"You can't put it off forever," she says, encouraging me to call the girl who threw me over for a human.

There's nothing I want to discuss with Ava.

But then my heart leaps, making a liar out of me. I haven't seen her or spoken to her in four months, and I miss her. I have to admit, if only to myself, I was quite attached to her—she's the closest thing I ever had to a friend. Maybe I even loved her in my own way. But not enough to give her what she was looking for. Ava wanted epic love, like what we witnessed between Lad and Ryann. She wanted no-holds-barred trust, and fairy tale romance, and family. Family. Ha. I have only the vaguest notion of what that is.

I'm not fit to be anyone's bond-mate, anyone's father. Ever. How could I be? I've never had a real father, or a real mother for that matter. The only thing I've ever been sure of is my ability to manipulate others using my glamour-enhanced looks.

Though her paramour is human and will die long before Ava will, I have to admit she still made the better choice.

"Give it to me," I growl, holding my hand out for the phone.

Chapter Three
Sunset

Brenna nods to a wide sliding glass door. *Take it out on the balcony. Just in case there are bugs in here. Don't worry—I'll look after Laney.*

Grabbing the phone, I follow her suggestion, sliding the door open and stepping out onto the oceanfront balcony. The air is cool, the sound of the waves soothing. The fragrance on the wind is a mix of salt and sea. I don't usually notice these details—it must be the influence of Laney's fresh perspective.

For a moment I stare at the touch screen, at Ava's name there. Then I touch the button to dial it. After a few rings there's an answer.

"Brenna?" Ava's voice asks.

The sound of it gives me a short, sharp pang. I hesitate, then respond. "It's me."

"Oh. Culley. It's so good to hear your voice. Are you okay?"

some cat food to go. Culley probably doesn't have as much as a can of tuna over there."

"You wouldn't happen to have an extra flea collar, would you?" I mutter, eying the dirty kitten in Laney's arms.

"I'll give you something even better—a cat shampoo that should take care of the problem and leave Cupcake smelling like his namesake."

She hands me a blue bottle and follows as I guide Laney toward the door and open it. "You know where to find me if you need anything, Laney. And I'll ask around about a cheap apartment."

"Thank you so much," Laney says with a genuine smile. "You've been so nice. I really appreciate it."

After the door closes, she asks me, "So, I guess you're taking me to a hotel now?"

I walk her a few steps away to my own front door, insert the key, and open it. "No. Right now we're getting some supper. We'll work out the overnight situation later."

I already know I can't trust her to stay in a hotel and not go spend the night on the beach or the street or something to "save money." Well, I suppose I could sway her, but I'm feeling strangely reluctant to resort to that with Laney. I'm not sure why.

It's never bothered me to sway humans before. I've swayed countless during my lifetime—at Eton, where naturally I got top marks from all my instructors whether I deserved them or not—anytime I needed to get out of a traffic ticket or disciplinary action or escape a particularly persistent admirer. It worked like a charm during my modeling gigs when a shoot went on too long and I got bored and ready to wrap things up. A bit of Sway sent the photographer's way and *poof,* we're done.

But swaying Laney feels different. For whatever reason, I like talking to her—the *real* her. She's interesting, and surprising, and so full of spirit and determination. And she has this quiet sense of dignity about her. The Sway will strip her of all that, of her inhibitions, her sense of self. She'll be a victim of my mind control, and I'm finding myself unwilling to victimize her.

She steps over the threshold into my condo. "We're in your place?"

"Home sweet home."

Taking a few tentative steps forward into the high-ceilinged great room, she bends to set the kitten down. It immediately darts across the room and under my sofa.

"I hope it's okay that he's in here? You're not allergic are you?"

"Not physically," I mutter. Louder, I say, "No. It's fine. We'll collect a pan of sand for him and set it up until I can get to the store for some kitty litter and stuff."

Laney doesn't appear to be listening to me. She's standing in the center of the room, turning in a slow circle. "Wow. It's so big."

"Pardon my asking, but how would you know?"

She gives me a tolerant smile. "I can tell by the echo of our footsteps and voices. Also, you don't have a lot of soft furniture or foofy decorations."

Her accurate perception makes me grin. "You're right. I'm a minimalist."

I follow her farther into the hard-floored, white-walled room, with its low, sleek furniture and the bare minimum of modern wall art. Directly opposite us, unadorned floor-to-ceiling sliding doors reveal the ocean-front deck, blue skies, and even bluer water.

Moving toward one of the open doors, Laney tilts her head back and lifts her arms to the side, clearly enjoying the breeze. "And you have an amazing ocean view."

Her choice of words has me burning with curiosity. "Have you not always been blind then?"

She turns toward the sound of my voice. "No. Only for the past two years. I was born with completely normal vision—as far as anyone knew. But when I was fifteen, my peripheral vision started disappearing. My parents took me to the doctor, afraid I might have a brain tumor or something. Turns out I have a hereditary condition called Retinitis Pigmentosa. It doesn't always lead to total blindness, but in my case, it will. It took about nine or ten months for most of my vision to leave me. Eventually, I'll lose it all. Right now all I've got left is a little bit of light and dark, some shadows, movement, vague outlines. At least the slow progression has given me a chance to prepare, to learn Braille and stuff."

"There's no cure?"

"No. There are some experimental treatments to slow the degeneration process but no cure. Not yet anyway. I'm always hopeful. I do miss seeing things like the ocean, the sky... fireworks."

"And people's faces?" I can't keep the bitterness out of

my tone. My whole life I've been acutely aware of how important appearance is to people's perceptions of others, mainly because they've always given me way more credit than I deserved. I've always been assumed to be smarter, more capable, kinder than I really am simply because of how I look.

"No, actually. I've always been so much more interested in what's inside of people." She stops and looks thoughtful for a moment, sad even. "Appearances can be deceiving."

"Yes." There is a sudden lump in my throat. I clear it before speaking again. "So… we should order some food. I've got several takeout menus here—Pan Asian, Italian, burgers and fries."

"Anything is fine. You order something, and I'll pay."

I can't keep a smile off my face. "You should hold onto that six hundred dollars a little more tightly, sweet."

"No. I insist. It's the least I can do after the way you helped me today."

I've got no intention of letting the girl pay for our food, and luckily, this issue won't require Sway. She won't be able to see me tuck a few bills into the delivery driver's hand and put her money back into that tiny purse of hers. If she ever takes it off her shoulder, that is. She's had it there the whole time we've been together.

That's when it occurs to me. I haven't seen any luggage. If she arrived in the city today, she should have some.

"Where's your suitcase?"

A deep blush colors Laney's face. "I… I'm not sure. I had one when I got off the bus, but a man offered to carry it down the stairs for me… and he disappeared. I thought at first maybe he left it sitting there in the station, somewhere near the loading area, but when I described it and asked a few people, they all said there was no unattended baggage around. I guess he took it."

Wanker. What kind of guy would steal a suitcase from a blind girl? The kind that lurks around L.A. bus stations, that's the kind.

"There was nothing really valuable in it," she says in a hurry, as if it's all no big deal. "Just clothes and a couple pair of shoes and toothpaste and stuff. I'll buy some more when I get a chance to go shopping. I was hoping there would be a Target or something near my new apartment— when I get one."

I mentally subtract the cost of a new wardrobe from the six hundred dollars Laney owns. Her housing possibilities are getting more dismal by the minute. "Thought it all through, have you?" I say. "So… how does Thai food sound?"

"Delicious," she answers, her hand going to her stomach. "And maybe we could put some of that cat food in a bowl for Cupcake. I felt his poor little tummy rumbling against my hand. I think he's still hungry."

"Sure."

Going into the kitchen, I look around for a suitable cat dish and settle on a small plate, open the bag, and pour some in, chuckling in disbelief. I'm *serving* the same little beast I scolded this morning about looking after himself.

As soon as the dish is on the floor, the kitten emerges

from under the couch and sprints over to it, gobbling the food so fast I'm worried he's going to choke.

"Is he eating?" Laney asks.

"I'm not sure if he's eating it or inhaling it, but yes, it's going in. And now to feed the humans."

I call the Thai place on my speed dial and order my favorites, hoping they'll appeal to Laney, too. The voice on the other end of the line informs me our food will be here in forty-five minutes. Hanging up, I look at Laney standing in the middle of my living room. What am I supposed to do with her now?

"The food will take a while to get here. Would you like to… go out on the deck? Or maybe walk on the beach or something while we wait?"

Her whole face lights up. "Could we? That would be wonderful."

"Sure. Let me change shoes."

I go back to my room for a pair of flip flops and return to the living area moments later to see Laney standing eagerly by the back door, barefoot.

"The sand might be a bit rocky," I warn.

"That's okay. I want to feel it," she says. "Oh—do we have to walk far on pavement before we get there? Maybe I should wear my shoes and then slip them off when we get to the beach."

Opening the door to the back deck, I grip her elbow lightly to guide her outside. "No. We're right on the ocean here. Just a few steps across the deck, past the fireplace and down a set of stairs, and you'll feel the sand. The sun's almost down now, so it should be cool to the touch."

We descend the steps together, and her tiny feet sink into the sand at the bottom.

"Wow. It feels great. Can we walk to the water?"

"If you like."

With my hand lightly placed on the small of her back, I guide her toward the ocean. The breeze picks up nearer the water, and Laney's sandy brown hair lifts and flies around her like ribbons, brushing against my arm as well. The red sundress is molded to her body in a way that makes the innocent article of clothing more revealing than she can possibly realize.

I look away as my breath quickens and my muscles tense and grow warm. I've spent the past few years working with the world's most beautiful women, and naturally found them appealing, especially after I turned eighteen and the Elven urge to bond kicked in. But something about this small human girl affects me like no one ever has.

I glance back at her, trying to figure out what it is. She's pretty—sure—but not remarkably so. Maybe it's the unashamed expressiveness of her features, or the simple not-trying-so-hard naturalness of her look.

We reach the water, and Laney gives a happy cry when the surf covers her toes. "It's so cold!"

She laughs out loud and drops her head back, turning her face to the sky, which is multi-colored, and now that I'm noticing it, quite stunning. I'm struck with a sudden wish that I wasn't the only one seeing it—that Laney could see it, too.

Before I quite realize it, I find myself describing the scene to her. "It'll be completely dark soon, but right now there's still a band of light on the horizon. It looks like a gold strip hovering above the water. Above that, there are streaks of orange cloud, intermixed with dark and light blue, sort of like a tie-dyed t-shirt. The shallow water directly in front of us is orange, too, reflecting the sunset. Just over our heads there are some breaks in the clouds and a few faint stars are showing."

I stop right there, my face heating, embarrassed at my impromptu narrative. I'm not sure what possessed me, but I must have sounded like an utter git.

I'm about to say so when I feel Laney's small hand take mine. She sighs—a contented, almost childlike sound.

"I haven't seen a sunset in so long, but I feel like I did just now. Thank you for that."

Something swells in my chest—a feeling like nothing I've ever experienced before. It's something like… pride, but not exactly. I'm not sure whether it feels good or awful.

"Can we walk down the beach a little?" Laney asks, tugging at the hand she's still holding.

"Uh… sure. For a few minutes. We have to be back before the food arrives. And before Cupcake turns my furniture into a pile of rags."

Laney lets go of my fingers and walks without my guidance, her path staying at the meeting point between wet sand and gentle surf. There's a bounce in her step, and her expression is so happy I can't seem to keep my eyes away from her face for more than a minute at a time. It's like there's some irresistible light coming from inside of her, and I'm a moth—or another equally small-brained and self-destructive insect.

"You must be so happy living here," she says, completely unaware of my unbroken study of her.

"Yes," I say in halfhearted agreement. I glance over the incredible view then back toward the condo, taking in the size and obvious *expensiveness* of it. In the garage beneath is parked my LaFerrari. Inside the condo itself is God only knows how many thousands of dollars in high-end furnishings and electronics. It's nothing new. I grew up with a similar level of luxury if not more.

And Ava was right—none of it has made me happy. No matter where I am or how much I have, I still feel... hungry. There's always this gnawing empty space inside of me, demanding to be filled. In spite of her lack of sight, Laney strikes me as someone who is *already* full. Like, if she were able to see, it would only enhance what is already a full life, while mine feels like a half-life. The thought makes me irritable. Angry even.

She must be missing *something*. Why else would she have left home and come here? I suddenly remember she told Brenna she was looking for something. For some reason, I *have* to know what it is.

"So are you going to tell me why you came to LA—other than your suicidal desire to volunteer at an S clinic in the city's worst slum?" My tone is harsher than it should be, but she seems unaffected, smiling serenely.

"I'm going to be fine working at the clinic. Nothing will

happen to me. You don't have to worry."

True. Because you're not going back there. Unseen, I smirk at her innocent confidence. Doesn't anyone comprehend how much this girl needs someone to protect her? She doesn't belong here in this city of users and predators and drug addicts. She doesn't belong here with *me*.

If Ava is right and my father is rounding up girls for European fan pods, she could easily have been snatched up already and be on her way to a life of enslavement and sexual servitude. Hell, *I* could have used her that way myself if I'd had a mind to.

Abruptly I stop walking, struggling for breath. Without warning, an image of Laney, warm and naked beneath me, crashes into my brain. I can almost feel her silky skin, hear her panting softly against my ear. Clenching my jaw and squeezing my eyes tightly, I will the rousing vision away.

I double my pace to catch up to her, arousal converting to anger as I do. "I'm not worried," I snap. "You're not *my* responsibility. But you must have parents somewhere. A family. Some friends. Why did they let you come out here by yourself?"

Her stubborn little chin lifts at my demanding tone. "For one thing, I'm eighteen—I'm no one's responsibility. No one can stop me from doing anything I want to. For another… my parents don't exactly know where I am. I left a note telling them I'm fine and that I'll contact them soon."

I'm no expert on good parenting, but even I realize they must be in a frenzy over the thought of their blind daughter out alone in the world somewhere.

"You'll call them when we get back to the condo. I'm sure they're sick with worry."

"No!" Then in a calmer tone, she says, "No, it will only make them worry more if they do know where I am. All they *do* is worry about me—all the time. They don't give me any freedom. They treat me like I'm still a child. If they find out where I am, I know exactly what they'll do. They'll get in the car and drive straight out here to bring me home. And I'm not going home until I've done what I've come to do."

"Which is?"

Laney walks a few steps in silence, then stops. "We should go back. The food delivery will be here soon."

Fine. She doesn't want to tell me. It only increases my resolve to find out. I have several bottles of wine back at the condo. I'll open one up during dinner, make sure she has a few glasses. She'll tell me.

If that doesn't work, I *will* use my Sway. Yes. I'll sway her like I've never swayed anyone before. She'll tell me everything I want to know, and then I'll put her in the car and drive her home *myself* if that's what it takes to get her out of this city.

CHAPTER FOUR
OVERNIGHT ACCOMMODATIONS

Laney doesn't drink alcohol. Not even one tongue-loosening sip.

"Overprotective parents, remember? I'm too tired anyway." She smiles sweetly. "It's been a long day."

If only Pad Ki Mow and pineapple fried rice had the intoxicating powers of wine, I would be golden because the girl can put down some chow. I've watched in literal awe as she inhaled about three-quarters of the food I ordered.

Finally full, she pushes away from the table. "That was so good. I hope you tipped the delivery guy well?"

"Yes. I put the change back in your purse." I smile at my cover story. What she doesn't know is I put *all* her money back in her purse and paid the guy myself.

"Good." There's a pause. "So, I guess it's time for me to

get going. If you take me to a hotel, I promise to spend the night there. Just… could we make it a cheap one? I really *should* start watching my budget."

Anticipating a battle, I let out a quiet sigh. "Listen, Laney… I've been thinking about what Brenna said. It really does make sense for you to just stay here tonight. There's a guest room. You'll save money… you'll be safe." Glancing over at the kitten sleeping on my sofa, his rounded belly turned up, I add, "Cupcake is already making himself at home here, and I doubt the hotels would take him."

Laney makes me wait for an answer, biting her lip and furrowing her brow, clearly debating it.

"Well… if you're sure it's not too much trouble. And I promise we'll be gone tomorrow."

Hopefully she *will* be gone tomorrow—back to her little hometown of Nowheresville. "I'm sure. It's no trouble."

She smiles. "Great. So, would it be okay for me to take a shower? Like I said, long day."

I stand abruptly, applying a chokehold to my overactive imagination, warning it not to go back to where it went on the beach earlier. My legs inadvertently bump the table and rattle everything on top of it.

"Of course. The guest room has a private bathroom attached. Follow me—I mean, come with me."

I put her hand on my arm and walk down the hallway. She is so much shorter than me that I can look down at the top of her hair, which, I have to say still looks and smells exceptionally clean. Even after walking around the city and out on the beach, Laney smells sweet like vanilla and peaches.

We reach the door across from my bedroom. It opens to a guest suite decorated in sand tones with turquoise accents—the choices of the decorator I hired over the phone before I ever even saw the place. I wonder if Laney would approve of the way it looks.

"Ooh, the carpet is nice in here," she says, causing me to glance down at her small, pink-tipped toes. "And it's so quiet. I might sleep all day."

I chuckle. "You're welcome to do that. There's nothing on the agenda tomorrow." *Other than getting you to spill the beans about where you're from.*

"Actually, I'm a fairly early riser, though I can't say what time I might get up with the time difference here in California. So I'll either be sleeping all day, or I might just be wandering around your house at three a.m."

Guiding her through the room, I say, "Well, however long you want to stay in it, the bed is right here. There's a table beside it. Sit here for a sec. I'll be right back."

Dashing across the hall to my own room, I grab a clean t-shirt from my bureau and bring it back.

"Here's something for you to sleep in. I'll leave it on the pillow. Okay, let me show you to the bathroom. Put your hand out to the side—yeah, like that—just walk straight down this short hallway here, and this is the bathroom. The sink is in front of you, the shower is to your right. Would you like me to set the water temperature or anything?"

She gives me a pursed-lip chiding expression. "No thank you. I can do it myself."

"Okay then, I'll leave you to it."

"Thank you. For everything."

I start to go but turn back when she speaks again. "Oh, would you mind giving me the address here? I need to find out where the nearest city bus stop is so I can plan transportation to the clinic tomorrow."

"I thought we'd already discussed this. You can't go back there." My frown is wasted on her, but she can probably hear it in my voice.

"Culley, I appreciate your concern—*and* you letting me stay here. But I have to go. It's why I'm here."

"You can volunteer at other places if you want to give back or serve mankind or whatever. There are plenty of soup kitchens and women's shelters."

"No. It has to be the S clinic—*this* one."

Her expression is so serious, so determined. I see that nothing I say is going to dissuade her. Well, nothing I say without Sway, anyway. Maybe I *should* go ahead and use it on her. My gut squirms uncomfortably at the thought.

Her insistence on this particular clinic does have my curiosity bursting, though. How do humans usually get each other to reveal information they'd rather not share? I have an idea. Putting one hand on the wall, I lean against it, looking down into her upturned obstinate little face.

"Listen, if you'll tell me *why* it's so important for you to go there, I'll drive you."

"Why do you have to know everything about me?" she asks with an aggravated sigh.

I blink. Blink again. It's a good question. I've never really concerned myself with the affairs of humans. In this case I chalk it up to too much forced proximity and an inquiring mind.

"Call it the price of cab fare for a ride over to skid row tomorrow."

She lets out a resentful breath. "Okay. I'll tell you. *After* my shower. Now go." She presses her hands against my abdomen and gives me a small shove, making me laugh.

"I'm going to hold you to that, you know."

"Go," she repeats.

Smiling, I make my way across the carpeted floor and out into the hallway, closing the door behind me as I hear the water turn on in the shower. My footstep sends something sliding across the hall's wood floor. I bend over to pick it up—Laney's red headband.

My first impulse is to return it to her. I spin around and grab the doorknob of the guest room but freeze before turning it. She might be undressing in there.

Down boy. Don't think about it.

I turn and resume my journey down the hallway toward the kitchen, rubbing the stretchy fabric band between my fingertips. I'll give it to her later. Spinning it around one finger, I go to the kitchen to clean up our dinner plates and glasses.

Under the bright kitchen lights I can see there's a light pattern stitched into the headband—hearts. I smile. Did she choose this? Or maybe her parents did, picking the sweet, childlike accessory for their sweet, childlike daughter. Only she's not a child. She might be innocent, she might be small, but Laney knows her own mind. She's independent to a fault, and maybe with good reason—she did manage to make her way out here from... well, from wherever she's from.

I lift the headband to my face, rubbing it against my cheek then pressing it to my nose. It smells like her, the sweet vanilla and peach scent sending a jolt straight from my head to my lower abdomen. I fold the headband, fold it again. Then I stuff it into my pocket, a mixture of shame and satisfaction bubbling in my chest. I am, for all practical purposes, a drug pusher—but I've never been a common thief—not until now. I won't be giving the hair accessory back to Laney. I want it. I'm not sure why.

Spotting the blue bottle on the counter, I decide to do something to take my mind off that unsettling question. It'll pass the time, not to mention preventing a flea infestation in my multi-million dollar condo.

"Cupcake. Come here, fella."

The kitten pokes his face out from under my couch, but as I walk toward him, he scrambles back underneath it, almost as if he knows what's coming. Getting down on my knees, I peer underneath the furniture, spotting the telltale gleam of two eyes deep underneath.

Dammit. How am I supposed to get him out of there? Too bad Sway doesn't work on animals. I'd have *no* reservations using it on this grimy little rat.

What do cats like? He's already eaten, so I doubt luring him with food will work. Maybe if I offer him a game of some sort? I haven't "played" since I was about ten, lacking any siblings, or pets, or any playmates who weren't adult servants on my mom's payroll. I'm not sure if I even know how to anymore.

Stretching out on the couch, I pull Laney's headband from my pocket and dangle it over the edge of the cushions near the floor, wiggling it around as if it were a live thing. A tiny paw emerges and swipes at it. *Ah ha.* Stretching my arm out farther, I repeat the enticement, imbuing the red headband with lively personality. This time the whole kitten dashes out and lunges for his prey. And I grab for mine, getting a hand around his skinny mid-section before he realizes what's happening.

"Gotcha. And now it's bath time, my friend."

Cupcake doesn't scratch or bite. Not until I try to submerge him in the sudsy sink water. Then it's man against beast. Unfortunately for the beast, I've got about a hundred eighty pounds on him and opposable thumbs. Unfortunately for me, this kitten has claws. It isn't easy, and I lose a decent amount of epidermis in the process, but I manage to soap and scrub and rinse him until I'm reasonably sure we are both pest-free. He certainly smells better.

I've just finished toweling him off when Laney emerges from the guest room and pads down the hallway on bare feet. She's wearing the t-shirt I left out for her, and my heart nearly stops at the sight of her in it. Her long hair is wet, her face fresh-scrubbed and shining. The t-shirt is huge on her small frame. It covers her decently, but it's still short enough to reveal a killer pair of legs, and the soft fabric draped over her body hints at a tempting shape beneath.

Laney's parents might still see her as a child, but *I* do not. In fact, at the moment she is the sexiest woman I have ever seen. It's a wholesome kind of sexiness, completely unintentional and unselfconscious.

I on the other hand, am sweating and probably look like I've been in a knife fight with a windmill. "Feel better now?" I manage to ask, my voice sounding a bit strained.

"Oh yes. That was wonderful. Your shower is much better than mine back in—" She catches herself before saying the name of her town, moving farther into the room with a rueful grin.

"I thought we agreed you were going to tell me where you're from."

"No," she chides. "I agreed to tell you why I'm here. Although, I'm not really sure why you'd care. I'm not sure why you're doing *any* of this—letting me stay in your home, feeding me dinner. Surely you have better things to do with your time than babysit a country bumpkin visiting the big city."

"As a matter of fact I do. I have a very important appointment with a bowl of ice cream. Would you care to join me for dessert?"

"Maybe a small dish," she answers. "I had a big supper."

I grin widely. "Really? I hadn't noticed. I'm sure you can find some room for Chunky Monkey. Here—there's a bar stool here at the kitchen island. Just climb up—there you go."

I move between the freezer and the counter, taking out bowls, spoons, scooping some ice cream for each of us. As I open drawers and cabinets, Laney waits patiently, following my movements with her face, if not precisely her eyes.

I set a bowl in front of her and sink a spoon into mine. But I don't actually eat any ice cream. Instead, I watch Laney eat hers. I'm struck by a sense of unreality. I have a human in my house. On purpose.

It's strange having *anyone* in my house—I spend most of my time alone and have since I went off to Eton at age thirteen. Even there, I had a private room. But having her here—it's hard to explain. She fascinates me.

Watching her is appealing in a way nothing else has ever been. Maybe it's because I can allow myself to *really* look at her, instead of taking a quick glance and then glancing away, which is what I usually do with humans and Elves alike.

Direct eye contact has always been uncomfortable for me—because of what I see in the eyes looking back at me. Desire. Admiration. Envy. Infatuation. All of it false. All of it brought on by my glamour.

That was one of the things I enjoyed about being with Ava. When she looked at me, there was an honest reaction there. Good or bad, I didn't care—at least it was real. Laney's even better. She is completely, one hundred percent unaffected by my appearance. And it relaxes me in a way I never thought possible.

She lifts the spoon to her plump pink lips, sliding it in between them and bringing it out again, wearing a small smile of private pleasure. My breathing quickens as my eyes roam over her face, cataloging the details—the brown eyes that seem to change according to the light, sometimes clear and bright, sometimes dark and deep—the soft arch of her eyebrows, the small, rounded nose, the pink tint of her cheeks that comes not from makeup but from within.

Maybe I shouldn't stare, but it's amazingly pleasurable to be able to look at someone closely like this, without the embarrassment of being caught at it. She doesn't know I'm doing it, so she won't read anything into it like any other girl would if she were to catch me studying her closely. If I stared at any other girl, she'd get up from where she was sitting and move toward me, leaving her friends—or her boyfriend—behind.

There's no expectation involved here. Unlike everyone else I encounter, Laney doesn't want *anything* from me. I can just enjoy her beauty without doing anything about it. And she *is* beautiful—so much more so than I even realized the first time I saw her. Is it always like that with people? The more you look at them, the more appealing they become?

"Why aren't you eating yours?" Laney asks, shocking me out of my perusal and private thoughts.

"Oh. I uh… I like to let it melt a bit first," I lie, looking down at the disgusting puddle in my bowl.

She wrinkles that perfect little nose. "Gross. Ice cream soup."

"Exactly. A delicacy. You should try it sometime."

"No thanks. I like my frozen desserts *frozen*." She pushes the bowl away. "I've had enough, though. I think I've managed to gain five pounds my first day in California."

She starts to get off the bar stool. "I'm pretty tired, so..."

My hand darts out and wraps around her wrist. "Oh no you don't. You haven't told me about this elusive *guy* you're searching for here in Los Angeles."

Sliding back to the center of her stool, she faces me across the counter, silent for so long I think she's going to refuse me and I'll be forced to sway her after all. But then she opens her mouth, closes it again then finally answers.

"I have a brother, Joseph. We're very close. He's not one of those annoying older brothers you hear about who torture their younger sisters or tell them to get lost. We're only eighteen months apart in age, and we grew up as playmates and best friends. We played pretend and Legos and built a tree fort together. We watched superhero movies and battled on the Xbox for hours."

As she describes her childhood, I picture Laney as a smaller version of herself, running wild through a suburban backyard, laughing and playing with this much beloved brother.

"Joseph was amazing when I lost my sight," she continues. "He was good at so many things, but he's always dreamed of being an actor. He's really talented—always the star of our high school's drama productions. He saved his after-school and summer job money for two years, planning to move to Hollywood to try to break into the film business. About a year ago he moved here, enrolled in acting classes, found work waiting tables. And then..."

My insides go cold, anticipating what's coming. A whirring noise begins in my ears as Laney continues her story. I almost don't want her to.

"At first we heard from him often. He was going on auditions, getting call backs. He had friends. He was so happy. Then he called and texted less and less. He stopped answering our calls. My parents were worried. They tracked down one of his roommates—Travis. After a lot of pleading from my parents, Travis admitted Joseph had tried S one night when they were out with friends. After that..."

She stops her story there, but I already know the ending. "And now he's missing," I say grimly. "You're here to find him."

"No. It's too late for that." She shakes her head, her voice breaking. "Joseph is dead. I'm here to find the person who killed him."

Chapter Five
Don't Mention It

For a moment, I'm actually relieved. Horrified, but relieved. "Your brother was murdered?"

"Yes—by the drug dealer who got him hooked on that awful stuff."

The relief evaporates, superseded by another, more visceral emotion. My breaths are harder to come by now—something heavy sits on my chest.

"He did… have a choice. He *chose* to take it," I say, feeling like the slimeball I am, even as the words leave my lips.

"No! It's not like him." She shakes her head vigorously. "Joseph was never a drug user in high school or junior college. He barely even drank. I know he was going out with his friends here to nightclubs and stuff, but according to them he never tried cocaine or pills, not even pot. I don't understand how it could have happened."

She stops, the frustration and grief seeming to steal her breath away. After sitting silently for long moments, she resumes her sad tale. "Anyway, it's too late to help Joseph. But I can help other people like him. I can work in the clinic, help people beat their addictions. And maybe by doing that I can gather enough information to find the person responsible and stop him from killing other people's brothers, and sons, sisters, and daughters... and friends."

A tear slides down one of her pretty cheeks, devastating me.

Why the hell do I care?

It's not like I didn't know people were dying of S overdoses. I avoid watching the news for the most part, but it's impossible not to see the destruction the drug has wreaked on the human population. I see junkies first hand on practically a daily basis, in the clubs and bars when I stop in to hand out "samples." I don't exactly like it, but I sleep just fine at night. I'm just doing my job, following orders.

But this—this feels different. I never met the guy, but after listening to Laney's description of him, seeing how much she cares for him, I feel like I knew him. Joseph. He had a name. A family. People who loved him, who miss him now that he's gone. And it's very possible I am the one who introduced him to the S that ended up killing him.

"I'm... sorry." The inadequate words hang in the air between us.

Laney wipes her face and gives an embarrassed laugh. "Aren't you glad you asked?" she says sarcastically. "I think I will go to bed now. I'd rather not sleep all day tomorrow, in spite of my threats earlier."

Rising from my chair I take her arm. "I'll walk you back to your room."

"Do you mind if Cupcake sleeps with me?" she asks.

"Well, he's certainly not sleeping with me. We just met—I'm not that kind of guy," I joke, and she laughs.

As if understanding our conversation, or perhaps sensing he's about to be left alone with the mean force-bather for the evening, Cupcake vacates his spot under my couch and scampers down the hallway ahead of us.

When I open her door for her, he shoots inside, and Laney turns to face me. "Thank you again for all you've done today. You really have been so nice to me."

"It's nothing." My face heats with embarrassment and shame. "Don't mention it." *Please.*

"It's *not* nothing," she insists. "You don't give yourself enough credit—you've gone out of your way to help a stranger without asking for anything in return. I may not be able to see things with my eyes anymore, but my heart sees a lot. And what it sees in *you* is a good person."

I have never despised myself as much as I do in this moment. I feel like chucking up. If the roof opened and lightning struck me, it wouldn't be half what I deserve for deceiving this girl—and for what happened to her brother.

"Yes, well... I'll see you in the morning," I mutter. "Sleep well."

"Good night, Culley Rune," she says with a sweet smile and goes into her room, closing the door behind her.

I'm not sure how long I stand in the hallway staring at

that door. What am I doing? What have I done? Suddenly I'm thinking back on my actions these past few months and seeing them through a different lens. I don't like the view— at all.

Slowly, I turn and shuffle to my own room for a shower and then bed. I'm not sure I'll get any sleep though. In the morning I'll be driving Laney to a drug addiction clinic so she can work to counteract the results of *my* actions. So she can ask questions and track down the person responsible for her brother's horrible untimely death.

Me.

Chapter Six
Pop In

The doorbell rings early. Way too early as far as I'm concerned. I roll over and ignore it, struggling to stay in the vivid dream that's put a smile on my face and convinced my body it's having a *very* good morning.

No one who actually knows me would come by this early anyway. They'd know my usual schedule includes staying out at nightclubs until the wee hours of the morning and sleeping in late. It's probably some sort of solicitor or maybe a package delivery.

The bell rings again. I bolt upright, suddenly remembering I have a houseguest. The noise might wake her. Scrambling from the bed, I grab a pair of shorts from the floor beside the bed and slip them on—it wouldn't do to parade around naked in front of Laney. Of course, she wouldn't be able to see me, but if we were to touch accidentally...

The thought is too reminiscent of my dream. I shake my head to dislodge the disturbingly appealing images then throw open the bedroom door. I'll get rid of whoever this is and hopefully be able to go back to sleep and re-enter the dream if I'm lucky.

Directly across the hall, the guest room door opens, and the star of my sensual vision stands there, looking sleepy and warm, her hair appealingly messy and those knockout legs taunting me from beneath my own t-shirt. The doorbell must have awakened her, exactly as I feared.

It rings again, longer this time, more insistent.

"What's going on?" she asks in a sleep-roughened voice. "What time is it?"

"Too early to get up. Go back to bed. That's what I plan to do as soon as I get rid of whoever's out there."

Striding down the hall, I stop just inside the door and peer out the security port, prepared to release the deadbolt and yell at the persistent mailman/charity collector/cookie-selling child. Instead, my hand freezes on the lock.

It's my father. *Shit.* The lingering pleasure buzz from my dream vaporizes, replaced by nerve-shredding unease.

He never visits my place, preferring to summon me to his downtown office or his luxurious home in Bel Air. What is he doing here?

Backing away from the door on silent bare feet, I crane my neck back to glance down the hallway and make sure Laney's safely tucked away in the guest suite. She's not. She's right behind me. I nearly stepped on her.

Shit shit. I spin around and grab her shoulders. "What

are you doing?" I hiss. "I told you to go back to bed."

Ding dong ding dong ding dong.

The bell is chiming in a persistent pattern now. Father is clearly growing tired of waiting. Bile rising in my throat, I twist to stare back over my shoulder at the condo's entry door. I won't answer. He'll assume I spent the night out and will go away. *No, that won't work.* He owns the building. He knows the code to my garage door keypad. If he opens it and sees my car, he'll know I'm home and let himself in.

Laney's face lifts in a knowing smile. "Why do you want to hide me? Is it a *girl?*" Her voice teases. "You didn't tell me you had a girlfriend."

I have no time for this conversation, no time to explain. I need to get rid of her and answer that door before Father—

The sound of the garage door opening sends a white hot slash of fear through me. *Shit shit shit.* He'll be in the house in a matter of seconds. My eyes go wide as I stare down at Laney. I can't let him see her.

Bending over, I sweep an arm behind her knees and lift her off her feet, poised to carry her back to her room. She lets out a little squeak of surprise.

"Be quiet," I order in a low voice. "I'm taking you back to your room."

Rushing out of the kitchen, my gaze catches on the sight of her purse on the countertop, her sandals beneath one of the bar stools at the kitchen island. *Damn.* I can't grab her things while carrying her. I'll have to come back for them.

I hear the door open from the garage into the kitchen.

It's too late. I won't be going back for anything. I can't pretend Laney isn't here. There's only one thing to do now.

Instead of carrying her into her own room, I veer into the master suite, tossing her onto the large bed then spinning and shutting the door. I dive for the bed myself, pulling Laney roughly with me toward the pillows and yanking the top sheet over us.

Laney gasps. "*What* are you doing?"

My words come out rapid fire, low and urgent. "It's not a girl. It's my father. There's no time to explain. Just go along with whatever I do—your life depends on it."

Her expression morphs from surprise to fear.

The soles of Father's highly polished Oxfords echo down the hallway, sending my pulse into a new galloping rhythm. As I hear the bedroom door open, I dive for Laney's neck, covering it with kisses and pulling her tightly against my body. A groan rises in my throat, only partly for effect. It's as if my dream is continuing without my having to go back to sleep.

Knowing Father is watching, I let my hand glide down her side, over her hip as my mouth continues its explorations. Under the covers, her small hand clenches my shoulder, though I'm not sure if she means to stop me or encourage me.

Hmm hmm.

The loud throat-clearing noise is my signal to end the act. I lift my head, then sit up, my shirtless chest shielding Laney's face from Father's eyes. I feign surprise to see him.

"Father. What brings you round this morning?"

He strides into the bedroom, not the least bit concerned that he's apparently interrupted a very private moment. "I came to see if you are all right. I was told that no one saw you out last night at your usual haunts. After you missed your delivery yesterday, I was concerned about you."

He studies me, running his hard gray gaze over my unclothed form. Instead of looking concerned, he appears irritated. "You certainly seem well enough. What's going on?"

"Going on? Nothing. Well actually..." I give him a sheepish grin and nod at the still female form lying beside me. "I took a night off. I was... tired."

His eyes glitter with amusement. "Tired, are you? I guess I know why."

Though my father is a high-powered celebrity attorney, not a celebrity himself, he used to keep his own small fan pod of human girls before Nox ended the policy and the fan pod system was dismantled by Alfred Frey, the Elven talent agent who created it. I've heard Father complain several times in recent months over the inconvenience of having random women brought to his home and then glamouring them later to forget what had happened during the night rather than having a ready and willing harem at his beck and call as he used to.

He leans slightly to the side, obviously trying to catch a glimpse of my bedmate. Squinting, he smirks as if entertaining an indecent thought.

Oh God—he's probably considering sampling the goods himself. *No! No no no.* My heart does a triple backflip.

I have to get him out of here—away from her.

Pushing away the sheet, I roll from the bed and saunter toward him. "Let's talk in the kitchen. Have you eaten? Care for some tea?"

He allows me to herd him out of the room. I close the door behind me with a decisive click. Hopefully Laney will lock it and stay out of sight. She certainly seemed to get the message, but of course she didn't see the lecherous expression on his face as he perused the shape of her body beneath the thin bed sheet.

Reaching the living room area, he stops and turns to face me, his eyes piercing in their intensity. "Be careful that you do not go too far, my son. Your lovely neighbors may be our kind, but none of them is suitable to be your bond-mate."

"I know. Don't worry."

But he's not looking at me any longer. Something has caught his eye. He strolls across to the island, leans over, and draws Laney's sandals from beneath one of the stools. He dangles them from the fingertips of one hand.

"And if you have a human girl back there…" He holds up the sandals, perhaps gauging the small size of them. "Well, you're welcome to your amusements—I can hardly point fingers—but it goes without saying that you must use ultimate self-control. I have *plans* for you. There is a bright side to your failure with Ava. It *does* afford us the opportunity to make an alliance with one of the like-minded rulers in Europe or Asia. I am in discussion with several of them regarding their daughters. We'll need unbreakable ties if we're to stand together against Nox and his allies."

"Yes, Father. I understand. This girl is… a pleasant distraction. I would never bond myself to her permanently. She's not even that appealing—just someone who was in the right place when the mood struck me." I swallow hard then school my expression into something I hope resembles lustful satisfaction.

The grin on Father's face is a mixture of viciousness and pride. "Very well, I'll leave you to it. But see that your *revelries* don't go on too long and keep you from your duties. Our plan is working, but we have to keep at it." Flicking his gaze toward the bedroom, he adds silently, *We cannot let up until the entire human population is either dead or hopelessly addicted.* He winks. *Or safely ensconced in fan pods for our enjoyment.*

Father goes to the front door and flings it open, glancing back at me with a look that's not quite a warning, but close. "I'll check in with you soon."

"Yes Father."

The door shuts, and I let out a long breath, sagging against it and staring at the tiles beneath my feet as my pulse slows to its usual pace. *That was close.*

I'm not sure what I would have done if he'd decided not to leave the bedroom, but to investigate my "pleasant distraction" for himself. No doubt he'd consider a beautiful girl like Laney a perfect addition to some European celebrity's private harem—*after* he'd had his fun with her.

And if Father realized she was blind, he'd be even *more*

thrilled. Without the ability to see, it would be harder for her to get away. He probably would have boarded her onto the first plane out of L.A., wrapped in a red bow as a special gift for his Italian or French counterpart.

The thought turns my stomach. Laney is far too innocent, far too sweet to even be in the presence of those depraved egomaniacs, much less living with them and obeying whatever sick whim they might have.

Shaking my head to dislodge the disconcerting mental picture, I lift a hand to massage one pounding temple. I'm not sure what's wrong with me. I'm not acting like myself. I've never thought twice about the human girls kept as glamour-bound playthings in the fan pods. I've never worried about the people my father cheated or manipulated or hurt. I've never cared about the humans addicted and damaged, and yes, killed by the S drug. They weren't—aren't—my concern.

The certainty of impending calamity invades my gut. I feel like a character in a disaster movie, living out the scenes just before the big catastrophe strikes. My thoughts are all confused, my nerves stretched as thin as angel hair pasta.

Intending to go tell Laney the coast is clear—and bundle her onto the earliest departing jetliner—I spin around. She's standing behind me again.

"God," I gasp, clutching my chest and staggering back a step. "You've got to stop doing that. What if he was still here?"

"I heard him leave." She shrugs. "So… that was weird."

She's obviously waiting for an explanation, but what can

I say? "How much of our conversation did you hear?"

"Not much. But the way he acted… why did you lie to him about me? Why did you pretend we were… you know?"

I stiffen and close my eyes. How can I explain such a depraved mindset to a wide-eyed innocent?

"My father is not… a good man. I didn't want him to get a look at you. I thought if he believed we were… busy… he might turn around and come back later. As you heard, he is not that easy to get rid of."

"But *why*? Why would you try to protect me? You just met me."

"I… I don't know."

"At first I thought you wanted to hide me because you didn't want your dad getting the wrong idea about a girl staying over. I thought he had some sort of high moral standards or something, and you didn't want to disappoint him. But then… you took me to your room… to your bed. And when he came in… it sort of sounded like the opposite."

"Well, you're partially correct. He does have certain standards. High morals have nothing to do with them though."

Staring down at her innocent face, her clean, straight hair, her tiny toes inches away from my vastly larger feet, I feel a surge of protectiveness. "Let me buy you a plane ticket," I plead.

Her expression of curiosity morphs into annoyance. "If you're so eager to get rid of me, why did you ask me to stay at your place? Oh right—I was 'in the right place when the mood struck.' Don't worry. I'll be leaving in a few minutes. Just let me get my clothes on, and I'll be out of your way."

My hand shoots out to stop her from marching away in an offended huff. Wrapping my fingers around her upper arm, I'm amazed at the softness of her skin. She's so vulnerable. In every way. Though she denies it, she needs someone to watch out for her, to keep her safe. She cannot be allowed to wander this city alone.

"You don't understand. L.A. isn't safe for you."

She whirls around and tilts her jaw up in defiance. "Is this about me being blind? Because if it is—keep your pity. I don't want it, and I don't need it. I'm through hiding and cowering. I'm going to *live,* or what's the point of it all? Besides, it's as safe here for me as it is for anyone else."

But you're not anyone else. "Which, as things stand with the S Scourge, is not very safe at all." The thought of something happening to her, at my father's hands or any others, lights an angry fire in my gut. My voice level ratchets higher. "Now which will it be—airport, train station, or bus terminal?"

"None of the above," she fires back. "I told you—I'm starting work at the S clinic today. Nothing has changed."

How can she say that? I feel like *everything* has changed in the course of the past twenty-four hours. "Do you really think it will do any good?" I smirk. "The S Scourge is rampant now, not only here—all over the country. What do you think you're going to be able to do about it—one little person slaving away in one run-down clinic? What difference do you really think you can make?"

Her lips flatten in a stubborn line. "At least *I'm* not afraid to try."

For a moment, I'm too taken aback to respond. "I'm not afraid."

The tilt of her mouth is soft, sympathetic. "Culley, you're about the most fearful person I've ever met in my life. You're afraid of getting too involved with people around you, afraid of caring, afraid of being hurt."

"That's ridiculous. You're daft."

"Okay, fine. You're not afraid of anything. That makes two of us. I'm going to get dressed, and then if you won't point me to the nearest city bus stop, I'll knock on Brenna's door and ask if she will."

I heave a weary sigh. "No. That won't be necessary. I promised to drive you to the clinic, and I always keep my word."

The corners of Laney's mouth curve into a wry grin. "Really?" she asks. "Always?"

I hesitate before answering. Why did I make such an asinine and blatantly untrue statement? "Yes. Starting right now."

CHAPTER SEVEN
STAKEOUT

Pulling up in front of the S clinic in Chesterfield, I cringe at the surroundings. The squatty painted brick building sits across the street from a pink liquor store, a smoke shop, and a closed-up appliance parts store.

"Well... we're here."

"This had better not be the bus station," she warns.

"No. That would have been *smart*. Instead, I've brought a helpless girl to spend quality time with junkies in the worst neighborhood in the city—just as you asked."

"I am not helpless." She frowns in my direction. "Are you sure I look all right? I'm dressed appropriately?"

After Laney retreated to the guest suite to shower this morning, Brenna stopped by with a shopping bag full of clothes for her. "Hope she doesn't mind hand-me-downs," she said. "I couldn't believe it when I got your text last night. Who would steal a blind girl's suitcase?"

"I dunno. Thanks for this." I took the bag's handles from her, my bicep popping at the surprising weight of it.

Obviously noting my shocked expression, Brenna explained. "I have a little shopping problem. I was glad to clear out some closet space. I hope they'll fit her. She's so much shorter. But the stuff like dresses and skirts and shorts should be okay. I know my shoes won't fit her munchkin feet, though."

"No worries," I assured her. "She's got a pair of sandals. I'll buy her anything else she needs to replace what she lost."

Brenna cocked her head to one side and gave me a funny look. "Ooookaaay. Oh—I talked to someone who knows someone who might need a roommate. I'll find out more for you today."

"Great. Thanks. She can't stay here again."

"Why? Does she snore?" Brenna guffawed.

My response was stern. "No. But I like my privacy." *And I'm having sex dreams about her which will only get worse after what happened in my bed this morning.* "Best case scenario is she doesn't need an apartment at all. I'm hoping to convince her to go home."

Brenna flashed me a wide grin. "Good luck with that."

When I closed the door, I went through the bag and discarded anything skimpy or provocative. Brenna has a great figure, and she's not shy about showing it. I had no intention of letting Laney parade her assets around—especially with the people she'd likely be working with today.

"You look fine," I assure her now, surveying the modest

belted shirtdress that hangs down past her knees, then get out to go around and open her door. By the time I reach her, she's already opened it and exited the car. I take her arm and guide her to the entry of the clinic. Part of me feels like I should go in with her, but then I reconsider. The workers might have seen me around the neighborhood.

"Well, thank you for everything—the ride, and last night. I'm glad…" she pauses here as if she's not sure she wants to say what she started to say. "I'm glad the first person I met in L.A. was you."

"Yes well…" I'm at a shame-fueled loss for words. "Have a good day with the S zombies."

She rolls her eyes toward her brow, smiling, and turns away from me, pulling open the door of the clinic and disappearing inside.

Very slowly, I stroll back to my car. Sitting behind the wheel, my eyes follow a wasted looking man as he staggers up the sidewalk and into the clinic. My knuckles tighten around the leather covered gear shift.

A beep from my phone alerts me to a new message. Glancing down at the screen, I scroll through the texts I ignored last night and this morning. And slip it back into my console. I have a full schedule today. Tonight's even busier, thanks to all the stops I missed last night. I should get started on my deliveries.

All right then. I nod and grip the gear shift to put it into drive.

* * *

Five o'clock. That's late enough. Laney has not yet emerged from the building, and after eight hours of sitting in my car in this same spot, I'm starting to feel like a pressure cooker that's about to blow. I couldn't bring myself to leave.

My patience is at an end now, though. I'm tempted to march into the place and demand to know what's keeping her. I know she's still in there, though I haven't caught sight of Laney all day—thankfully she and her co-workers did not leave the building for lunch.

The thought of lunch unleashes a loud growl from my belly. I didn't think to bring any snacks with me, and it feels like my stomach is starting to eat itself. I glance at the clock on the dashboard again—5:05. *Where is she?*

The only thing worse than the hunger pangs is the unrelenting boredom. Every time some unsavory character walks down the street in front of the clinic, my muscles tense, but actually, it's been a very quiet day in the neighborhood. The most interesting thing to happen was several hours ago when some street punks—who apparently couldn't see me sitting behind the tinted glass of my windows—started removing my lug nuts in an apparent attempt to steal my tires.

I jumped out of the car and scared them off, putting a big helping of Sway into my instructions not to come back. At least I got some exercise. Swiping the ignore-call button on my phone doesn't really count. I finally had to turn it off, it was ringing and notifying me of texts so often.

Finally, Laney emerges from the door of the clinic, turning back to smile and wave at someone inside. I throw open my car door and approach her.

"Have a nice day at work?"

She jumps, her hand coming to the base of her throat. "Culley. You scared me. What are you doing here?"

"Picking you up after work." I take her other hand and tug her toward my car.

She stumbles along with me, babbling her protest. "You don't have to do that. I told you I'm fine. My co-workers gave me directions to the bus stop and some suggestions about where to look for a low-cost apartment."

"You won't be needing those suggestions. Brenna told me she's found a place for you." I throw the half-truth out there in a soothing I've-got-this tone, hoping she doesn't dig her little heels in and refuse to get into my car. "We're going to see her right now. She'll tell you all about it."

I open the car door and wait for her to take a seat, but she doesn't immediately. She stands there, a medley of thoughts parading across her face. "Fine, but you really didn't have to come back for me. You must have better things to do than babysit me."

"No, not at all," I say, powering my phone up again and wincing at the number of calls and texts I've missed. I *will* need to get Laney into an apartment and out of my condo soon. Now that Father's come by my place once—I know there's at least a slim chance he'll do it again. "So, what did you do all day?"

"Oh, I met so many people. The clinic director, Shane, let me be the greeter and pass out forms and do the intake interviews."

"Sounds wonderful."

"What did you do today?" she asks.

Sat in my car watching the clinic door. "Oh, this and that."

"You never told me what you do for a living."

Well, I'm a drug dealer and a lackey to my Dark Elf father who's plotting to take over the world and enslave all the humans.

"I'm a model."

"Ha ha." She nods her head side to side in a silly bobble head doll way. "What do you *really* do?"

I smile, tickled at her skepticism. "You don't believe me?"

"How many people in the world are *actually* models? It might work as a come on line for most girls, but I'm not buying it."

"All right. You got me. What do you *think* I do for a living?"

"Hmm… well, you came here from Australia, obviously. And I'd say you've also lived in England. So… you travel for your work."

"You have a good ear."

"That tends to happen when you lose one sense—you rely on your others more strongly. You also wear very expensive cologne and clothing," she continues compiling the clues.

"How can you tell about the clothes?"

"I felt the fabric yesterday, when you were leading me to your car. Also… your bedsheets are very nice."

She blushes deeply, making my grin grow even wider.

"All right then, Miss Detective. What's your best guess?"

"Your father has a sophisticated, rich-guy way of speaking, and he mentioned 'duty' when you two were talking, so I'm going to say he's the head of some company, and you work for him. Either that or you're some kind of socialite heir, and you don't work at all."

"You've just accused me of being a lazy, free-spending parasite. I think I'm insulted," I tease. "You're very close, actually. I do work for my father. He's the head of a big law firm, and I do a variety of things for him."

"He didn't sound Australian," she observes. "Why not?"

I breathe a sigh of relief. Out of all the questions she could have asked regarding my father, this is the simplest to answer.

"He's lived in lots of places over the years, but since my birth he's been here in America. My mother and I moved to Australia when I was a baby. I rarely saw him when I was growing up. More often lately. What about your parents? Are you close?" If I can get her talking about them, she might let a clue about their names or location slip.

"We are. Too close, if you ask me. Don't get me wrong—they're wonderful people. They love me. They've actually been there for me in every possible way. I can't say that about everyone. The blindness... well, not everyone has been able to handle it. Home has been sort of a sanctuary for me since my sight started failing. That was good at first. I think I needed some time to adjust emotionally. But lately the sanctuary has started to feel more like a prison."

"At least your parents care where you are and what you're doing." I try to keep the bitterness out of my voice but don't quite manage. Laney notices.

"And yours don't? Your father did come to check on you this morning."

"Not out of fatherly concern," I mutter.

"Right. He said something about a plan—in addition to duty."

"I thought you said you didn't really hear anything."

"I said 'not much.' I can't see people obviously, but I do have a pretty good sense about them. You said your father is not a good man, and from what I've heard, I'd have to agree. But you're so nice. How did that happen?"

Nice. I let out a single sardonic laugh. She may be the first person I've ever met who's labeled me as "nice."

"Listen, I don't really want to talk about my father, okay? We're not close. Actually I'm not close to either of my parents. Do you think yours are looking for you?"

"Probably. I left that note, but knowing them they're asking everyone I've ever met if they know where I've gone. I'll let them know when I'm settled. Speaking of that, you said Brenna has a lead on a place for me?"

I nod. "She told me she talked to someone who might need a new roommate."

Her shoulders sink against the seat. "Might."

"You'll find someplace—don't worry. Or… you could let me send you home."

"Why are you so determined to ship me back to—ooooh—you almost made me say it that time. What difference does it make to you whether I'm there or here?"

There are so many answers to that question. For one thing, *there* is far away from the epicenter of the S Scourge. *There* is where Laney's family is, eager and ready to take care of her and keep her out of trouble. *There*—is where my father and the Dark Elves like him are *not*.

"It doesn't make any difference to me," I lie. "I'm just putting it out there as an option."

"Well, no thank you. I haven't had quite enough California sun yet." She feels along the armrest, hits the button to lower the passenger side window, and sticks her arm out, letting it float on the current of air alongside the car.

"Or enough BFF time with drug addicts?"

"They're just like you and me, you know," she scolds. "Regular people. Only they made a bad choice, and now they're finding it hard to extricate themselves from the consequences."

I want to laugh. I'm all too familiar with bad choices— and their consequences. We pull into the condo's parking lot and my garage, entering the condo through the door to the kitchen.

"We're in your house," Laney says with apparent surprise.

"Yes. How'd you know?"

"It smells like you."

"Oh really. And how do I smell?"

"Like citrus, and amber, and fresh water. With a little bit of caramel."

I blink in surprise, my breath suddenly going shallow. "That was very... specific."

"I'm into fragrances. You said we were going to see Brenna." Her tone is suspicious.

"We are. Have some patience. Aren't you hungry?"

"No. I want to go see Brenna. I want to hear about the apartment."

"Fine. Come on then." I hold out my hand and she walks toward me, reaching out until our fingertips touch. Wrapping my fingers around hers, I steer her through the kitchen toward the front door and down the walk to Brenna's place. "Let me knock. *And* talk. She has guests, remember?"

"What do her guests have to do with anything? Oh— you mean we might be bothering her? Should we just call instead?"

"I don't like talking on the phone."

I ring Brenna's doorbell, and within moments the door pulls open.

"Oooh Culley. Ow are you?" The girl speaks with a strong French accent. I know I've met her before—in Manhattan I think it was—but I can't remember her name.

"Hello. Is Brenna in?"

"Culley, it's Estelle. Remember me? We met at Cielo in New York—a few months ago when you were betrothed to Ava. Remember?"

"Oh, yes, right." I glance to the side to see Laney's reaction. Her expression hasn't changed. "Good to see you again. You're visiting? Or are you staying here now?"

Her puffy lips pull together in a pout. "No. Unfortunately, I am only here for the week. Come in please. We can catch up."

She still hasn't acknowledged that I'm standing beside a girl. Hasn't even looked at Laney really. Which is probably for the best. If I want to keep Laney under my father's radar, I don't need to go introducing her all around the Dark Court. Brenna isn't into the whole political scene or the Council's plan to overthrow Nox and dominate the humans. I can't say the same for Estelle—I don't know her well enough.

"I can't stay, I'm afraid. I'll wait out here—just need to chat with Brenna for a minute."

The pout turns into a sullen sniff, and Estelle quirks her pretty pointed chin to the side indignantly. "Very well. I weel let er know that you are eere."

She spins on her heel and disappears down the entry hall. Inside, the sound of a TV turned up high mingles with other chattering voices. Brenna's visiting dancer friends, no doubt.

"You dated her?" Laney asks.

"No. I barely know her. Why?"

"Nothing. Just the sound of her voice." Laney pauses. "She likes you."

"Nah." I dismiss her assertion as Brenna walks toward us smiling.

"Oh Laney, that dress looks great on you! Did Culley tell you the good news?"

"Yes, I'm very excited," Laney says. "You have an

apartment possibility for me?"

Brenna grins. "Yes. I talked to one of my friends who has a place in Los Feliz. One of her three roommates is moving out at the end of the month. You could move in on the first and take her place. And you wouldn't even need a down payment. Plus—they allow pets."

Laney's face lights. "Oh wow. That's amazing. Thank you so much. Do you know how much my share of the rent would be? I need to figure out how much I'll have left over to pay for a hotel room until then." She touches the tips of her fingers to her thumb, doing mental math. "Let's see... that's five nights, so I'll need to divide it up—"

Brenna interrupts. "Hotel? Can't she stay with you? It's only a few more days. You have so many rooms over there, I was thinking of forking off some of *my* company on you." She laughs loudly. "Don't worry—I'm only kidding. I know how you *like your privacy*. But you and Laney managed just fine last night, didn't you?" She gives me a wink.

My mind immediately flashes to the scene this morning in my bed. "Fine" is not the word I'd choose. Though I've kissed my share of girls, and gone much farther with all of them than things went with Laney, nothing has ever affected me like those few minutes. The thought of spending another night alone with her—not to mention five more nights—has me tense and sweating.

"I'll pay for the hotel," I say. "Don't worry about that."

Laney's chin lifts into the air, and I know I'm in trouble. "No. Absolutely not. You've done too much already. I will not take your money." She doesn't stomp her foot, but she might as well.

"Look, be reasonable. As you pointed out earlier, money is not a problem for me. It's really no big deal."

"It is to me," she argues. "I won't take it. Point me to the street, and I'll go find a place on my own. If you force me into your car and take me to a fancy hotel and try to pay for it behind my back, I'll walk away as soon as you leave and let the room sit empty."

Shooting a beleaguered glance at Brenna, I roll my eyes. *I'm going to have to sway her.*

Or... you could respect her wishes and just let her go.

My eyes narrow in a stubborn glare. *Oh sure, let the little country bumpkin wander off to some cheap, bedbug-ridden motel within her "budget," which I'm sure will be in a **lovely** neighborhood. Shall I pin a "Mug me" sign to her back as well? Oh—and did I mention, she's BLIND?*

You don't have to shout, Brenna responds.

I'M NOT—Oh. I was shouting. I never do that. *Sorry.*

What is it with you and this human chick anyway? Brenna's eyes roam over Laney, assessing her head to toe. *I would never have guessed you'd be a sucker for the pure and innocent type.*

"I'm not!" I snap, unconsciously saying the words out loud. And shouting. Again.

"What?" Laney asks, jumping back a bit.

"I'm not," I repeat at a much lower volume. "... going to force you to take money. Of course not. But let me take you to a hotel—a decent one. You can pay me back later after you find a job."

85

"No."

I throw my hands up in aggravation. Ugh. This girl. She infuriates me and makes me sick with worry all at the same time.

Okay then, one serving of Sway coming up. I have no choice now. Lacing my words with the strongest Sway I can manage, I say, "Laney—you *will* stay at a hotel of my choosing until your apartment is ready to move in. And you'll like it."

For a few moments, she doesn't say anything. She stands, expressionless, blinking up at me.

Swayed.

Then she says, "*No.* I'm not sure which part of that word you don't understand, but it means, 'I will not.' Did anyone ever tell you, you are super bossy?"

Shocked, I glance at Brenna's equally wide-eyed face. *It didn't work. My Sway didn't work.*

She shakes her head, clearly baffled. *Maybe it only works if they can see your eyes?*

I don't know. What now?

Now, Brenna says with a smirk, *You ask nicely.*

"Um…" I begin. "Yeah. I may have heard that a time or two. Listen, Laney… you're right. I have been a little bossy… but it's only because I'm concerned about you. You know that, right?"

She makes a noise that sounds kind of like *hmmph,* clearly unimpressed.

"Please. Please just stay at my place until your apartment opens up. It's silly not to. As Brenna said, I have plenty of room. I'm gone all day and out most every night." I grimace. "I'll hardly even notice you're there."

What a lie. If I become any more aware of her presence, I'll be a stalker.

Indecision coats her face. "I don't know. I've put you out too much already."

"Five nights in even a cheap hotel will put a serious dent into your cash supply. You know your way around my place already. Cupcake loves it there. Brenna's right next door in case you have questions about… girl stuff or whatever. I'm tired. You must be tired. Let's just go home—I mean to my place— and order some dinner, open up the windows and let the breeze in…" I'm casting around for anything I can think of to entice her. "There's more Chunky Monkey in the freezer."

"Hey! You told me you were out of ice cream, you big liar," Brenna says.

Laney laughs out loud, and my heart leaps with hope.

She bites her lip, twisting her mouth to one side as she considers it. Then she smiles. "Well… since you asked so *nicely*, I would be happy to accept your invitation. You're right. Financially, it's the smartest thing to do. And I do like Chunky Monkey."

"Well, all right then…" Trying to restrain myself from jumping up and doing a fist pump, I place a hand on Laney's shoulder and steer her back toward my own front door.

"I'll ask how much your share of the rent will be," Brenna calls after us. For me alone she adds, *Have fun. But not too much fun—not unless you're in the market for a Mrs. Culley Rune.* I can almost hear the wink.

Chapter Eight
Adult Experiences

In my whole life, I could probably count on one hand the number of times I've been nervous. This is one of them.

Leading Laney back into my condo, I am jumpy, my skin ultra-sensitive, all my senses heightened as if there's a threat nearby. But there is none. There's just a small human girl who can't even see me, for God's sake. *What is my problem?*

"So, what sounds good for delivery tonight? Want to try some Mexican this time? Italian?"

She stops walking and faces me, a hopeful smile on her face. "Maybe we could go out somewhere? A restaurant near the ocean, with outdoor seating? My treat—I can never repay you for all you've done for me. But I can buy you a nice dinner."

"We can't go out," I blurt.

Every time I'm out in the city, someone takes a picture

88

of me. Often it's a paparazzi. Normally I don't mind all that much—it's good for my modeling career. But I can't be photographed with Laney—can't take the chance my father will see the pics and the asinine captions that are bound to accompany them—New Lady Love for Culley Rune? Who is the Mystery Woman on Culley's Arm?

Her forehead wrinkles in concern. Or maybe disappointment. "Why not?"

"You're tired. It's been a long day. And there'll be a long wait at anyplace we go."

The furrow deepens. "I already said I'm not that tired. Working today actually energized me. It was good to feel useful again, to be treated like an adult. And I don't mind waiting. I want to experience the city a little bit." She pauses. "What's the real reason? Do you not want to be seen with me? Is there something wrong with the way I look?"

"No. Of course not. You're beaut—I mean—you look fine. It's just…" *Being seen in public with me could put your life in danger.* "… it's been a long day for *me*. I'd really rather stay in. If you don't mind. And poor Cupcake has been alone all day. We can't leave him."

"Oh. Of course. That's fine."

Her crestfallen expression makes me want to take it all back and put her in the car to head for Curtis Stone's hard-to-book Gwen restaurant on Sunset Boulevard. Then I get an idea.

"How about this? Why don't we order in from Gwen? Ever heard of it?"

"Of course. It's famous—the chef is on TV. Won't that be expensive?"

"Not so much—I'll select some menu items that are on the lower end of the price scale." Which doesn't really exist since a meal for two there runs about two hundred bucks. "Sound good?"

She lifts her narrow shoulders and lets them fall. "Okay. You'll have to read the menu to me."

I guide her to a chair in my living room and go to my desk where my laptop sits open. Calling up the Gwen's website, I give her the choices—and the prices—subtracting a healthy amount from the real number of course. I also neglect to mention the exorbitant delivery fee I'll be paying to get that gourmet food all the way from Sunset out to Malibu.

"I would have thought that place would be so much more expensive," Laney says. "It all sounds so good. I think I'll have the handmade Orecchiette pasta and the dry aged rib steak. What about you?"

"Same. I'll make the call. Want to wait for it out on the deck? We can do our own seaside dining. I'll bring out some drinks in a minute."

She stands, and I cross the room to take her arm and lead her to the back door. When she feels my touch, she pulls her arm away with a smile.

"It's okay. I don't need your help. I know the way."

Blinking in surprise, I withdraw my hand. "You do?"

Laney strides confidently to the door and puts her hand on the handle. Turning back toward me she says, "Don't be so surprised. I told you—I'm fine on my own. I'm also used to being underestimated. *That's* why I didn't tell my parents where I was going. *They* don't believe in my abilities either." Then she opens the door and walks out onto the deck, closing it behind her.

"What a bloody little fool," I say to the empty room. She might have learned her way around my condo quickly and managed to navigate the S clinic today, but she's still nowhere ready to live on her own in a place like L.A.

When I call the restaurant I give them not only my address, but my credit card number to pay for the food—and explicit instructions about what the driver should say when he comes to the door. When there's a big enough tip in it for them, the hopeful actors and starving artists who work those kinds of jobs are willing to go along with almost anything.

Then I hang up the phone, pour a glass of tea for Laney and grab a beer for myself, and head out to the deck. When I sit down opposite her, I am contrite.

"I'm sorry I've been treating you like you're helpless. I can see that you're not. You are, however, short on funds. So I'm glad you agreed to let me help you out with a place to stay for a few days."

Laney's tone is conciliatory as well. "I'm sorry I snapped at you. I'm probably over-sensitive about my disability—it's still pretty new, you know?"

"Understandable," I say, taking a long pull from my bottle.

"I wasn't wrong about one thing though—you really don't want to be seen in public with me. Is it because of Ava?"

The beer in my mouth goes down the wrong pipe, and I choke, coughing to clear my airway. "What?" I cough again. "Why would you ask that?"

"Estelle mentioned you were engaged before—to a girl named Ava. Actually she said 'betrothed.' I'm guessing she hasn't been in the country long, though I have to say her English is a whole lot better than my French." She smiles. "Do you not want word to get back to Ava—that you're out with another girl? Are you hoping for a reconciliation or something?"

Frowning at the tide rolling onto the nearby shore, I answer honestly. "No. There is no chance of that. She's with another guy. They're deliriously happy I guess."

"I'm sorry. You must have loved her very much."

No, actually. I don't believe in love. "I don't really want to discuss it. What about you? Anyone special waiting back on the ranch?"

She laughs. "I don't live on a ranch—nice try." Her tone turns wistful. "No, there's no one. There was once. Brandon. My first love. We dated for most of high school. But he broke up with me when it became apparent I'd be permanently disabled. He just wasn't up for that kind of responsibility. I don't blame him. What high school guy would sign up for that? Even most older guys would take a pass."

She pauses. "So, you must be older than I first thought. Your voice and the feel of your skin made me think you were around my age. But you were engaged already, so..."

"I'm nineteen." I answer her unspoken question but

there's no way I can explain to her that I'm actually a year *older* than the majority of my people when we typically select a bond-mate.

Bonding age in the Elven world is eighteen. That's when the powerful drive to bond kicks in, and it becomes almost physically painful to deny it. Of course we can't bond with just anyone to satisfy the need. We only get one shot at it— one partner for a lifetime. For us that means eternity.

Needless to say I walk around daily with a *considerable* amount of discomfort. A stiff breeze and I'm pretty much ready to go. I've even started turning down bookings for swimsuit and underwear ads lately. The ad agency would be getting a lot more than they bargained for in those photographs.

"What about you?" I ask.

"I'm eighteen. Old enough to vote and run away to California. Not old enough to buy beer. You've obviously found a way around that. You've got a fake I.D.?"

"Something like that." I chuckle. "I look older than I am." *Plus I'm rich and famous and have the ability to sway anyone I choose—except for you.* "I think I hear the doorbell. If you'll excuse me, I'll go get our food. We can eat out here if you'd like. There's a table."

She pops out of her chair. "Oh no you don't. I'm paying for this."

"Right. I know. Well come on then, moneybags. Buy me some dinner."

The delivery man performs flawlessly, sticking to our agreed upon script. "That'll be forty dollars."

Laney hands me her purse. "Take out fifty please and give it to him."

"You're the boss." Handing two twenties and a ten to the man, I say with a wink, "Here you go mate. Don't spend that tip in one place."

With the actual price of the meal and the delivery cost, fifty dollars isn't an outrageous tip—it's about right. The restaurant agreed to put the cost of the meal itself on my card, which of course Laney doesn't know.

I feel bad allowing her to spend even fifty dollars of her precious little cash on this meal, but I'm also starting to feel bad about the way I've been taking advantage of her blindness to deceive her about things like money, even if it was done in the name of protecting her.

We eat our supper on the deck. It's a beautiful night, and the food's amazing. But I'm finding it hard to concentrate on anything other than Laney's face. She makes this blissed out expression when she tastes something good, and her whole face lights up as she talks, telling me about her bus trip to Los Angeles and the people she met at the clinic. Things get a bit less entertaining when she starts quizzing me about my life.

"Tell me about your family."

I clear my throat, experiencing a sudden flood of awkwardness. I don't usually feel awkward. Then again, I don't usually talk about myself.

"Well, I've already told you my parents are separated. My father has lived here all my life. I grew up in Australia with my mum. At least until I was thirteen and I went off to boarding school."

"What's your mom like?"

"Um… I don't know. Busy. She has a pretty important job, and it takes a lot of her time. She travels a lot."

Laney's smile decreases by about seventy-five percent. "Oh. What does she do?"

Well, you see, she's the ruler of the Dark Elves in Australia. "She… runs a company."

"Wow. Your parents are pretty impressive. My dad's a pharmacist, and my mother is a stay-at-home mom."

"That sounds nice, actually."

It sounds more than nice. I can't even count the number of times I wished my mom was actually at home—when I had a problem at school, or had a question I was too embarrassed to ask anyone else, when I just needed to talk.

On the upside, I became very good at solving my own problems. Maybe a downside was that I learned to just *not* talk—about anything of importance anyway. But really, who wants to hear all my crap? At least I never got into the bad habit of counting on anyone else. When you rely on yourself, no one can ever disappoint you.

"You don't have any siblings?" she asks.

"No. Just me."

"Sounds lonely."

I don't like the note of sympathy in her voice. I don't need it and definitely don't want it. And I don't want to talk anymore. It's too early to go to bed. *What the hell am I going to do with her all evening that doesn't involve talking?* In answer to my own question, a racy image flashes through my brain, and I quickly tamp it back down.

"Want to watch a movie?" I suggest, then immediately backtrack. "Oh God. I'm sorry."

"Why? I love movies. Do you have some or should we stream something?"

Relaxing again after what I thought was a fatal faux pas, I say, "Whatever you want. If you have any favorites, we could download one of those, or we can search for something neither of us has seen."

"Have you ever watched the *Lord of the Rings* movies? Those are my all-time favorites."

I laugh inwardly. She *would* want to watch a film about Elves. "No. I've never seen them. It's early yet—we could have a movie marathon and maybe see all three." *And not have to talk anymore at all.*

"Well, I don't think three is possible in one night. They're pretty long. But we could watch them all this week. The Hobbit, too. I don't love that one as much, but it's still good."

I locate the first movie, and we settle in, each of us at opposite ends of my leather sofa. Laney curls her legs under her and hugs a throw pillow, bouncing a little as the opening strains of the movie's score begin.

She smiles widely. "I'm so thankful these came out before I lost most of my sight. I watched them so many times I can still see the scenes now in my mind. Trust me, you will love this."

She's right—the film is well done and quite enjoyable. I've avoided watching them or even reading the book series because I anticipated rolling my eyes at the inaccuracies of the scenes involving Elves. But when the Hobbits arrive at Rivendell, my breath is taken away at the similarities between the Elves there and the Light Elves who live in Altum.

Of course real Elves don't have pointed ears, but the tranquil elegance of them, the ancient way of life that still exists there in the underground kingdom is very similar to the movie director's portrayal. If the movie is true to the books, then Mr. Tolkien was a very clever fellow. Makes me wonder if perhaps he actually even met one of our kind at some point in his life.

Though the film is good, I'm fighting the same compulsion I did during dinner. My gaze is constantly drawn away from the screen to Laney. She's so into the movie, reacting to the dialogue and music, and perhaps the images painted by her mind. Her expressions are fascinating, and entertaining, and... adorable. She's a beautiful girl.

Cupcake is curled in her lap, purring as she strokes his fur. Lucky bastard. I'd be purring, too if those pretty fingers were petting me in that gentle, rhythmic way.

By the time the fellowship of friends reaches Lothlorien, I realize I've unconsciously moved closer to Laney on the sofa. Her bare toes are nearly touching my leg, and I feel the most powerful urge to reach down and touch them, to wrap my fingers around her dainty ankle. And then I picture sliding that hand up her calf, past her knee...

"Did you like it?" Her voice shocks me out of my dangerous thoughts, and I realize the movie has ended.

"Oh. Yes. It was very good—better than I expected."

"I told you." She beams. "There are some movies, like love stories, that I don't want to watch again and again, but I can never see these enough."

"You don't like love stories? I thought most girls were into chick flicks."

"Oh—well, I *do* like them, but you know… they kind of just make me sad now."

"I see," I say, though I actually don't. "Because of your ex-boyfriend? Brandon?"

She wrinkles her nose at the sound of his name. "No. Not exactly."

There's a long exhale as she seems to consider what to say—or how much. "After I lost most of my sight, I went through this long period of time where I sort of withdrew from the world. All I did was watch those movies. And cry. And mourn the loss of my love life."

She lets out a small laugh that sounds more sad than happy. "I was living vicariously through movies and books. But now… I feel like I've turned a corner or something. I don't want to just live through fictional characters—I want a *real* life—of my own. I want to live life *fully*, you know? To go places and meet people and experience things, to taste all life has to offer. I was sixteen when I was declared legally blind. It was like my life was arrested in childhood. But now I'm an adult. I want to *live* like an adult, have all the experiences adults have."

"I understand."

I sound so wise, so caring. But actually I'm a total heel

because as soon as she mentioned "adult experiences" my mind went there—you know, *there*. I shift uncomfortably, rearranging my pants to accommodate the natural end result of those thoughts.

Laney continues. "That's why I had to leave home. If I hadn't left to come here and help at the clinic, it would have been somewhere else. There are so many things I've never gotten to do. I mean, I've never even driven a car. I've never rollerbladed, never been to a karaoke bar."

I laugh out loud. "You're not missing anything there, sweet."

"You've done Karaoke?"

"Me? God no. I can't carry a tune in a backhoe."

"I don't believe that. You've got a great voice—I love listening to it. I'd like to sing a duet with you."

Hearing her say that about me causes my heart to flip, and I'm filled with a warm, buzzing sensation, as if I've swallowed a whole hive of happy little honeybees.

"Don't hold your breath for that one. As for roller blading—I've never done that, either. Sliding around out of control and busting my tailbone is not my idea of a good time."

"Well, maybe not, but the point is, I want to try it all for myself—to challenge myself and do things I've never done—that no one thinks I'm ready for. I've never tasted champagne. I've never been skinny-dipping. I'm still a virgin, for goodness sake—I'm probably the only one in L.A."

"Not quite the *only* one," I assure her. I stop short of

admitting that I'm a virgin myself, though *goodness* has nothing to do with the reason why. She'd probably never believe it anyway.

Laney doesn't seem to hear me, going on with her impassioned story. "When Brandon came over to give me the 'Dear Laney' speech, we went to my room to talk. He was stammering and clearing his throat as he started making his case, and I could sense what was coming. I... well, I felt desperate. I'd lost so much already that the thought of losing him too was overwhelming. I begged him not to break up with me."

She rolls her eyes. "Because *that* always works so well. Nothing more attractive than a weeping, desperate girl." Her sarcastic amusement dissipates as she goes on in a more subdued tone. "I offered him the opportunity to, you know—go all the way. We'd been kind of working up to it for a while."

Mesmerized, I watch the pulse beating in the side of Laney's smooth neck, the blush that pinkens her cheeks over the intimate subject matter, the way her fingers smooth over the surface of her nails again and again.

"He turned me down," she says. "He said he couldn't 'do it with a blind girl.' And then he left."

She stops there, and the room is silent except for our breathing. I realize I've drawn even nearer to her. Our faces are close now, mine hovering just over hers.

My voice is low and scratchy when I reply. "Well, he's obviously a total twit. Any rational guy would count himself damn lucky to get a chance to be with you."

Her response to my words is unexpected. She surges upward, bringing her mouth into contact with mine.

At first I'm in shock. The feel of her soft, warm lips, the sweetly seductive movements of her tongue, the heady peachy-vanilla scent surrounding me—all of it is setting off small explosions throughout my body and over the surface of my skin. Then my mind goes blank, and the stroke of my tongue matches hers. My body is getting with the program, eager for more contact with her soft skin, with the little hand that is moving from my shoulder to my side to my abdomen, leaving a trail of fire.

I hadn't planned on kissing Laney—not now—not ever. But now that it's happening, it's the most exciting, most erotic thing that's ever happened to me. I feel like there's a wild animal inside of me lunging against the restraint of a collar and chains, roaring in demand to be set free.

As my arms wrap around her and pull her onto my lap, the beast roars in a new way—a sound of satisfaction blended with even more demand. Laney is making the sweetest, sexiest little noises I've ever heard in my life, squirming in my lap and kissing me with near desperation.

Without my permission, my hand moves to the front of her dress, making quick work of the top two buttons and greedily slipping inside—and then I stop.

What the hell do I think I'm doing?

Where do I think this is going to lead? I know where—right down the hallway to that oversized bed of mine. And I can't take her there. I can't take anyone there—not unless I want to be bonded to them for eternity—and that means

Laney shouldn't be anywhere near my bedroom. Or near me.

Withdrawing the hand as if burned, I slide Laney from my lap and get off the couch, standing beside it and breathing in long, winded pulls. She looks like a kid who's just fallen from the merry go round—dizzy and dazed—and not too happy.

"What happened?" She blinks in confusion and turns her head side to side, perhaps listening to see whether someone else has entered the room.

Her unbuttoned dress gapes at the top to reveal a satiny pink bra. I close my eyes and spin away, my body throbbing in frustrated fury at me.

"Button your dress," I bark at her, my voice coming out much harsher than I intended. Everything in me is amped up at the moment, and my vocal chords are only the least of it.

Glancing back over my shoulder, I watch Laney doing the buttons, her kiss-swollen lips forming a pout. Her hair is mussed and beautiful, and the bottom of her dress is disarranged and pushed up to the tops of her thighs.

Oh God. I have to turn away again. I need to get out of here, or I'm going to be back on that couch, running my greedy hands over that beautiful body. Or worse—scooping her up and carrying her down the hallway to my room. The mental image is so compelling, I literally cringe with the pain of not acting on it.

"I have to go," I growl. "It's late. You should go to bed—don't wait up for me."

Several long strides take me to the back door. I fling myself outside and literally leap off the deck instead of taking the stairs. Breaking into a run, I head down the beach and away from the savage temptation that even now calls to me and tells me to return to her and finish what I started.

Chapter Nine
Look Inside

The brisk Pacific breeze is at least moderately effective at cooling me off, and the impromptu run down the shoreline has taken the edge off the unspent energy charging through my body. Now all I need is an ice cold shower, and I might—*might* manage to fall asleep tonight.

When I get back to the condo, I see a light still on. *Damn it.* Of course, it's possible she followed my order to go to bed and left the light on for me, but not wanting to take the chance, I don't go inside. Instead, I keep walking toward Brenna's deck. There's a candle burning on the outdoor table, and faint music comes from inside.

"Hey there, neighbor. Getting some air?"

I smile at the sound of Brenna's voice and the dark silhouette of her form sitting in one of the deck chairs. "Yes, you could say that."

"You're welcome to join me. I'm taking a break for a

minute from all the craziness inside. Remind me never to have forty-five hundred houseguests again, okay? Of course, you're welcome to join them if you'd rather. There's a pretty entertaining game of charades going on in there."

I ascend the steps and drop into a chair next to her. "No thanks. Crowds aren't really my thing."

"That sounds pretty funny coming from a guy who spends all his nights in dance clubs and bars."

"Yeah well, work is work."

"Did you work tonight?" she asks.

"Nah." I nod toward my place. "Didn't think it would be right to leave my 'houseguest' alone."

"You like her, huh?"

"No. It's not like that. She's human. And... well you know."

"Ava's with a human."

I snort a laugh. "Thanks for the reminder." Standing up, I say, "You know, I think I will join the party. I could use a drink."

Brenna slides from her chair and walks to the door, opening it and letting the sounds of raucous laughter and clinking glasses out into the night. "Me, too. Maybe it'll help me forget that I've got two more weeks of *this* ahead of me."

Laughing, we step inside together. I help myself to the bar and lean against it as the next performer takes the floor. Two horrendous pantomimes and another drink later, I'm about ready to call it a night and slip back into my own condo when Brenna approaches me, her cell phone in hand.

"It's Ava."

I let out a weary breath and take the phone, bringing it to my ear with a surly, "What is it?"

"How are you Culley?"

"Lovely. What's going on Ava?"

"Brenna told me you've been helping that human girl—and she's staying at your place. Do you have feelings for her?"

"Of course not—not that it's any of your business."

"It would be completely natural if you did, you know. You're nineteen. Remember in New York when you told me all you could think about was kissing me? Well, I think that was not really about *me*. It was about being ready for a monogamous relationship, ready to bond. It's time, Culley. All you need is to find the right girl."

"Yes, well, thank you Oprah, but I'm not really in the mood for relationship advice from the girl who dumped me—"

"Are you sure she's fully human? She's not part-Elven or something?"

"What? No. She's tiny. She's *blind*. Why would you ask that?"

"Well, if you're attracted to her, I thought maybe... okay, well, here's why I wanted to talk to you." She takes a breath, and there's a long pause. "Asher is half Elven."

My heart jumps into my throat. "What? How is that possible?"

"We just recently figured it out. He's not susceptible to my glamour, which I always thought was weird, and I think he looks Elven, but after hearing about how Asher's mom met his dad—and what he was like—the pieces connected. They were never married. She had a brief love affair with him when she was eighteen and got pregnant. And get this—I think he's a Dark Elf."

"Do you know who he is?"

"No—all we have is a first name—Hagen."

"That's extremely common. I know at least six Hagens. It means 'firstborn son.'"

"I know," she says. "It doesn't help much. She met him when he was passing through her family's property on his way to Altum for the Assemblage almost twenty years ago. She thought she loved him. I'm not sure if she was swayed or not. Since then, he's been in and out of Asher's life, seeing him only a few days a year—always here in Mississippi, never at his own home. He claims he's always moving around so Asher can't come visit him. He *must* be in the Dark Court. He knows he'd be punished for bonding with a human."

"How does Hagen get past the iron barrier at the farm?"

"He doesn't. He always has Asher meet him somewhere else, and they talk and have lunch or supper at a restaurant."

"He never told Asher?"

"No, but he's been trying for a while to get Asher to leave the farm, to move away from Mississippi. I think he wants more of a relationship with him. We're trying to find him. If he is in the Dark Court, he could be an ally for us in the battle against the S Scourge. He obviously doesn't hate humans if he bonded himself to one—and he must care about his son or he wouldn't bother visiting him." She pauses. "We need all the help we can get. Of course you know we'd love to have yours."

"I've already told you—"

"I know what you said. But you're going out of your way to help a human girl when there's nothing in it for you. I don't think you want to see them all destroyed."

"I don't really care what you think."

"Culley. All I'm asking is that you think about it. Look inside your heart. About helping us—and about Laney."

Suddenly my skin is broiling. My head feels like it's going to pop off my neck like some kind of pressurized cork.

"I've got to go. Don't ask Brenna to put me on the phone again, okay? If I want to talk to you, I'll call." I hang up the phone and leave it on the counter, heading for the door. I might need another midnight run on the beach.

A couple hours and a shower later, I'm still thinking of Ava's words. *Look inside my heart.*

I don't know about my heart, but my hand is on the doorknob to Laney's bedroom, and my mind is spinning between two opposite points.

One side is telling me to put my idiot arse in the bed and get some sleep. The other feels like it's possessed by a powerful sorcerer, impelling me to turn that knob and open her door. I just want a quick look at her. I won't wake her. I need to make sure she's okay, that she's comfortable, and that she's still *there* after the rude way I pushed her away and left her earlier tonight.

The sorcerer wins, and I enter the bedroom, taking care

to make no noise, drawing close to the bed in the darkness. The sound of Laney's slow, even breathing assures me she is in fact there and she didn't hear the door open. She's left her drapes open, and moonlight streams in, illuminating the shape of her body under the thin coverlet. One of her little bare feet sticks out of the covers, tempting me as always.

Cupcake is curled into a furry ball on her pillow. He's doing a terrible job of guarding his mistress. Instead he's completely zonked out, looking content and happy to be near her, the lucky bugger.

Laney's face is peaceful, serene. The moonlight gilds her smooth cheek until it resembles white silk. I want to reach out and stroke her skin with a fingertip, to feel that softness and gain some of that innocence for myself through osmosis. As she dreams, the corners of her mouth turn up in a sweet smile, and I find that I'm smiling in response.

I've never seen anything more beautiful than this girl— this foolish, trusting girl who doesn't know any better than to fall into a deep sleep and leave her doors unlocked in the house of a monster. It's like the tale of *Beauty and the Beast* come to life, only the beast is a male model—his ugliness is hidden on the inside where it can't do the very necessary job of warning people away from danger.

I need to send her away. It's the only way to save her. Keeping her here within my reach is the cruelest, most selfish thing I've ever done. Though I've pretended to fight it every step of the way, I suspect that in some secret place deep inside, I wanted it. The worst part is—I think she wanted it, too. I think she's starting to like me.

God, I hope not.

My gut does a weird fluttering thing at the possibility. Getting on my knees, I kneel beside the bed and study her face—for what? Clues to her dreams? Tear tracks?

What did she think after I stopped our kiss so abruptly and left the condo? *Did* she cry? Did she get angry and vow to pack her bags and leave at daybreak? The thought causes my blood to race with a mixture of fear and relief. It would be much better if she *isn't* attracted to me, if she hates me now. I won't really know until morning.

If she does, we can just keep our distance over the next few days in the condo and go about our separate lives until her new place is ready for her to move in. Simple. Sensible. *Miserable.* But that won't solve the bigger problem here—she's not safe in this city. Eventually I'm going to have to get back to work, and I won't be able to watch over her every minute. There's no end to the trouble she could wander into.

The only truly safe place for her is back home. And there may be only one way to convince her to go. Ava's plea pops back into my head. *We need all the help we can get.*

It's crazy. It's terrifying. But I may have no other choice.

If I were to help Ava and her friends stop the S Scourge—stop my father from eradicating most of the human population and subjugating the rest—there would be no more reason for Laney to remain here in Los Angeles. She'd go back home—voluntarily—and she'd be safe. I could go back to my normal life.

Laney stirs in her sleep and murmurs something that

sounds like, "I need you."

Heart thrashing, I rise to my feet and back slowly away from the bed. Who is she talking about? Dreaming about? Her idiotic ex-boyfriend? Her parents?

Me?

The stupid exhilaration the idea sparks in my heart drives me to take action. I ease the bedroom door open, slip out into the hallway, and close it again. Getting my phone out of my pocket, I hit a contact button I haven't used in a long time.

The surprised-sounding feminine voice answers. "Culley?"

"All right, Ava—what do you need me to do?"

Chapter Ten
Morning Person

The next morning my hearing is on high alert for sounds of Laney rising and getting ready for the day.

She must have set an alarm or something because the shower turns on shortly after seven o'clock. Feeling like I haven't slept at all myself, I pop out of the bed and out of my room, heading for the kitchen. I'm prepared for any sort of mood from her this morning—irritation, annoyance, sullen silence, outright hostility. In the past, girls have reacted rather badly to me rejecting them. Maybe a fresh cup of coffee and a hot breakfast will smooth things over a bit and at least keep things civil between us.

Naturally, I'll offer to drive her to the clinic again. I know enough about her stubborn nature by now to realize she'll go there even without my help, whether it requires a bus, a cab, or even hitchhiking. A shudder passes through me. A cold-shouldered thirty minute drive of silence is nothing compared to the horrors of what *could* happen.

Laney's bedroom door opens as I'm spooning scrambled eggs onto a plate for her. It's one of the few things I know how to cook. Ordering takeout is my finest culinary skill. I could have servants if I want them—a chef, a maid—but preferring privacy to convenience, I've declined so far.

Adding a piece of toast, I set the plate onto a placemat before one of the stools and turn to pour coffee into a mug.

"Good morning!" Laney's bright, cheerful voice is nearly a song. It's so startling, I spin around and slosh hot coffee out of the full mug onto my hand.

"Ow. Shit," I yell then hastily add, "Good morning."

She laughs. Her face is clear and happy, her smile wide and genuine. "That's a strange greeting. Are you okay?"

"Yeah. I'm all right. Just a spill." I grab a towel, mopping up the floor, and turn on the cold water to run over my hand. I give her an assessing glance. "How did you sleep?"

"Wonderfully. Mmmm… I smell coffee. And toast?"

"Yes, I whipped up a little breakfast." Squinting, I search her face for signs of hurt, anger, falseness or at least some missed sleep or late night tears. No, the cheer seems to be real. *What the hell? Did last night have no effect on her at all?*

"Thank you. I'm starved," she says, feeling for and sliding onto the stool at the counter. "I want to give you some grocery money, okay? I can't stay here and not at least help with expenses."

"Oh yes—you're going to eat me out of house and home." I snort. "It's a few meals, sweet. It's not going to break the bank. Okay, coffee's on your right. Want anything in it?"

"Some artificial sweetener. And milk if you have it. I know you're Mr. Made-of-Money and you don't need my contribution, but I want to do it anyway—for my sake—not for yours."

Remembering the things she'd told me about how eager she was to start living as an adult and not be taken care of like a child, I say no more about it, changing the subject instead.

"So, I assume you'll want to go to the clinic again today?"

"Yes." She smiles. "But I don't need you to take me there. I downloaded an app last night called Nearby Explorer. It tells me where all the mass transit locations are and gives me walking directions to get there. So you see—I can take care of myself."

My head snaps back in shock. "Oh."

I haven't seen her use a phone yet. I sort of assumed she didn't have one because how could you dial or text on a screen you couldn't see? She must keep it in a pocket or that ever-present purse of hers. If I'd known about that earlier, I'd have snatched the device and searched it for her contact information already.

"How did you download it?"

She rolls her eyes and gives me a tolerant smile. "The same way everyone does silly. From an app store. But I use the voiceover feature with my phone to tell it what I'm looking for or what to do instead of typing it in like I used to do."

"Oh," I say again, feeling supremely stupid for not

realizing she'd be using adaptive technology. "Well, you won't need the... Explorer or whatever to get to work today. I'm going that way anyway on my way to work, so it's no trouble to drop you off."

She tilts her chin, tensing her forehead in the way someone does when they're not sure you've told them the facts. Finally, she says, "Okay. If you don't mind. But this is the last time. Tomorrow, I'm going to get myself there."

Tomorrow, I'll have already gone through your phone and notified your parents of your whereabouts.

"Very good. Well, what do you say we leave here in an hour?"

I have no intention of dropping her off and leaving her there unsupervised. Just as I did yesterday, I plan to stay outside the clinic all day and wait for her. Laney agrees, and we start the drive from my posh neighborhood to the clinic.

I'm still baffled at her attitude this morning. It's as if she doesn't care at all about my bizarre broiling-hot-then-ice-cold behavior last night. Maybe the kiss didn't affect her as much as it did me? She did say she had a serious boyfriend before and they'd been working up to "going all the way." Maybe his carnal skills were a lot more developed than mine.

Maybe she doesn't like me as much as I thought she did.

"Would you describe the scenery to me?"

Her question yanks me out of my brooding thoughts. "You want to know what I see?"

"Yes please. I've made this trip several times now, and it would be nice to know what's between here and there. I am sort of a tourist after all."

"Well, you're pretty far from the touristy areas right now. You know I live in Malibu. From there we drove through Pacific Palisades and Santa Monica on the way to I-10. Those areas are pretty nice—ocean views, wide streets, lots of green spaces, shops, and restaurants, and big homes. From the highway you can't see much that's interesting. Just a lot of buildings and cars. Off in the distance are the San Gabriel Mountains. You can't always see them, but today's not too hazy." I hum a low laugh in my throat. "I don't usually see them even when it's clear. I'm so used to them being there."

"Sounds pretty. We don't have so much as a big hill where I live, much less any mountains. I wish I'd come to California years ago."

Glancing away from the road to take in Laney's face, my heart tugs at the forlorn expression she wears. As we exit the highway, I renew my efforts to describe the surroundings for her. Unfortunately, there's not a lot I can say that's complimentary.

"We're in South L.A. now. There are... houses... trees. A market. A church."

We pull up to the front of the clinic, and I put the car in park. "And we're here. I'm not sure you *want* to know what the clinic looks like."

Laney releases her seatbelt and turns in her seat to face me. "Thank you for playing tour guide for me." She pauses, then adds, "You really do have a very nice voice."

Wham. My heart slams against my sternum then rolls up

to my throat, blocking it. "Uh, thanks," is all I can manage to force out. Why do a few kind words from this girl affect me so much? It's ridiculous. It's like my brain has reverted back to adolescence and the first time a pretty girl spoke to me at a middle school party. That was a *long* time and many miles ago.

There's no way I'll be able to sit here in my car all day with nothing for my mind to do but wander and torment me with images of something I'll never have—something I shouldn't even want.

It's time to get back to work. Time to go see my father.

Chapter Eleven
Angel of Death

Father's in his office in downtown Los Angeles where he conducts his legitimate business with the human world.

His entertainment law firm represents a huge number of Elven and human actors, models, musicians, public speakers, and athletes. The office also serves as the headquarters of the Dark Council. On any given day he could be negotiating a contract with a movie studio or professional sports team or assigning someone to handle damage control after an Elven celebrity has a particularly public bad day. Today he'll no doubt be giving an ear bashing to his only son about shirking his duties as a drug pusher.

I check in with the receptionist, and she lets my father know I'm here—right after she lets me know, in no subtle terms, that she's available if I'm interested in an evening or two of *everything but*. Giving her a wink, I head down the corridor toward Father's office and promptly forget about her. If I took up every woman who put out that offer, I'd never have time to do *anything but.*

"Well, well, look who's here. I trust you had a refreshing break?" Father sneers.

"Yes. Sorry about that. I guess I'm not quite used to working full time yet," I lie.

"You're an adult now. It's time to get up to speed—in your work and every other area. Speaking of which, I've been in contact with the Dark Council leader in Italy. His daughter Alessia is about to turn eighteen. That could be a good alliance for us."

Inwardly, I bristle at his mention of marrying me off. On the surface, I am all unconcern and cooperation. "Whatever you wish, Father."

"I hear she's quite beautiful. But if you find she doesn't interest you in that way, don't be concerned. You may still keep up your activities with humans on the side after the wedding, as long as you don't attempt to go too far with it. You could even retain your little *plaything* from the past couple of days as part of your household staff if she appeals to you that much."

My heart freezes to an abrupt stop then assumes a panicky beat. Did he get a look at Laney? Is there any chance he's found out anything about her?

"No," I say in a casual, almost bored, tone. "She's nothing special. I'm finished with her."

"Good, because we're moving to the next level of production in our S facilities." He gives me a steely-eyed grin. "I need all your focus and attention now. We're almost ready to expand beyond the major coastal cities into the heartland of America."

"What would you like me to do? Shall I go and inspect the new facilities for you?"

Father waves a hand dismissively as he stands at his desk, leafing through papers. "I like you where you are—you're doing a good job as a brand ambassador for us, encouraging S experimentation."

"But I want to play a larger role. I'm ready for more responsibility. As your son and heir, I think I should have a more visible role, don't you? Any number of Elves or attractive humans could take my place as pushers. I'm ready for more."

Father looks at me speculatively. He nods his head, a smile sneaking across his normally severe face. "Perhaps you're right. I *am* rather busy today with other matters. I'll have you go to our local facility and inspect things in my place. Our healer will accompany you—he needs to make sure the proper proportions of ingredients are present in the drug to foster maximum addictiveness in human users. After you give your report, I'll determine whether to send you to our other facilities."

He touches a button on his desktop intercom. "Frida, my son is leaving now. Please send in my ten o'clock appointment."

Releasing the button, he steps from behind his desk and approaches me with catlike grace, his icy eyes sparking with pride or maybe with the anticipation of father/son world domination. He places a hand on each of my shoulders and squeezes, facing me eye to eye.

"I'm pleased. Very pleased. I haven't been sure you were totally on board with this. But the two of us working together can accomplish anything. Along those lines, I want you to keep an eye on Hakon for me today."

"Why? You think he's incompetent?"

"No. Not incompetent. His talent is above reproach. It's his... enthusiasm I question. He's changed since we've begun the S initiative."

"I'll watch him."

He hands me a business card. "Here's his number. Pick him up and then drive to our facility north of the city in the foothills. He knows where it is."

It's interesting. All the time I lived in Australia and England I thought of my father as all powerful and pictured his subjects—formerly Davis's subjects—as loyal and completely under the control of the Dark Council. But Ava disobeyed him and defected. Now there's another possible dissenter in his ranks.

How many more might there be? Could Ava be right? Can we possibly count on more allies to aid our cause? And I do consider it *our* cause now. Stopping the S Scourge is the best—and possibly only—way to get Laney to leave the city and go back home. The sooner that happens the better.

The healer gives me his location, and I put the address into my car's GPS. Hmm. Pretty sketchy neighborhood for a doctor to live or practice in—Elven *or* human.

When I reach the building it's apparent he doesn't live

here. It's a homeless shelter. A line of people stretches down the sidewalk. Baffled, I park in a metered spot, lock my car, then go inside, seeking out someone who looks official.

A woman sits at a table in the building's front room, surrounded by stacks of papers, talking on the phone. She tucks the receiver against her shoulder and asks, "Can I help you?"

"I'm looking for Hakon?"

"Oh yes. Doctor Hakon is back in the med clinic." She points over her shoulder. "Just follow the signs. Are you here to volunteer?"

I almost choke in shock. "Uh, no. I..." Shaking my head, I walk away quickly, following the signs to the shelter's medical clinic.

Is that what Hakon's doing here? Volunteering? Surely not. Maybe this is where he pushes the S—there are certainly plenty of addicts here. Kind of seems pointless to me, sort of like preaching to the converted, but who am I to question Father's methodology. It's working well enough.

I spot Hakon as soon as I open the clinic door. He's the only one here who looks even remotely Elven. A broad-shouldered, black-haired man, he is middle-aged and handsome. Actually, he might be older than middle-aged—that's as far as any of us get when it comes to appearance.

But no, he doesn't have the wizened, cynical eyes characteristic of the truly old ones like my father. Hakon's green-blue eyes are rimmed with faint laugh lines, but they still hold the bright spark of someone who's seen less of the world and still has the capacity to enjoy it.

"Culley?" he asks.

"Yes," I confirm.

He smiles and holds up a finger. "I'll be with you in a minute." He turns his attention back to the patient sitting on a chair in front of him, speaking to the skeletal old man in a gentle tone. "All right now—I want you to promise me you'll keep eating, Mr. Jackson. You need to regain some weight, build up your strength."

"I will, doctor. Thank you, doctor."

"Good man." Hakon claps him on the shoulder and starts walking toward me, saying a few words to an assistant before we leave together.

Once outside, my curiosity gets the better of me. "I didn't realize you treated humans as well. You have a medical degree?"

He smiles and shakes his head. "I'm a 'holistic' medicine doctor as far as the shelter directors know. They're not picky. Regular volunteers are hard to come by at this place. And the patients don't care. The vast majority of them have no insurance and no money to pay for treatment. Anything's better than nothing."

"So what's the old man's problem?"

"Cancer. The tumor's gone, but he's weak. He's got a few months of recovery ahead of him. He'll be okay," he adds as if I was truly concerned about the old geezer.

"It's gone… you healed him?"

Hakon winks and holds a finger up to his lips, though I'm not sure whether it's the humans or my father he wants to hide his extracurricular healing activities from. His next words answer the question.

"I'd appreciate it if you didn't mention to Audun exactly where you picked me up today. It's my day off, but I still don't think he'd be thrilled."

Wow. The guy has a pair, I'll give him that. In spite of his rather off-putting concern for underprivileged humans, I feel a grudging respect for the man. Anyone who's not quaking in fear of my father is either extraordinarily brave or just plain stupid, and the healer doesn't seem like a fool to me.

"So… you've been to the factory before?" I ask.

"A couple times. At initial setup and then once more recently to tweak things with the formula."

"Seems like it's pretty effective."

"Yes," he answers in a grim tone, turning away from me. "Do you want to take your car or mine?"

"Let's take mine. I don't want to leave it here."

Taking a last look back at the clinic and the collection of human misery that surrounds it, I pop the door locks and climb in, pushing the air conditioner button immediately to get some relief from the heat that's collected inside.

With the ever present L.A. traffic, the drive to the factory takes about two hours. Hakon and I make small talk along the way. Father is right—he doesn't seem particularly enthusiastic about his work on the S project. Maybe he just prefers dealing with patients. It would be natural for a healer to be more interested in healing than manipulating a drug to cause the most possible damage to people—kind of goes against the whole doctor's code thing I guess.

The factory is located in the outskirts of Simi Valley, north of the city, a large, dilapidated looking building that Father must have acquired cheaply. Doubtful there was even any permitting done before production began. The cracked concrete parking lot is dotted with patches of weeds sprouting from the broken spots. Surrounding it is a warped, rusted chain link fence. There are only a few cars in the lot. I pull mine right up to the scarred metal doors and park it.

As we get out, Hakon advises me to follow him and walks toward the building at a let's-get-this-over-with pace.

"What are we looking for exactly?" I ask.

"They've been given enough raw saol to increase production. So we'll make sure they're working up to speed, meeting the quotas Audun has put forth. We'll also find out how their efforts to produce saol itself are coming along."

"They're having trouble?"

"It's not as easy as it seems. There aren't as many old growth trees here as there are near Altum. We've been sending harvesters up to the redwood forests on the northern coast and the giant sequoias in the Sierra Nevada to gather sap from their root systems, but that's not the only problem. Something is going wrong during the distilling process. Perhaps you can advise us on it. I haven't been to Altum and seen it in person for almost ten years myself."

"Of course. I'll try. So… for now you're relying solely on the initial saol samples I brought back?"

"Not solely, but mostly. So far that's the most viable and

effective active ingredient we have." From the sound of it, the last word seems to leave a sour taste in his mouth. "Without you, there would be no S production at all."

As he walks, he glances back over his shoulder as if to see how the information strikes me.

I don't show him. It actually hit me like a sucker punch to the gut, but I don't know for sure whether Hakon's sympathies are with my father or with the innocent human population so I can't let him suspect the traitorous thoughts spinning through my mind.

Without me, Laney wouldn't have ever come to L.A. Her brother would never have died of an overdose. He'd be alive. She'd be safe and happy. It makes me feel like the Angel of Death. How could I have ever thought she'd like me?

"Okay, here we are," he says, pointing around at the various work stations in the busy, whirring room. "This is the tableting room. The raw active S is kept here. The chemists cut it with a bulking agent and a binder here. The ingredients are blended over here and put into a granulator. Then they go into the tablet press. These machines can produce thirty thousand tablets an hour. You'll recognize these." He grabs a handful of pills and lets them spill back out of his palm into the bin.

His expression is easier to read this time—definitely judgmental. My hopes rise, detecting his disapproval of the drug itself and of me. Maybe this is the ally we're looking for. Even if I'm wrong and he's all for the world domination plan, it occurs to me I should at least pump him for information—maybe some of it will be useful to Ava and Lad and Ryann and Nox and Vancia as they work toward a solution on their end of this mess.

"Why are they wearing masks and gloves?" I nod toward the workers at the far end of the table where the raw S is handled. "You're not afraid of giving the humans *germs*, I assume."

He gives me a wan smile. "No. It's for the workers' protection. As you know, the substance is highly addictive."

My eyes go wide. "Elves are affected by it as well?"

He nods. "Yes. Unfortunately. We've had to get rid of some of our chemists because they became useless and began stealing our supplies to satisfy their own habits. Then Audun put out word that any of our people caught using S would be severely punished—you remember. We've had no problems since then."

"Right. I'm surprised the Light Elves have been able to have it so close for so long without ill effects."

His brows draw together. "I've wondered about the same thing. Obviously something is different about their constitutions. Or maybe it's environmental. I'm not sure. I'd ask, but I doubt I'd have any luck getting answers on that one. My communication with their healer is limited. When I am there for the Assemblage, Wickthorne and I don't exactly discuss state secrets."

"How do you test the final product for efficacy? If it's so addictive?"

His gaze slides off to the side then comes back to meet mine. "I can't test it on myself, obviously. I use… volunteers."

"Humans."

"Yes," he says grimly.

"Swayed?"

A terse nod. Then his glance slides over to me. *Why are you here? Did Audun send you to test me?*

No. I came to check on the factory. To learn. Why do you ask?

I don't think he trusts me.

Should he?

He doesn't answer my question, only asks another of his own. *Do you share his glamour gift?*

No. I inherited my mother's.

A grin cuts across his face and he shakes his head. *If you did, you'd be able to lie to me anyway, and I'd never know.*

Why do you think he doesn't trust you?

He shrugs noncommittally. *He's had me followed. Audun trusts no one.* One of his brows lifts as he repeats, *No one.*

Something in his bright aquamarine eyes alarms me. Is he warning me that I might have been followed in the past?

The thought sends a jolt of adrenaline through my body. *Laney.* I've taken her from my condo to the clinic more than once. Could Father's lackeys have followed us there? Could one of them be there right now, watching Laney, perhaps posing as an S addict to get close to her? Or maybe he's waiting outside the building for her to emerge when her work hours are through. Suddenly I fear I've made a very grave error leaving her there alone all day. Slipping my phone out of my pocket, I check the time and blanch.

"I've seen enough," I bark. "I need to get back to the city."

CHAPTER TWELVE
BUCKET LIST

By the time I drop off Hakon and return to the clinic in Chesterfield I've broken every speed limit ever conceived by the LAPD and the CHP as well. My face is covered in a sheen of sweat, though I've had the air blasting the whole way.

Right at five o'clock, Laney emerges from the clinic looking serene and happy—and beautiful. Of course.

I get out and walk around to the passenger side of the car, opening the door before she can tell me not to. "You called for a limo, lady?"

She stops in place. "Culley—I told you—I don't want you picking me up every day. I'm fine."

"I know. I'm only here because… there's somewhere I wanted to take you."

Her face contracts in suspicion. "Where?"

"You'll see. Trust me."

"Fine." She blows out a breath and walks toward me, feeling for the car as she gets close.

Once we're inside and on the road, I come up with a plan to transform my excuse for picking her up from lie into truth.

Smiling to myself, I turn up the radio. "It's going to take about forty minutes to get there."

"Where are we going?"

"Be patient. Good things come to those who wait."

When we arrive at our destination, I park the car but leave it running. "Okay, get out."

"We're here?"

"Yes. And we're going to switch places."

She freezes, her hand on the door pull. "What do you mean?"

"I mean you're going to drive. So get out and come around to this side."

"Culley—are you serious? I can't do that."

"Why not? You said you wanted to do things that challenge you, to experience things you've never done. Today, you're going to drive. We're in the parking lot of the Rose Bowl. Apparently, lots of native Angelenos learn to drive here."

"But…"

"It's empty, Laney. And it's huge. There's nothing for you to hit. And if you do get close to something, I'll tell you to hit the brakes."

"Oh my gosh," she says, her voice shaking. But then she smiles—a wide, genuine one. "Okay."

She gets out and makes her way to the driver's seat. I shut her door and go around, climbing into the passenger side, strapping on my seatbelt and making sure she's done the same.

"Okay now, you said you played Xbox with your brother, right?"

She nods.

"Ever play any driving games?"

"Yes, but there were no pedals."

"Okay, well the steering wheel action is pretty much the same. But you're going to use your right foot to operate the gas pedal as well as the brake. Brake's on the left. Go ahead and press down on it—I'll shift the car into drive for you."

"I'm scared," she says.

"Me too," I admit and we both laugh. "Just kidding—you're going to be great. Remember the brake is on the left. Okay, it's in drive. Give it some gas."

"Wait, Culley—how much did this car cost?"

I glance around at the interior of my four and a half million dollar LaFerrari and smile. "Not so much. Now go ahead. You can do this."

Laney gingerly applies her foot to the pedal, and we ease forward, then she presses harder, causing the car to speed up. It jerks to a sudden halt, and she giggles nervously. "Sorry."

"No problem. Don't worry about hitting anything. There's nothing ahead of us."

After a few more stops and starts, Laney gets the hang of the gas pedal, and I begin to give her calm, intermittent directions. "Turn left. Okay good. All right now, left again. You're driving along the perimeter of the lot, doing great."

She beams as she drives, sitting high in the seat and still clutching the steering wheel in a death grip. "This is fun."

"You're a natural," I say. "So, take your next right out onto the surface road—you can go ahead and drive us home."

She slams on the brake. "What?"

I laugh out loud at her horrified expression. "I'm only joking. I think that's enough for today. Besides, I have somewhere else to take you before we lose daylight altogether."

"The sun's still up? What time is it?"

"About six-thirty." I shift the gear stick into park. "Okay, Danica Patrick. I'll take it from here."

Before she unfastens her seatbelt, Laney turns to me. "Thank you, Culley. Really."

"Sure. It's no big deal." But I can tell to her it was a big deal—that I had faith in her, that I didn't treat her like a helpless child. And honestly, it was kind of a big deal to me, too. I haven't made a regular practice of doing things just to make someone else happy. It feels good.

We listen to the radio and chat about her workday as we make our way through city traffic to Venice Beach, not far from where I live in Malibu.

When she gets out of the car and smells the air, Laney says, "Are we back at your place?"

"No. Different beach. Come on. Do you trust me?"

She dips her chin in a "duh" expression. "I drove a car—blind."

"Right." Slipping on a pair of sunglasses and a ball cap first, I lead her to a sidewalk store called Jay's on Oceanfront Walk. "What's your shoe size? Like, a four?"

"Four? That's what children wear! I'm a six," she says proudly.

"Oh, okay." I can't wipe the amused grin from my face even as I approach the rental counter. "Two sets of rollerblades, please. A *ladies'* size six and a men's twelve."

I turn back to Laney to see her mouth has dropped open. "We're rollerblading?"

"We are. You may be sorry later when you're having to play nurse to me because of all my broken bones."

She starts hopping on her toes. "Oh my gosh, I'm so excited—rollerblading at the beach! It's like a TV show or something."

Now my smile is so wide it's hurting my face. This girl makes even impending bodily harm fun. We take a few minutes to get the blades on and tightly laced, then we both stand and get our balance. Laney starts to move forward on her skates.

"Wow—you're not even shaking," I say. "My ankles are wobbling around like overdone noodles. Sure you've never done this?"

"No, but I ice skated a few times when I was younger. This feels sort of like that. Of course I could *see* then. You're going to have to go first and hold my hand—I don't want to plow into anyone."

"Great. This will *really* be like the blind leading the blind—no offense intended." I take her hand and move out onto the sidewalk, wobbling a bit still but feeling more stable as I pick up speed.

"None taken," she says. "It will be kind of nice to do something where you're not infinitely better than me."

"What are you talking about?"

"Well, you're so good at everything, so worldly. You've been all these places, and you find it so easy to navigate a big city. Not only am I a country mouse, I'm one of the three blind ones."

"Don't sell yourself short. I think you're pretty amazing. You're an incredible driver, for one thing."

She laughs. "Oh yes. My skills are matchless."

"And you're damn good on these rollerblades—you're holding me up, you know—which means you're also fearless—hey watch out."

A kid on a bike is coming straight toward us down the sidewalk, and I have to yank Laney toward me to prevent a collision. The sudden movement knocks me off balance, causing me to fall to the side onto the beach and pull Laney right along with me. My back hits the sand, and she falls on top of me, our chests colliding and our limbs tangling.

"You okay?" I ask, straining my neck to get a look at her face. When she doesn't say anything at first I'm worried. Then she starts laughing. And doesn't stop. Pretty soon we're both lying there, our rollerblades buried in the sand, our chests and stomachs pressed together and shaking with uncontrollable laughter.

Finally Laney regains enough composure to speak. She does a pushup over me, trying to untangle herself. "You...

you really are bad at this, aren't you? I thought maybe you were kidding or just trying to make me feel better."

I help her off of me then struggle to my knees and then my feet, brushing sand from my clothing. "Well, I'm glad my incompetence amuses you so much."

She beams. "It really does."

The rest of the hour goes much smoother with no more collisions or mishaps. By the time we turn in the rollerblades to the rental shack, my muscles are sore and my heart feels lighter than it has in years.

Laney and I walk back to my car, hand in hand. I open her door for her, but she doesn't get right in. Instead, she reaches up and wraps her arms around me in a tight hug.

"Thank you for today," she whispers against my neck. "It was one of the best I've ever had."

I've heard people say before something made their hearts "melt." I never knew that was a real thing until now. My heart feels all soft and gooey to the point it's affecting my eyes. I blink them rapidly to hold in the moisture that threatens to leak out.

Patting her back awkwardly, I mumble, "You're welcome," and rush around to the driver's side to get in.

I've backed out of the parking spot and we're heading for home when Laney says, "You know, there's only one thing that could make today better."

My nerves go on instant alert. Is she going to ask me to kiss her again? If so, I am in no emotional condition right now to refuse the temptation. *Please don't ask me Laney.*

"What's that, sweet?"

"Karaoke."

I laugh, partly from surprise, partly from relief.

"I'm serious. It's not that late. Let's go. Wouldn't that be the perfect ending to today?"

This request I have no trouble refusing. "Believe me, you do *not* want to sing a duet with me. My rollerblading skills? *Olympic caliber* compared to my singing. Besides, it *is* getting late. We should get home."

"That's okay," she says brightly. "We can do it tomorrow."

"Tomorrow my singing voice will be as bad as it is today. You can ask every day for the rest of our lives, and that's not going to change."

I cringe after the words leave my mouth. I've just accidentally alluded to some sort of future with Laney. Which is impossible. For one thing, the rest of my life is going to be considerably longer than hers.

"It doesn't matter you know. You don't have to be perfect. I am your friend, and I'm ready, willing, and able to forgive anything you have done, or will do, wrong. Including painfully bad singing."

She means her remark as a joke, but it sort of spoils the mood for me. All I can think about now is the things I have done wrong—and the fact that if she knew them she definitely would *not* forgive me, or want to sing a duet with me, or do anything at all with me ever again. A driving lesson and an hour of rollerblading don't make up for a lifetime of bad behavior.

"Listen," I say. "In all seriousness, I know you are smart enough—and certainly gutsy enough—to get yourself to and from the clinic every day. But I'd really appreciate it if you would allow me to keep driving you. Just for the next few days until you move into your apartment. It would make me feel better—as your friend. And... well, I kind of enjoy it."

She gives me a gentle smile. "That is a very nice, non-bossy offer. And I accept."

"Great." I smile widely.

"Great."

Chapter Thirteen
Neighbors

For the next two days we cohabit peacefully. As friends.

I sit a safe distance from her on the couch as we watch movies each night. I don't wait outside the clinic all day long, guarding the door. I don't sneak into her room at night to watch her sleep. And I don't kiss her. It's killing me.

But it's for the best. She's getting more comfortable in the city. I've seen her navigate the city's bus routes, riding along to make sure. She's secured a part-time job at a shop near the apartment where she'll be living. She doesn't need me anymore. Which is good. Our time as "roommates" is almost at an end. It's almost time to let her go.

On the Friday before she's scheduled to move into her new place, I drive her to the clinic as usual. According to our agreement, this will be the last time. And when I pick her up tonight, that will be the last time. I'm quiet and moody on the drive, thinking about it. I've gotten rather used to our routine—and to having her in my place.

Maybe she senses my morose mood because when we arrive at the clinic, instead of getting out of the car as expected, Laney continues to sit there, facing me. Her expression is... what? Expectant? Mischievous? A little of each maybe?

"Did you forget something?" I ask.

"Did you?" she replies in a teasing tone. There's definitely a glint of mischief in those hazy brown eyes.

Despite myself, I feel the corners of my mouth turn up. "Not that I know of."

She gives a saucy little shrug. "I just thought maybe you'd like to kiss me good-bye."

All the air leaves my lungs at once, pounded out by hard-driving shock. Meanwhile my mind instantly starts up the mental reel of that scene between us on my couch. The same scene that's played in a constant loop in my brain for the past week as I struggled to banish the erotic images and go to sleep, as I lay awake until the wee hours imagining Laney's soft curves under her coverlet in the next room. The same scene I re-live nightly in dreams that leave me aching and sweating, desperate for her touch.

"What?" I gasp.

"A kiss—you know, lips and tongues, and—"

"I *know* what a kiss is," I practically roar.

She flinches at the increased volume of my voice, and her happy expression morphs into displeasure. "Why are you getting so agitated? It's only a kiss. I keep waiting for you to kiss me again. It's our last morning drop-off, and I'm moving out tomorrow... and we've been having a really good time together. Your heart beats really fast when we're close. I just thought you might... never mind."

Fumbling for the door handle, she starts to get out.

I open my own door. "Hold on. I'll get that for you."

"No," she snaps. Then more quietly she says, "No thank you. I can do it myself. Thanks for the ride. Have a good day."

She gets out and makes her way around the front of the car to the curb then the sidewalk, taking even, confident steps toward the entrance of the clinic. She's obviously learned the terrain already and feels comfortable here. And she's obviously mad at me for turning down the invitation to kiss her again.

I sit stock still in my car, hands gripping the steering wheel to the point of pain while the lower half of my body aches with longing. Eyes closed, jaw clenched, I fight to master my racing thoughts. *Stop thinking about it.* Stop thinking of *her* that way.

If she only knew how desperately I want to take her up on her offer—and so much more. But it's best that she doesn't know. Tomorrow she begins her new life here in L.A. One that doesn't involve me.

I do *not* have a good day. In fact, it's torture. I keep seeing the look on her face when I declined her offer of a kiss. I keep wondering whether I made the wrong choice.

No. Stay strong. One more day. You can do it.

I'm a wreck by the time five o'clock rolls around. I get

to the clinic early, just to make sure she doesn't decide to take the bus home after all, still angry—or maybe hurt—at my refusal of her innocent temptation.

At 5:05 I open my car door to get out then shut it again. It's Friday. They're probably all in a weekend mood and chatting it up in there.

By 5:10 my patience is gone, and I'm down to a minute-by-minute battle for self-control. I shouldn't go in there and make myself known to the clinic employees. I'm supposed to be keeping a low profile. As the minutes tick by, my imagination starts going crazy. Maybe she did leave early and take the bus already. Maybe she never made it to the bus stop at all and is right this very minute in the lair of some local gang or worse—in my father's home.

No longer concerned about being spotted or identified by the clinic workers, I turn off my car and leap out, striding directly into the middle of the small facility.

Laney's not here.

Turning one way then another I confirm my initial assessment. She's gone. But where? My Sway is fired up to full power when I pepper the clinic workers with questions. They stare at me, wide-eyed.

"Where is Laney? You didn't let her leave on foot, did you? You didn't let her take a bus?" They better not have allowed her to accept a ride from some stranger as she did with me the day I met her.

The friendly face of a young man breaks through the smog of panic surrounding me. He smiles, which serves to double his crunchy granola do-gooder handsomeness. Tan and golden blond, he looks like he should be in a commercial for hiking boots or suntan lotion or something. He approaches me with his hands up in a calming gesture, as if he's soothing a skittish unbroken horse in a training ring.

"Calm down, friend. I'm Shane, the director of Starting Steps. Our Laney is just fine. We let her go this afternoon, and a young woman named Brenna came to pick her up—she said they were friends. I believe they're neighbors, in fact."

Neighbors. Friends. Brenna. The violent beat of my heart begins to slow, allowing me to breathe normally again. My whirling hurricane thoughts calm to the point where I'm able to ask rational questions.

"You personally saw her get into the car with Brenna?"

Shane nods. "I walked her to the curb myself and opened the door. Are you a friend of hers?"

The guy eyes me in an evaluative way, as if he's taking my measure—sizing up a threat... or a competitor. He's not much older than Laney and me—mid-twenties I'd guess. When she mentioned "Shane" in conversation this week, I pictured a much older, much less attractive man.

What did he call her? *Our Laney?* It seems a little familiar and way too early for him to have taken ownership of his new volunteer. How much time could they have possibly spent together as they were both working here? The clinic looked to me like it always had a steady flow of human suffering in and out of the doors all day long. And he looks like he spends more time on a surf board than inside a dingy drug treatment facility.

"She lives with me," I say, taking a step closer to the guy and narrowing my eyes.

"I see," he says calmly, but I can tell from his expression he's not thrilled with that piece of information. *Good.* "Well then, all you'll have to do is go home and knock on your neighbor's door. I'm sure you'll find her getting ready for the gala."

"What gala?"

"The Stop the Scourge Gala tonight at the Jonathan Club. Dinner, dancing, a silent auction. It'll be attended by a who's who of the film and music industries and scores of wealthy philanthropists."

He gestures to the other clinic workers—most of whom are female, all of whom are staring at me with their jaws hanging open. "Laney said she had nothing to wear, and we've got things covered here, so I sent her home early to allow her time to shop or to borrow something."

It finally registers to me that Laney is safe. She's either at Brenna's place or out shopping with her. Both options are worlds better than the horrors I imagined when I first realized she'd left the clinic without me watching over her. I let out a long breath and nod, backing toward the door.

"All right then. Thank you."

The guy dips his head in acknowledgment. "You're very welcome. Should we expect to see you there tonight? Every checkbook is welcome—as long as you can afford the price of admission."

I don't like his smug face and knowing tone. "Don't worry yourself on that account, mate."

The guy breaks into a grin. "Well, if you see Laney, let her know my offer to come and pick her up tonight is still good."

"Yeah." I scowl. "I'll do that." *Right after I rip your highlighted Malibu Ken doll head from your shoulders and stuff it down the nearest storm drain.*

Stalking out of the office, I slide behind the wheel and stomp the gas, eager to get to Laney and confront Brenna over her failure to contact me about this unscheduled pickup. I'm not sure where along the way she switched from being my ally to Laney's, but I don't like it. Not one bit.

Chapter Fourteen
Gala

"Okay, okay, hold on."

Brenna's irritated voice is audible before she even unlocks the door to her condo in response to my pounding. When she pulls it open, she gives me a *What the hell?* look. "Where is the fire, neighbor? Did you blow up a frozen dinner in your microwave or something? Are you out of sugar?"

"Where's Laney?" I demand. "Is she here?"

Brenna's scowl relaxes into a smile. "She's almost ready. Want to come in and wait?"

"Ready?" I step into the condo, lifting a hand in perfunctory greeting to Brenna's ever-present house guests and hangers on. "What have you done to her, Brenna? And why didn't you let me know you were picking her up?"

She laughs. "I offered to kitty-sit tonight, and Laney mentioned she had nothing to wear to a black tie event. So

I'm playing fairy godmother. You sound like you think I'm torturing her or something. I promise you, she came here of her own free will. No humans were harmed in the course of this makeover."

"Be quiet," I hiss. "She'll hear you."

Brenna rolls her eyes. "She doesn't know *anything*. She can't even see us."

"You'd be surprised," I mutter. "She sees more than you think. And she doesn't even need her eyes to do it."

"Well, you might want to prepare *your* eyes because when you see her in the—"

Laney steps out into the living room area, and all conversation ceases. *This* is why Brenna didn't tell me she was picking up Laney and what they'd be doing.

A sleek, metallic evening gown flows over Laney's body like molten silver, flashing in the light of the room as she moves and turns. It's cut low in the front, revealing a hint of cleavage and molding to her shape in a way that makes my eyes bulge from their sockets and my mouth go dry.

Her long hair is styled into softly flowing waves, reminiscent of a classic old Hollywood starlet, and her skin glows, perfected by a pinkish blush at the tops of her cheekbones. Her perfect, plump lips turn up shyly at the corners.

"Do I look okay?" she asks, waiting as the silence extends. I'm unable to answer or say anything at all, overwhelmed by the sight of her. I want her so badly it literally hurts. The pain radiates throughout my body, its epicenter in my groin.

Apparently taking the lack of comment as disapproval, Laney falls back a step, her timid smile vanishing. She moves to flee back into the room where Brenna has been getting her ready.

I step forward and catch her, finally locating my voice though it comes out in an odd, strangled sounding manner. "Laney—you look... very nice."

"Nice?" Brenna barks a laugh. "She looks freaking amazing. I. Am. A genius."

"So am I." A deeply tanned brunette steps forward, her chest swelling with pride. "I altered that Amazonian dress to fit this little squirt."

"Culley," Laney whispers. "What are you doing here?"

"I... well, I've come to give you a ride to the event tonight." Before walking in here and seeing her looking like this, I had no intention of attending the gala. But now... now I think she needs a bodyguard.

Her pert nose goes up in the air. Yep—still mad at me. "I don't need a ride. Shane has offered to come pick me up. I'm sure you have other plans—you've already spent too much time babysitting me."

"As a matter of fact, I *don't* have other plans. The Stop the Scourge gala has been on my calendar for weeks now. Everyone who's anyone will be there. You don't expect me to miss the charity event of the season, do you?"

She blinks a few times, resembling a confused baby owl. "Oh. I guess I should have realized you'd be there because of your position with your dad's company. But you never mentioned anything about it."

"It never came up. How was I supposed to anticipate your sudden interest in stuffy charity events?" I study her more closely, perusing the glamorous makeup and hair and the sexy dress. "Why are *you* going? Is this your boss's idea?"

She throws her shoulders back. "Why shouldn't I go? To answer your question, yes, Shane did ask me to attend. He thinks I could be helpful."

"Helpful? How?"

"He asked me to speak to the attendees—about Joseph—to tell them his story. He thinks it will put a face on the S epidemic and cause people to be more generous."

"So in other words, he's using you."

"I wouldn't put it that way."

"I would. He wants you to share your sob story so they'll pull out their wallets and checkbooks and write a big fat number down."

She tightens her jaw and turns her head away from me, giving me a close-up look at the smooth, touchable waves of her hair. "You are so cynical."

"You have no idea, sweet"

"Well for your information, Shane told me I was still welcome to come even if I didn't decide to speak. Happy now?"

This information does *not* make me happy. It makes me quite annoyed in fact.

"I need a few minutes to shower and put on a tux. Wait here—I'll be back soon."

I can tell my domineering tone doesn't sit well with her. Her mouth turns down with a stubborn slant, and she folds her arms across her chest. Finally she says, "Fine."

Moving like I've got wildfire at my heels, I exit Brenna's condo and go to mine. I don't really need a shower for cleanliness's sake. However, after seeing Laney in that body-hugging dress, I do need a little *alone time*, and the shower seems the perfect place for it.

I've got to get over it. I cannot let myself look at her that way tonight. I need to wipe my mind clean of the thoughts that filled it the moment I saw her looking like a bombshell temptress, like the movie stars and celebrities she'll be mixing with at the gala.

Twenty minutes later I'm back at Brenna's door, armed with renewed determination and a couple of bracing drinks I downed quickly as I donned the monkey suit.

You're fine. She's just another girl. Not even your type.

The door opens, and Laney stands there looking like *no* other girl in the world. And *exactly* my type.

I have to swallow hard before speaking. "Ready to go?"

She nods and turns to give a wave to Brenna, who waits behind her to zing me with a knowing look.

You gonna be all right there, cowboy?

Shut up. I glare at Brenna but it does nothing to dim her gloating.

Laney reaches for me, and I offer my arm. Together we proceed in silence to my car, get in, and start toward the city's downtown business district and the exclusive Italian Renaissance style club where the gala will be held.

Though I'm doing my best to keep my eyes on the road, they keep drifting over to take in the sight of her. She is radiant.

"So…" She finally breaks the silence. "Thanks for bringing me tonight. You really didn't have to. I mean, Shane seemed like he was completely fine with picking me up."

"It's nothing. I'm going that way anyway, so no need to trouble your boss."

"It's… well, I thought maybe I scared you off this morning or something."

"Me scared? Of you?" I take a breath to calm my suddenly racing heart. "Nah."

"Okay, so I guess you just didn't *want* to kiss me then."

And here we go. This is my opportunity to put an end to the nonsense between us once and for all. I can no longer deny the attraction, but acting on it again is out of the question. I should make it clear there's no possibility of anything happening between us, in case she was hoping for it… or something.

My stomach goes into a nose dive at the thought. *Is* she hoping for it? Stupid stomach. I jam a fist into my midsection, pressing hard to stop the idiotic butterflies that are clearly lost because they've never taken residence there before—not once in my whole life. What is it about this girl?

"Listen… Laney—you're a lovely girl. I can't deny I'm attracted to you. I mean, obviously you know that after the… incident the other night. But my life is pretty complicated right now. I can't… get involved… with you."

She keeps her face pointed straight ahead, not inclining toward me, not showing me any reaction. "I see."

"Besides, you're moving into your new place tomorrow. You'll be busy with your new job and your clinic work. I've got a critical time coming up at work myself. It doesn't make sense. I think it's better if we keep things as strictly friends from now on."

Again, a stretch of silence. Finally she nods. "Okay then. Thank you for telling me how you feel. I certainly don't have any interest in pursuing someone who's not interested in me. Been there and done that one already. Friends it is."

Well, that was easy.

I'd expected hurt feelings or pouting, maybe even shouted accusations of leading her on. Instead, Laney rides serenely beside me in the car, not looking the least bit bothered. Which makes me feel... weird.

I'm still troubled by it when we arrive and I hand off the keys to the valet at the entrance of the club. Lightly taking Laney's arm, I escort her into the club, falling naturally into a description of our surroundings.

"We're in the foyer. It's very large, very swanky. A long carpet runner goes through the lobby and up a set of stairs. There are wide columns on either side of us, oil paintings on the walls, lots of fancy flower arrangements, big chandelier, the works."

"I wish I could see it. It sounds beautiful."

"It's not bad."

The club is steeped in old money elegance, but the most beautiful thing in the place—by far—is Laney. And I'm not the only one to notice. As we make our way through the lobby toward the ballroom, I see the eyes of every man we pass, whether he's alone or with someone, land on her and stay there.

I've gotten pretty good at reading faces over the years, and I recognize desire when I see it. By the time we reach the gala, my insides have heated to the boiling point. I'm ready to shoot laser beams from my eye sockets at the next guy who stares at her, which is a bad thing because when we enter the ballroom, several dozen sets of male eyes turn to us—to her. I'm going to have to stay right at her side all night to keep her from getting swarmed by all these jackals.

"Do you see Shane?" she asks. "I want to let him know I'm here."

Tamping down my annoyance long enough to glance around, I survey the room for the head jackal. "I don't see him. But don't worry. I'm sure he's on the lookout for you. Want a drink? A soda or something?"

"Do they have champagne?"

"I thought you didn't drink."

"I don't. But tonight feels… I don't know, special or something," she explains. "And I've always wanted to try champagne. Besides, I'm kind of nervous about speaking in front of everyone. It might help."

"The bar is this way."

I accompany Laney across the empty wood-topped dance floor where a bar is set up directly opposite the small orchestra. As we make our way through the crowd surrounding the bar, several women offer hellos. Some of them I've met before, and I'm obligated to stop and exchange a few air kisses and words with them. At least the

Elven women in attendance are subtle about their reactions to my appearance. The humans—are *not*. Sometimes I'm amused by their gawking. Tonight it's annoying me to no end. I just want to reach the bartender and get Laney her first glass of champagne.

Finally I gain his attention. "Dom Perignon please."

"Sir, the Dom Perignon is—"

I know what he's going to say—the Dom Perignon is not complimentary. The champagne they're serving gala guests is a less expensive brand. But it's Laney's first time tasting champagne.

The three hundred dollars I lay on the bar in front of the man silences him. He nods and turns to enter the wine storage area, coming back seconds later with a bottle. He pops the cork and fills two tall crystal flutes.

"As I was saying sir, The Dom Perignon is an excellent choice for tonight. Enjoy. If you'll point out your table, I'll have your bottle sent over."

"Wow, that's nice," Laney exclaims. "This really is a fancy event if they're giving away bottles of champagne to the guests."

"Yes, it's top shelf. So what do you think?"

"It's good," she says. "Sweet."

"Another one to cross off your bucket list."

"My what?"

"That list of things you've never done but always wanted to try."

"Oh, right. I can thank you for helping me with three of them now."

Looking down at her beautiful smiling mouth, I'm acutely aware of the last item on that list—skinny dipping. There's one I *won't* be helping her with. Which leads me to the thought of somebody else filling that role.

Suddenly hot and uncomfortable, I tug at the neck of my tuxedo shirt and glance around at the crowd. "Do you know if you have an assigned table?"

"Yes, Shane said Starting Steps has a table for ten. I'm supposed to sit with them. Does your father's company have a table?"

"I'm not sure. I forgot to ask," I lie. "Perhaps I'll just sit with you. Our company table is bound to be full of stuffy millionaires with shallow pockets."

"We can ask Shane. I'm sure he'll be happy to have you if there's room."

Oh, I'm sure. I grin and guide her toward the perfectly scruffy blond man waving wildly from an elegant cloth-draped table near the stage. The ballroom is all done up in white, from the flower arrangements atop each table to the candles glowing around them to the white-leaved potted trees placed at intervals around the room.

As we near his table, Laney's boss gets a closer look at her, and I have no doubt he would like a *closer* "working relationship" with Laney. I can't blame the man. She's stunning.

"Laney—wow," he exclaims, his gaze roving up and down her body. "You look sensational." He steps forward and kisses her cheek, wrapping his hand around one of her wrists.

A bright smile lights up her face. "Shane, you're such a flirt. I'm sure you've said that to all the girls from the clinic here tonight."

Looking around, I see none of the other women who were there today when I went in searching for Laney.

"Actually…" He hems. "It's just you and me tonight. We're sharing a table with several other non-profits, so there wasn't room for the whole clinic staff."

Laney's expression clouds. "Oh no, I feel bad. Someone who's been there longer should have come instead of me."

"No, I need *you* here. You have an important role to play, remember? As I've told you before, you walked into my life at the exact perfect moment—like it was meant to be."

Shane's challenging gaze lifts to meet mine for the first time.

Unaware of our silent exchange and apparently of the undercurrent of her boss's words, Laney says, "Well, I sure hope my speech will live up to your expectations. And I hope I don't sound like a hick up there—my accent comes out when I'm nervous."

"No need to be nervous. You'll be wonderful. Just be your sweet self, and I know everyone will love you as much as I do," he gushes. "Well, shall we take our seats? I think they plan to serve soon."

Shane slides an arm behind Laney's back, effectively pulling her away from me. "Culley, I assume you have your own table? We'll see you later perhaps. Thank you for driving her here tonight. Enjoy the gala."

It's clear Shane means to dismiss me, but Laney turns back to face me.

"Is that okay, Culley? You see your group?"

She's concerned about leaving me alone. Even after our talk in the car. Even after my rejection.

That does something to my chest. It's tight and sore as Shane pulls her farther from my reach and settles her into a chair on the other side of him.

"Yes, of course," I mutter, frowning at his self-satisfied expression. *Speech, my ass.* It's painfully obvious he asked her here as his date.

In actuality, no one will be here from my father's firm. The very last thing Audun Rune is interested in is raising money to fight the S Scourge. I'm beginning to realize I may spend the evening wandering the club's gilded hallways when a curvy blonde runs over and flings herself at me, nearly knocking me into one of the empty chairs at Shane's table.

"Culley Rune! Where have you *been*? You said you were going to call me, naughty boy." She laughs loudly. "I didn't know you did the charity circuit. Want to sit with us at the studio's table? I want Daddy to meet you. He's looking for a male lead for his new YA book adaptation. I've been telling him about you—you have the perfect look. You've acted before, right?"

Casting one last look at Laney, I allow the babbling girl to drag me toward her table. Her name escapes me. All I remember is her father is a movie producer and she's taking acting lessons. I met her at... I don't know... one of the clubs around here several weeks back. They all run together in my memory—the clubs *and* the girls.

"See you later then," Laney says softly, and I lift a hand in a good-bye wave she cannot see, feeling like I'm letting something fragile and irreplaceable slip through my fingers.

Chapter Fifteen
Tribute and Tears

Our tables are far enough apart I can't hear Laney's conversation with Shane. I can tell they get along well, though. She smiles at him as they talk and occasionally throws her head back in laughter. He leans close, draping an arm across her chair back.

It's a challenge to keep my attention focused on Nicole—that's the hopeful actress's name—and the rest of my table mates. Their lively discussion of the movie industry does not interest me in the least. Same goes for Nicole's flirtatious body language and the blatant way she keeps touching my hand, my arm, my shoulder. I can't help but sneak looks in Laney and Shane's direction.

As the evening moves along, he edges his chair incrementally closer to hers. By the time dessert is served, he's sitting close enough to her that their knees touch. According to the programs on our table, her speech should begin soon. I've already decided the minute it's finished, I'm taking her home. It's been a long night already, and she needs her rest. Besides that, the bartender was true to his word and sent the bottle of Dom to their table. I've counted three glasses Shane has filled for Laney so far.

"Ladies and gentlemen…" There's a ringing noise I realize is coming from the tapping of a silver fork on a crystal glass. A fit man with thick dark hair and hipster glasses stands at the podium, smiling and speaking into the microphone. "If I could have your attention. It's about time to begin our program. Hasn't this been a lovely night so far?"

There is applause from the attendees who seem to be making a concerted effort to wrap up the numerous conversations going on.

"I'm Jack Soderman, news anchor at Action News, and I'm your emcee for the evening. We'd like to start off by thanking some people who've made this beautiful night of hope possible."

The guy rattles off a list of names and corporations, all of which draw polite applause, and then he starts Laney's introduction. Suddenly, my stomach is filled with swarming bees. I can't sit still, so I get up and go to the back of the room where I can pace.

"This young lady is a last minute addition to our program, but once you meet her, I think you'll see why the night would not have been complete without hearing from her," the emcee says. "Laney recently arrived in Los Angeles, and her first stop was the Starting Steps clinic in Chesterfield."

Murmurs filter through the audience as attendees no doubt express their shock, admiration, and perhaps dismay over Laney's decision to visit that infamous neighborhood.

"I don't need to tell you this young lady is fearless. But her courage doesn't stop there. You see, Laney came to the city alone, without a place to live, without knowing a soul, not because she wants to be a star or pursue fame and fortune, but because she wants to help stop this epidemic we've come to know as the S Scourge. Perhaps most impressive... she's done all this, without... being able... to see."

A gasp rises from the crowd.

"Come on up here, Laney—I'll let you tell them the rest."

Laney stands, and Shane guides her to the stage and up the two steps toward the podium. As she steps into the spotlight, there is another collective gasp, this one for a very different reason. Her silver dress dazzles in the bright light, and the glow seems to extend to her hair and face, as if she's in the center of a halo.

Her eyes, her skin, everything about her is beautiful, and I'm clearly not the only one who thinks so. Nicole's producer father leans to the man next to him—an Oscar-nominated director—and whispers something, gesturing toward the stage.

"Hello everyone." Laney's voice is shaky. She gives a tremulous smile that only makes her more appealing. This crowd probably hasn't seen much humility lately. She's got them eating out of her hands already, and she's only said two words.

"Thank you for letting me come here tonight. I'm grateful for the chance to tell you about someone who means a lot to me."

She tells the audience about her brother Joseph. I've heard some of the story already, of course, but this time she adds more details, tells more about their shared childhood. As she speaks, pictures of Joseph—with her, with her parents, hamming it up for the camera with silly faces and big, All-American boy smiles—appear on the video screens around the room. She must have allowed someone, Shane perhaps, to download them from her phone.

The thought irks me. She hasn't let me get near the thing. Of course, Shane isn't trying to send her home at the earliest opportunity.

Laney has the audience mesmerized, alternately laughing and tearing up. Then her voice gets quiet, and she speaks close to the mic. The rest of the room goes silent.

"The last time I ever talked to my big brother was on the phone. He sounded sad, and I remember being worried about him. I thought maybe he'd auditioned for a part he didn't get or had some trouble with a girl or something, but he was never one to talk about problems. He kept them to himself and always tried to stay positive. Right before he hung up he said…" Laney's voice grows thick with unshed tears, her pretty eyes glistening in the spotlights. "He said… 'I'm sorry baby girl.'"

She stops and swallows hard. "When I asked him what for, he told me he had to get off the phone—and that he loved me. He said he wanted to make sure I knew that."

Laney pauses and lets the words sit there a minute before continuing. "I will never get over losing Joseph. My parents will never get over it. Our home is a different place without him. We are different people without him. The world is a little less bright without him. He was the kindest, most generous, most loving person I've ever known. And he is gone. Forever."

The pain in her voice is so real—the emotion on her face so raw, so unguarded. I'm battling an overwhelming urge to run up to the stage and grab her, to whisk her away somewhere private where she's not so exposed. But I can't. We are on opposite sides of an unbridgeable gulf.

She is purity and light. I am darkness. And I am frozen in place, completely powerless to stop this heart-wrenching display of grief and suffering. Or the lethal damage it's doing to my soul.

I haven't cried since I was thirteen years old. But there is an aching pressure building behind my eyes, and the lump in my throat grows more painful with every word Laney says.

"Joseph wasn't perfect. My brother made a mistake by trying S—like so many young people do. But one moment of bad judgment should not be deadly. It shouldn't destroy so many lives. Recreational drugs have existed probably as long as human beings have. This one is different. S is merciless. It is sneaky. It is *evil*."

Standing in the back of the room, I feel as if her unseeing eyes are staring directly at me. A shiver passes through my entire body.

"If this evil substance can steal the life of a smart, kind, good, loving guy like Joseph, it can get to anyone, anywhere. *No one's* family is immune. *No one's* friends are safe. I ask you to consider that and do whatever you can to help stop it before it reaches yours."

The room bursts into raucous applause and chants of "Stop. The. Scourge! Stop. The. Scourge!"

Laney smiles and holds up a silencing hand, leaning in close to the microphone once more. "Thank you. I'd like to say one more thing." The crowd goes quiet again. "I've only met one other person in my life who's as kind and generous as my brother, and I can't leave the stage without thanking him. He has done more to help me since I arrived in L.A. than anyone could reasonably ask…"

No.

"… without expecting anything in return, and I truly don't know what I would have done without him."

No. No. No.

"Without him my personal fight against the S Scourge would be absolutely nowhere. In fact, I probably wouldn't be *here* tonight if not for him… and I certainly wouldn't be wearing such a pretty dress."

She gives a winning smile as my heart sinks to the soles of my Brooks Brothers wingtips. "My friend… Culley Rune."

Oh God no.

Chapter Sixteen
Dance With Me

I have never felt so dirty in my life.

I want to slink from the room like the snake that I am, slithering between the pairs of designer shoes to the exit door. Around the ballroom, heads turn, searching for the paragon, this shining example of altruism.

Unfortunately, Nicole stands and points directly at me, beaming and then clapping her hands above her head, gesturing for the rest of the gala attendees to do the same. To my utter mortification and shame, they do, rising from their chairs one by one then en mass to give me a standing ovation.

I feel like I'm standing alone on the fifty yard line of a football stadium in front of a capacity crowd. At the Super Bowl. Naked.

Thankfully, the emcee steps back onto the stage and takes the mic. "Isn't she something? Another round of applause for Laney."

The crowd turns and faces the front of the room again, shifting their adoration back to where it belongs—on the truly kind and selfless girl standing there.

"If Laney can overcome her own challenges to make a difference for the S victims in our community and around the nation, I think the rest of us can make some time in our 'busy schedules' to help, or do our part by finding a few extra dollars to contribute to the fight," the emcee says. "The silent auction tables will be open until eleven, and there are envelopes on your tables if you'd like to make a direct contribution. Our live auction will take place at ten. The band is getting into place, and the dancing will begin soon, but first, I'd like to ask you to direct your attention to the screens around the room for a short video presentation put together by another generous benefactor—Mr. David Turgeon."

Nicole's father lifts a hand and dips his head in humble acknowledgment, the room goes dark, and I take a direct line to the hallway.

Locating the men's room, I knock the door open with a forearm and go inside, enter a stall and lock it behind me, then turn and lean against the door, tipping my head back and breathing hard, battling a surge of queasiness.

I hate myself.

Out of all the times in my life I've felt like a fraud—and there have been many—this is the worst. No contest.

It's one thing when people look at me and see an illusion. That's the curse I was born with. It's another thing altogether to have fooled this sweet, trusting girl into somehow thinking I am a good person.

How did things get to this point? What am I even doing here with her? *How* did I let myself kiss her and even *think* about going further with her? The very last thing Laney needs is to be shackled for life to the likes of *me*.

I should leave. I should let her spend a pleasant evening with Shane, talking, getting to know each other, dancing.

That's the mental picture that propels me out of the bathroom and back into the ballroom. As much as it sickens me to think of degrading her with my touch, I hate the idea of *him* touching her, holding her close, even more. He's too old for her. Too smooth. And too... whatever. He's not right for her, and she's probably too innocent to even realize he's making a play for her.

Entering the ballroom I spot Laney immediately. She's surrounded by a group of people, and Shane is close by her side—of course. I reach the group, pushing through the throng none too gently.

"It's time to go," I say into Laney's ear.

She jerks her head back. "Culley—wha—why?"

"It's late. You've done your speech. Let's get out of here."

"And go where?"

"I dunno. Home. Cupcake has been alone too long. We need to check on him."

One of the women who was crowding Laney turns her attention to me. "Culley? What are you doing here?"

Her eyes flare with a look I know all too well. My mind ricochets to the past, searching desperately for how we met, for what happened between us, and how far it went. Her cat-that-ate-the-canary smile makes me fear it was pretty far.

"Don't you look yummy in a tux?" she purrs. "The last time I saw you, you had on much less—"

"Excuse me," I interrupt. "I need to have a word with my friend."

Dragging Laney to the side, I say, "I'll get the car from the valet. Tell all your new fans good-bye."

"Why are you in such a hurry? Afraid of a cougar attack?" Her teasing tone drops as she pulls back from me. "You can go if you want to, but I'm staying. I've never been to a fancy party like this. The band is good, and I want to dance."

Something in her tone concerns me. It's too free and easy, and her words have become softened around the edges, slurring slightly.

"How much champagne have you had?"

"I don't know. Shane poured it for me."

"I'll bet he did," I mutter. "Come on. We're leaving."

I pull at Laney's arm, but like a baby mule being forced back into its pen, she digs her heels in and refuses to walk with me. "I told you—I want to stay. I want to dance."

She reaches out for my other hand, and unable to resist, I give it to her.

"Dance with me Culley," she pleads and leans back, pulling me toward the band.

"I don't dance," I inform her. It's painful to be even this close to her. Full body contact and rhythmic tandem motion will put me right over the edge.

Her lower lip juts out. "Okay, fine. I'll ask Shane. Where is he?"

She won't need to search for him. Glancing over her shoulder I see the wanker heading this way.

"Fine." I heave an exasperated sigh. "We'll stay a bit longer." Sliding an arm behind Laney's back, I attempt to draw her away from the dance floor toward a table in the corner. "Let me get you something *non*-alcoholic to drink, and then we'll sit and listen to the band a while."

"I. Want. To. Dance," she insists. Then she calls out, "Shane! Where are you?" in a sing-song, very tipsy voice.

As if conjured from thin air, Shane appears and takes her hand. "Did someone order a dance partner?"

"Yay!" Laney throws her arms around his neck, and they leave me, heading for the dance floor.

Standing at the edge of the parquet floor, I watch them find a spot and begin to move together to the beat of the Latin-inspired song the orchestra is playing.

He's good. Of course he is. He couldn't just be a clean cut, handsome Good Samaritan, he also has to be trained in ballroom dancing.

As I watch the two of them turn and spin across the floor, talking and laughing, a strange new feeling comes over me. A blend of resentment and unease, the discomfort of it is nearly unbearable. With a startle, I recognize it as jealousy. I've never experienced that particular emotion before, but that has to be what it is.

Laney and Shane are made for each other, two of a kind, both do-gooders and activists, both self-sacrificing and generous. Both human. They even *look* good together—a matched pair.

I hate him.

I hate this man I barely know with a ferocity that's almost fanatical. As I stand fuming and fermenting in bitterness, other party guests approach me and make conversation. I greet them and strive to be polite, to act interested, to laugh at their meager attempts at humor. But my mind, my body, my entire being is concentrated on the dance floor. On Laney. It alarms me to realize how much of my attention she commands.

Oh shit. I think I love her.

This is what Ava was talking about. *This* is the way Lad and Ryann feel about each other, the way Nox and Vancia feel. It *is* real.

This discovery does not make me happy. I've never *wanted* to love someone. And yet here it is. Everything that's ever seemed important, everything I've ever desired, valued, or enjoyed is like worthless refuse compared to the way I feel about Laney.

It takes all my self-control to act calm and unruffled. My hands literally shake with the desire to march out there and grab her and carry her away from all these people—from Shane—like some kind of belligerent caveman.

The sane, levelheaded, more *evolved* part of me orders me to stay on the sidelines, let her enjoy his company, get to know him better, to bow out and let her be with someone who's better suited to her. It's not like she's my bond-mate or even my girlfriend. I should leave her alone. I should let her make her own choices about whether to stay in L.A. or go home, about whom to dance with and talk to, and even whom to go home with.

Screw that.

Striding out to the center of the floor, I tap Shane on one shoulder. "Mind if I cut in?"

"Actually—"

"I thought you'd never ask," Laney interrupts. "You don't mind, do you Shane?"

His scowl defies his amenable words. "Of course not. I'll go refresh my drink. Would you like more champagne?"

"Oh, that sounds good—"

"She's had enough," I say and pull Laney close, sweeping her into a simple waltz box step and leaving Shane standing alone in the center of the floor wearing a very perturbed expression.

"If I want more champagne, I'm going to have it," Laney informs me. "You are not the boss of me."

I can't help smiling as I speak right next to her ear. "*You* are a very stubborn girl—maybe even a brat. Has anyone ever told you that?"

Her cheek rises to meet the side of my mouth as she grins. "Maybe," she says. "And *you*—are a big, fat liar. You said you couldn't dance."

"No, I said I *don't* dance."

"You do now." She giggles.

As irritated as I feel, I laugh along with her. I can't help myself. "Apparently so. *You're* an excellent dancer by the way."

"Eight years of lessons," she says with a triumphant smile.

Taking one of Laney's hands in mine, I spin her, then pull her in close again. It's just as bad—just as good—as I knew it would be, being close to her like this. We move together easily, fit together perfectly.

She's just as soft, and warm, and delicious smelling as ever, but now, she's also relaxed in my arms instead of tense, thanks to the champagne. She laughs freely, molds herself to me as we move across the floor, sighs with pleasure as our cheeks touch.

Her lack of inhibition is doing terrible things to me. I find myself responding to her every motion, matching them with moves of my own. We're in the middle of a charity gala, in the middle of a crowd, but the dance feels... intimate. I can't seem to stop myself from imagining this same level of closeness *without* all the observers, without the layers of evening wear. If our rhythm is this good on the dance floor...

Stop. Just stop it.

Consciously putting some space between our bodies, I search for something to say, words that will break the dangerous spell that has fallen over us, a virtual bucket of cold water.

"You seem to get along well with your boss," I sneer.

"Yes, Shane's a really nice guy."

"He's a wanker."

Laney retracts her head. "What? No he isn't."

"Trust me. He is. You don't know guys like him. He's

been trying to get a look down your dress all night."

"Really?" Her tone and smirk express her disbelief. "Well, at least *he's* not publicly announcing he's slept with me."

My feet stop moving as if I've hit a brick wall. I can barely force the words from my constricted throat. "You *slept* with him?"

"No!" She laughs loudly. "No—I'm talking about *you*— and that woman who was drooling all over you a few minutes ago. Clearly you two had a 'relationship.'"

"I wouldn't call it a *relationship.*"

"You had sex with her."

"No. I did not."

"Are you sure? I've gotten pretty good at reading voices. That lady was certainly convinced you two had a thing going on. Maybe you've forgotten."

"Um… I'm quite sure I'd remember that. Wait—are you *jealous*?" Her answer matters more to me than I'd like to admit.

"Are *you*?" she counters. "You were pretty unfriendly toward Shane."

"As I said earlier… wanker."

"You *are* jealous, aren't you?" Laney bites her lower lip, smiling, and moves closer to me, wooing me into resuming the dance. "Your heart is beating a mile a minute," she whispers against my throat.

I'm not sure if it's the post-speech high or all the attention she's received from Shane or just the champagne that's making her so brave tonight, but her closeness is working for me, ratcheting up my heart rate and breathing until I feel like I've run an Olympic hundred meter sprint. And this new confidence she's displaying is incredibly sexy. I've only seen the shy Laney, the stubborn Laney. But this girl—*this* Laney is feeling her power over me. I don't want it to show but somehow she sees it anyway.

She knows I want her.

And she seems to want *me.* Oh God this is bad. She's supposed to go back home where it's safe, where Father can't get to her, where *I* can't get to her. It's pointless to deny I want her. I've never wanted anyone or anything so much. And marrying some strange girl halfway around the world definitely does not interest me. I want Laney and *only* her.

But I can't do it to her.

I can't bring her into my dangerous world. And I could never sleep with her and send her away. She's too precious for that. She's already had one dick boyfriend who didn't appreciate her properly and broke her heart. I'm not going to be the next on that list. I've got to stop this. I have to pull this runaway train off the tracks before it slams into the explosives waiting down the line.

"I'm not jealous," I lie. "I have no proprietary feelings toward you at all. I don't... see you in that way."

"Which way is that?" she demands, her tone belying her skepticism. "The way you see the girls you kiss and caress and—oh wait—*we did that.*"

Her lifted brows and the challenging set of her mouth await my answer.

I make sure she feels my shrug under her fingertips that rest on my shoulders. "What happened between us was no big deal. I kiss a lot of girls. As you've pointed out, women hit on me all the time. I have my pick. Daily."

"I see," she says, her tone going frosty as she pulls her hands away. "And that's what you like? Kissing a different girl every day? Being with a different girl every night?"

Gritting my teeth, I force out the next lie. "Of course. What guy wouldn't want that? Variety is the spice of life, as they say."

She's finally heard enough. Her body stiffens. She stops dancing entirely. Laney steps back from me, blinking furiously. Her face has taken on a new pinkness, and her bottom lip trembles.

"Maybe I should let you go then. I'm sure you don't want to waste any more time with me when you could be locating your next target for seduction. Thank you *so much* for the dance."

She turns and stumbles away from me, right into the waiting arms of Shane, whose expression is all solicitous concern.

"Ready for that champagne now, darling?" he asks.

"Lead the way," she mutters, and together they move away from me through the happy throng of dancers.

Well, that worked brilliantly. *Are you happy now, asshole?*

I am not happy. In fact, I have never felt less happy in my life. There is a sinking sensation inside me, and I close my eyes to steady myself against a sudden bout of dizzy nausea. Then I open them again and head for the exit.

This is the perfect out. If I leave here now, Laney will spend the rest of the evening with Shane and his charity friends. He'll comfort her and cheer her up, escort her safely from the gala, and perhaps drive her to a hotel. He might even have a sister or female friend who could put her up tonight until her new apartment is available tomorrow. Or perhaps he'll offer her *his* place for the night.

I stop in my tracks and clench my fists into tight balls, closing my eyes. *Breathe. Walk. Don't think about it.*

She's better off with him. She doesn't need me. She's proven she can and *will* make it on her own in this city. I've only continued to help her because I wanted to keep her around—I can admit that now.

So why can't I leave? I'm standing inside the front doors of the club, where it's nearly deserted and relatively quiet compared to the happy cacophony of the ballroom. On the other side of the doors I can hear muffled laughter and snatches of conversation between the waiting valets and smell the drifting smoke from gala guests who could no longer contain their nicotine cravings.

I lift my hand and flatten my palm against the inside of one door, intending to push it open. But my feet don't move. Why can't I make these stupid, uncomfortable, shiny shoes simply walk outside and down the sidewalk to my car and just go? It would be the best thing for Laney by far.

Dropping my head in defeat, I turn back around. I can't leave her here. She has something of mine—something I can't live without. My heart.

Somehow in the course of a week, I've gone from

desperately wishing to finish my business here in America so I could leave and be alone again to being unable to picture living the rest of my life without someone. Without *her*.

Finally breaking my inertia, I walk back to the ballroom again. The open bar has taken full effect now, and the crowd inside is rambunctious, their voices loud and their pockets no doubt much looser than they were earlier this evening.

The emcee steps up to the mic. "Ladies and gentlemen, if I could ask you to find your seats once again, the live auction is about to begin. We have some incredible packages here, vacations, sporting events, a private dinner prepared in your home by a celebrity chef whose name I'm sure you'll recognize…"

I scan the room, searching the dance floor, the bar area, and the various tables for a flash of silver beading, for the top of Laney's honey-colored hair.

She's not here.

Where would she have gone? Not out the front—I had that exit covered, so to speak. I step back into the central hallway and look one way then another, spotting the elevator doors. The rooftop terrace. That's where she'll be— unless she's in the ladies' bathroom—or in some private alcove with Shane.

Fury stabs my gut at that mental picture. What an utter ass I am. I can't believe I hurt her feelings like I did, suggesting she was no more special to me than any other girl. I have to find her, to explain that I didn't mean it. That the truth is the exact opposite of what I said.

Pressing the elevator's call button repeatedly, I battle a growing sense of dread. Maybe she *is* up there—with Shane. Maybe he drew her out to listen to the city's night noises and feel the evening breeze. Maybe right this minute he's saying all the *right* things, all the things any *rational* man would say if he were lucky enough to find himself alone in Laney's presence.

Then a horrifying thought strikes me—maybe they're not talking at all.

The elevator doors finally open, and I pace inside until it reaches the roof level. Bursting through the doors at a near run, I startle a couple on the other side who appear to be making their way back to the party after an obvious makeout session. What little lipstick remains on the woman's face is smudged, and the guy's hair is in total disarray. He's clearly having a better night than I am.

"Excuse me," I blurt.

The amorous couple shake their heads and get on the elevator while I charge out onto the veranda. There she is, standing at the far end against the white balustrade with her back to me, her head tilted back as if she's enjoying the sensation of the night air on her skin.

She's alone, and I'm overcome with the impulse to go to her and take her in my arms and describe the beautiful surroundings to her, to paint a mental image of the glowing city skyline, the white curtains billowing from the corners of the vine-covered arbor above our heads and the tiny white twinkle lights that adorn it as well as the potted trees that dot the perimeter of the terrace. I want to help her see this place—and every place she goes in the future.

I approach her soundlessly, nearly mesmerized by the way the wind lifts and plays with her long curls. She is achingly beautiful in the glow of the city lights. It gilds her skin and makes her beaded dress sparkle like the stars high above.

Before I draw close enough for her to be aware of me, Shane crosses the terrace, carrying two flutes of champagne. He comes to a stop way too close to her, leans in, and appears to nuzzle her cheek as he says something that makes her laugh.

A red haze drops over my vision, a surge of violent energy filling my veins and stiffening my muscles. Before I quite know what's happening, I'm striding toward them. Shane must hear my rapid approach because he lifts his head and turns back to see who's coming. The smile drops from his face when he spots me.

"Culley," he says with a terse, apprehensive nod.

"Why are you here?" Laney whips around to face me, her mouth drawn tight. "I would have thought you'd be busy locating your evening's entertainment. Or have you already had all the women at the gala? I think I hear some people leaving a restaurant down on the street. Perhaps there's some fresh meat for you there if you don't mind hurrying to catch them."

"Laney…" The word is a hopeless plea. "I need to talk to you. Alone."

Her chin lifts. "There's no need—you were quite clear about your feelings. I think you've said everything that needs to be said."

"Not everything. Please, Laney."

For a moment she says nothing. Her face shows no reaction. Then she turns to Shane, placing a gentle hand on his arm. "Do you mind giving us a few minutes? Culley and I need to say good-bye." Her last word is a growl exiting her mouth. I've never seen her so angry.

"Are you sure?" Shane asks, eying me suspiciously.

"Yes. Yes, I'll be fine," she assures him. "I'll meet you back downstairs in a few minutes."

Laney and I stand, silent and tense, facing each other as we wait for Shane to cross the terrace and get on the elevator, the doors closing quietly on his very displeased expression.

"Well?" she demands once he's gone. "What do you want?"

I stare at her, unable to give voice to the word screaming inside my brain.

You.

Chapter Seventeen
Ugly Truth

Now that I've got her alone, I don't know what to say. I can't grab her and kiss her—which is what all my instincts are demanding. I can't tell her I want her for myself. *That* is impossible. But I also can't tolerate the idea of leaving her out here alone with *Shane* and his perfect hair and his perfect manners and his bottomless champagne glasses.

I'm at a complete loss, so I blurt out the thought at the top of my mind. "I am an ass."

Laney leans back against the terrace railing, folding her arms across her chest. "Yes—you are."

"Yes. I am. I shouldn't have said what I did in there on the dance floor. It was rude, and I apologize. But I need you to understand… there is nothing here for you… with me. I'm not the kind of guy a girl like you should set her sights on."

"A girl like me?" she asks.

"Sheltered, innocent…" *Human.* "And neither is Shane," I add. "How well do you even know that guy?"

"Shane has been a perfect gentleman this evening and every day since I met him—which is more than I can say for some people."

"Good manners and pretty words mean shit. You barely know him. You don't know *who* you can trust in this city. That's why you need to go back home where you'll be safe."

She stamps one tiny, glittering shoe. "I don't want to be safe! I've *been* safe. I've been babied, and stifled, and kept safe my whole life, and I'm sick of it! If you don't want me that's one thing, but don't try to force me back into that pathetic excuse I had for a life."

My voice drops to a low whisper. "You don't think I want you?"

"Well, it's pretty obvious. You clearly regret kissing me the other night. You practically jumped out of the car when I tried to kiss you this morning. You pushed me away when we started to get close on the dance floor tonight."

I stare at her incensed expression, my heart hammering. "Damn it, Laney—I'm *trying* to protect you."

"From what? I don't need your protection, and I don't want it. I *don't* need a chaperone. I think this crusade to protect me is just an excuse to get rid of me." Her angry tone morphs into a speculative one. "Or maybe… you're trying to protect yourself?"

She takes a step toward me, grips the lapels of my tux, and draws herself against me, shocking me by pressing her body all along the front of mine.

A waft of vanilla-scented air meets my nostrils, making me instantly ravenous. She tilts glistening eyes up to me. I'm grateful they can't see how much I'm struggling not to jerk her up to my mouth and claim her right here and now. My hands shake with the effort of restraint.

"Why?" she demands in a harsh whisper. "Why are you so afraid?"

Her question catches me off guard. Compared to the humans all around me, I am powerful. I'm wealthy, good looking, and even moderately famous. I have every advantage, including ones they could never understand—my father is in charge of the Dark Council and soon to be in charge of all of their lives. What would I have to be afraid of?

Her. She is right. But I can't let her know that.

"You're afraid you *do* want me," she says, the light of understanding shining in her big brown eyes. "And you don't like losing control."

I huff a short, uncomfortable laugh. "I know you like to think you have X-ray vision into people's souls, but you don't know me."

"I think I do," she counters. "You never let yourself count on anyone for anything because the people in your life have disappointed you. You've been alone so long you've forgotten what it's like to let someone get close. And you're afraid that if you do, they'll reject you. I won't reject you, Culley. I care about you. I like you—just as you are."

Instead of warming my heart, her words send me into a state of near panic.

"I've been lying to you," I say bluntly.

She inhales a sharp breath then blinks several times. Her voice is very calm. "About what?"

"Everything. For one thing—my job. I really am a model."

"Well, that's terrible," she deadpans. "What a tremendous turnoff. How dare you not be up front about such a horrifying personal detail."

"And I *do* work for my father, but not at his law firm." A raw, desperate laugh escapes my throat. "Want to hear my job description? I've told you that Father was rather uninvolved in my life? That changed around about the time I turned eight, when it became apparent I took after my mother instead of him. He decided my particular genetic 'gifts' could be *useful* to him. He's always believed in the old adage 'money is power,' and he'll do anything to increase his own power—and wealth."

Swallowing hard, I force myself to admit the shameful things Laney needs to hear, the ugly truth she needs to understand about me. "First he had me work with the grieving parents his firm came across—only the well-to-do ones of course—get close to them, let them become attached to me, so they'd be willing to sign over their life savings and all their investments to the little boy who reminded them so much of their own lost child. When I got older, he assigned me to use my 'other' forms of appeal… to women. You meet a lot of rich women working as a male model—single, divorced, widowed… married."

All the color leaves Laney's face. "You slept with them?"

"Didn't need to. They handed over their money without it going that far. But I wooed them. I lied to them. And I stole from them. There were other women. Father wasn't interested in them for their money, but for... other reasons. I helped him... procure them. Sort of like a living bait and switch scheme."

"They went home with you and ended up with him?"

My throat fills with bile. "Exactly."

I don't mention the worst of it—my role in the S epidemic, my possible role in her brother's addiction and death. She's already repulsed by me—rightfully so. Something in me can't bear to take that final step and have her see the full ugliness of my soul. Watching her unreadable expression, waiting for her reaction is torture.

"Culley," Laney finally says. "Why are you telling me all this? Are you trying to disgust me? You don't. Your father is a different story. He's beyond horrible for using his child like that. But that's not *your* fault. If you're trying to make me hate you, you can just stop. I could never hate you—no matter what you've done. What do you want me to say?"

I grab her shoulders and give them a little shake. "I want you to say you'll leave L.A. Tomorrow. Tonight if possible. As long as you're here, you're in danger—from the S addicts, from my father, from me most of all."

Instead of pushing her away as I should, I drag her closer to me, wrapping her tightly in my arms. She feels perfectly right. The softness of her skin, the sweetness of her scent, the sound of her rapid breathing—it's almost more than I can bear. The torment of wanting what I cannot have is the most painful thing I have ever felt.

Speaking into her hair just above her ear, my throat aches and my voice is a ragged whisper. "Go home, Laney. *Please*. Because if you stay, I'm not going to be able to stop myself from ruining you, from hurting you. I want you too much—in every possible way. I've tried to stop, but I can't."

"I don't want you to stop. I want you, too," she says eagerly.

"*No*," I growl. "You don't understand. My wanting you is not a *good* thing." I take a deep breath and let it out. "I hated seeing you dance with Shane tonight. Because he's not a wanker. He's a good guy. He's everything I'm not. I couldn't stand seeing you give him all your attention when... when I want it for myself."

I pull away from her and face the mirrored windows of the high rises surrounding the terrace, gripping the white painted railing in front of me as I continue. "I've never met anyone like you. You challenge me, you amuse me... and yes, you scare me. But we *can't* be together. I'm not right for you. Believe me—if you only knew—you don't want to get stuck with me."

"*Stuck* with you? You're perfect for me. I think you're *the one*, Culley."

"No," I blurt. "I'm not."

Can I tell her? It may be the only way I can get her to see the impossibility of this. "I'm not what I seem to be, Laney. We're... not even the same race."

She laughs out loud. "Is that what this is about? Do you really think I'd care about that? It doesn't matter."

"I'm not referring to skin color or country of origin. This goes beyond that—"

"Culley," she interrupts. "I love you."

"What?"

"I love you. No matter what your race or what you've done, no matter what other 'terrible secrets' you have up your sleeve. In spite of what you believe, I *do* know you." She places a tiny palm on my pounding chest. "I know your heart—and I love you. I won't leave you."

I am immobilized, stricken by her words and the stark honesty behind them. For the first time in my life, someone cares about me—*me*—not my looks or what I can do for them.

But it isn't real. It can't possibly last.

I choke out a response, stamping out a ridiculous surge of joy. "You don't love me. You can't. You don't know the whole truth. If you did, you'd never say that."

"Well then *let* me know you, Culley. Let me in. Just *tell* me… what is this truth you're so terrified to admit?"

"You…" I falter, then try again. "You are so convinced I'm a good person. Well, the kicker is this—I'm not even a person at all."

CHAPTER EIGHTEEN
GENEROUS BENEFACTOR

Laney's eyebrows knit in confusion. "What does that mean?"

"It means I'm not human, Laney. I'm something else—something else entirely. I'm Elven. You know, Elves? Like *Lord of the Rings* and silly Christmas movies—only real."

For a moment there is total silence. And then she moves into my arms, laying her cheek against my rapidly beating, rotten, inhuman heart.

"Thank you," she whispers. "Thank you for your honesty. I've always known you were different. I knew there was something special about you. But your heart—it may beat faster, but it's the same—it's like mine."

My heart clenches with a sweet pain at her words. How I wish they were true. "No." I tighten my hold on her and whisper into my hair, "Your heart is pure and good. No one is like you."

"You could be, Culley. You could be good. But even if you never change one single bit... I love you the way you are. Nothing will change that."

My heart thunders, clinging to her extraordinary words, wanting desperately to believe them. "Laney." I breathe raggedly. "I've been alone for so long."

"Not anymore. I want to be with you—always."

No one has ever said anything like that to me. I can hardly think over the whirring of my own pulse in my ears. Shaking, starving, I lower my head and bring my lips to hers, unable to resist their sweetness any longer.

Laney rises on her toes, meeting me all the way. We wind together, my legs bracketing hers, trying to contain the surfeit of emotion and energy between us. Her hands go to my chest, my shoulders, sink into my hair, stroking and soothing, and yet with each touch I grow more impatient to touch and kiss and possess every part of her. Now. Tonight. Just one night with her would be worth having the mark for eternity—Hell, my hair's so blond it's practically white already.

As we pull out of the kiss, we're both trembling.

Shit. What have I done?

And how soon can I do it again? Now that I've opened up to her, now that I've admitted my unholy attraction to her, I don't want to shut that door again. I don't even think I can. How could I lie to her and myself and pretend not to care, pretend to be unaffected by her sweetness, and her beauty, and her inexplicable belief in me?

"Let me take you home," I urgently whisper against her

lips. "I want to be alone with you."

"Yes," she answers. "Yes. That's what I want, too."

We practically run to the elevator and kiss all the way to the first floor until we hear the ding indicating the doors are about to open.

"I need to get the car," I say. "Do you want to come with me? Or wait inside?"

"I'll go to the ladies' room and meet you in the lobby in a few minutes, okay?"

"Yes." I kiss her thoroughly. "See you in a few. God you're beautiful."

She giggles and pushes at me. Grinning like a dolt, I head for the front of the club, having to restrain myself from whistling aloud. A happy tune floats through my brain, though, as I pass my claim slip to the valet and stand in the cool night air.

Oh, my jacket. I left it in the ballroom.

"I'll be right back," I say to the guy manning the valet stand. Re-entering the club and ducking back into the ballroom, I spot my jacket hanging on the back of the chair at Nicole's table on the other side of the room. I'll have to time my retrieval mission in between live auction items. Right now, a trip for two to Napa Valley and San Francisco is up on the block. The emcee does a fine job of hyping the romance and sophistication of the getaway, and I find myself wondering if Laney would enjoy a trip to Northern California.

As soon as the wine lovers' getaway is going, going, gone, I slide across the room, intending to snag the jacket and say some hasty good-byes to my table mates. Most of them are so far into their respective wine glasses they won't remember my leaving early.

"And now, ladies and gentlemen, the premier offering of the night... a romantic two-week getaway to beautiful Rome, Italy. Perfect for an anniversary celebration, marriage proposal, or a honeymoon. We'll start the bidding at ten thousand dollars. Do I hear ten? Ten thousand?"

"Ten thousand!" Nicole's father stands and puffs his chest out as he announces his entry in the auction. People around the room clap in approval.

Another gala guest stands—a tall, angular woman—the CEO of something by the looks of her. She directs a challenging smile at the movie producer, indicating the game is on. "Eleven thousand."

"Twelve thousand," he counters.

There is more applause, more laughter as the rival philanthropists are jeered and cajoled by their respective tables to keep going.

"Fifty thousand dollars."

An audible gasp ripples across the ballroom, and heads turn to locate the source of the outrageous bid.

I don't have to look. I already know who the "generous benefactor" is. Chills streaked down my spine as soon as I heard his voice. My father—Audun Rune.

The emcee seems at a loss for words. Maybe he's trying to decide if this newcomer to the gala is for real. The sight of the other patrons rising from their seats and giving Father an ovation must convince him because he finally fumbles the microphone up to his mouth.

"I believe we have a winner here. Fifty thousand going once... going twice... sold for fifty thousand dollars to the big-hearted man in the Gucci suit there. Sir, S victims in this community owe you a huge debt of gratitude. Thank you for your amazing contribution to the Stop the Scourge cause." He claps his hands and nods toward one of the volunteers who move through the room collecting information from the bidders. "Could you... get his...yeah, thanks."

The woman rushes for Father, eager to write down his name and payment information. I want to run for the door, grab Laney, and sweep her away from this place. But I know that's out of the question. Father is here for a reason—other than being seen publicly supporting this *worthwhile* cause. He'll want to speak to me.

After he's finished shaking hands with the other bidders and accepting kudos from party guests, I stroll over to him.

"Father. I see your altruistic spirit is alive and well."

He gives me a shark-like grin. "Oh yes. Never let it be said that Audun Rune doesn't care about his fellow man. This isn't *your* usual sort of venue, though. I trust you've enjoyed the party?"

"Yes, I thought it would be worthwhile to... connect with some big influencers." I toss my head to the side toward the table where Nicole and the people from her father's movie studio are beginning to stand and gather their belongings.

"I see," he says. "Someone told me you were here with

the loveliest girl. I believe she was one of the speakers?"

Tilting my head, I squint upward, pretending to think. "I did dance with a girl, but she's here as her boss's date. I'm alone tonight—but I don't intend to be for long."

For father's sake, I shoot a direct and very lewd glance at Nicole. She does a surprised double-blink, but then responds in the expected way. Smiling, she begins to move toward me.

"Well. I must have heard wrong then. I must be off— busy night. Enjoy *your* evening and your amusements while you can. I bought that Roman vacation package for you and your new bride."

My gaze whips from Nicole back to him. "What?"

His satisfied grin stretches wide. "Yes, it's all worked out. You're to be a groom. Alessia's father is the Dark leader in Italy. Are you pleased?"

"Of course. Come, I'll walk you out, and you can tell me about the plans." I want to get him out of here before Laney tires of waiting and comes looking for me.

"What about your lady friend?" he asks, eying Nicole.

"Yes, right." I stop in place, waiting for her to reach us.

"Hi Culley," she says, almost shyly. "Who's this?"

"Nicole, this is my father, Audun Rune. He's an excellent entertainment attorney, in case you're ever in the market."

"Charmed to make your acquaintance," he says, taking Nicole's hand and bringing it to his mouth, pressing his lips to her knuckles and keeping them there for an inappropriately long time as she giggles and blushes.

If I actually cared anything about the girl, I'm sure I'd be annoyed. As it is, I'm only aware of the valuable seconds ticking by. We need to get out of here.

"So, would you like to come back to my place for a drink or something?" I ask Nicole. "We didn't get much of a chance to catch up tonight."

Her eyes pop wide with surprise and excitement. "Oh. Yes, that would be great. Let me tell my father goodnight, and I'll be right back."

She steps away just as Shane walks by. He's turning side to side, craning his neck, obviously searching for Laney.

Reaching out, I catch the sleeve of his tux. "If you're looking for your date, I believe I saw her in the main hallway." Imparting a dose of Sway with my words, I add, "She's probably waiting for you to take her home."

He stands and blinks at me for a second before responding. "Oh. Thanks. Hey, good to see you tonight. Thanks for supporting the cause."

"You too, mate. You all right to drive?"

"Yeah, I'm good. Only had a couple of drinks."

Shane heads for the hallway where I presume Laney is waiting for me. He's going to have a hell of a time convincing her to leave with him after what just transpired between us. And he'd *better* be sober.

I'm trying to figure out how to call a cab for the two of them when Father asks, "Since when are you interested in the blood alcohol levels of humans?"

Meeting my father's curious gaze, I shrug. "The guy seemed a bit bombed out."

"Aren't you the concerned citizen?" Father says, his eyes narrowing in scrutiny.

"Well, we have to get on the road with the mug. You recall what happened to Ava's father, I'm sure."

Nicole returns, saving me from further interrogation. "Here she is," I say grandly. "The belle of the ball. Ready to go, love?"

She nods eagerly, and the three of us head for the door. I'm glad I've already given the valet my ticket. The car will be ready and waiting for my escape.

Unfortunately, when we reach the club entrance, Laney is standing there just inside the doors, arguing with Shane. Can I slip past her without being detected and without Father overhearing any damning conversation? The last Laney knew, she was meeting me at the front doors and we were going home to make love. Now Shane is absolutely convinced she's his date and going home with him.

"I can't," she says, turning her head side to side, wearing a desperate expression.

"But the party's over, sweetheart. Everyone is leaving."

"I'm not your 'sweetheart,'" she argues.

Good girl. Oh, but it's not good. I tamp down the satisfaction that arose when she denied him. I *need* her to leave with him. Her life could depend on it.

"Ah, trouble in paradise," Father quips. "Perhaps she'd like a *different* companion for the evening." He eyes Laney's figure in the tight silver dress with far too much interest for my comfort.

I turn to him abruptly. "Would you mind escorting

Nicole to my car for me? I need to visit the bathroom before we leave." I'm hopeful the distraction will work—only a few minutes ago, he gave Nicole a similar once-over. I have to get him outside and far away from Laney before disaster strikes.

His eyes go back to the blonde bombshell standing between us, and a lecherous grin sneaks across his face. "Not at all. Come along my dear. Now tell me about yourself. A girl as beautiful as you *must* be an actress."

He pulls her along, out through the doors, leaving me in relative privacy with Laney and Shane. I know what I have to do, though it might kill me. As soon as Father spotted her tonight, I knew. *I can't be with her.* My intention to take her home and bond with her was a foolish fantasy. It would have ended in calamity for both of us. But she's so determined for us to be together. She thinks I'm *the one*.

I have to do something to change her mind.

"Culley." Baffled hurt is evident in Laney's voice. "What is going on?"

"Going on?" I repeat blithely. "Nothing. I ran into an old friend of mine—she's an up and coming actress—stunning girl. We're going to go back to my place to 'catch up.'"

I elbow Shane and give him a you-know-what-I-mean look. He laughs as I knew he would.

"You're taking *her* home? To your place? Right now?"

"I know, right? Lucky me. With this ugly mug, I've got to count my lucky stars for scoring such a babe."

Shane laughs even louder.

"Oh," I add as if it's a secondary thought. "You might want to stay with Brenna tonight. Or old Shane here. Unless you'd like to listen in... or join." I deliver the disgusting words in an offhand tone. Inside, I'm dying.

"Hey," Shane says in offended protest, clearly coming out from under the Sway spell I laid on him.

Laney lifts a hand. Though she can't see my face, she makes direct contact with a loud, stinging slap.

I force out a laugh, rubbing my smarting jaw. "I guess that's a no then. Well, I'll be off. You two kids have fun tonight. Don't do anything I wouldn't do." *Like sleep with Shane because you're so angry with me. Or show up at my door later to verify I'm actually with Nicole.*

I have no intention of taking the actress back to my condo. I may have to glamour her brains out to forget I suggested it, but I don't care. I don't want anyone around tonight.

By the time I make it out to the curb, I see my problem has been solved for me. Father has his arm around Nicole's waist, whispering in her ear as the two of them lean against my car.

"Ah Culley. Listen, you don't mind if Nicole and I take a drive do you? We've just started getting to know each other and have found we've quite a lot in common. We could use a little more time to *chat.*" *I'll be happy to drop her off at your place afterward*, he adds silently.

Don't bother. I'm tired anyway, I respond. Out loud I say, "Of course. And considering I'm engaged to be married, it's probably for the best."

Nicole's eyes widen in horror. "You're engaged?"

I smile bitterly. "A recent development. It was good to see you again. Take care... and good luck."

With that, I slide behind the wheel of my car and slam the door, speeding away into the night. No doubt I shouldn't have abandoned her to my father like that. She'll wake up tomorrow morning wondering how she spent her evening and assuming she had way more to drink than she realized at the gala. She might even end up in a European fan pod somewhere.

I force the distasteful thought from my mind. I can't save all of them. I *can* save Laney—and I will. If it's the last thing I do, I'll protect her from Father... and myself.

I can't believe how close I came tonight to throwing all caution to the wind and bonding with her. If he hadn't shown up when he did, that's exactly what would have happened.

My body warms at the thought of it, tightening into a frustrated knot. Images of Laney in that dress—*out* of that dress—moving wantonly underneath me, smiling seductively, making noises of pleasure—torture me all the way home. I pull into the garage, slam the car door so hard the windows rattle, and charge into the house and down the hall to the shower.

Standing under the scalding spray, I try desperately not to imagine those same salacious scenes starring Laney and Shane. My belly turns with furious revulsion. How could I have sent her off with him?

How could I *not* have? It was the only way I could come

up with on the fly to protect her from my father. All I can do is hope the fact she was not swayed will keep her from giving in to whatever advances Shane might make toward her.

"You selfish bastard," I mutter, pressing my forehead to the wet tile and letting the water attempt the impossible—nothing will take away this excruciating tension.

I'm not going to be with her. The certainty sits in my gut like a stone with sharp edges. But I still don't want Laney to give herself to Shane. I *am* selfish. I cannot have her, but I don't want anyone else to. *She's mine.* It doesn't make any sense, but everything in me screams it—she's mine, mine, mine.

I don't know how I'm going to live with this, how I'll continue going through each day.

The doorbell rings as I turn off the water.

Shit. Is Father finished with Nicole already? I hope he didn't disregard my instructions and bring her here anyway. Maybe it's Brenna bringing Cupcake home. Charging into my bedroom, I rummage through the drawers, yanking on the first pair of shorts I come across. I stride to the front door and look through the security port.

All my breath leaves me at once. It's Laney. She's standing alone, and she appears to be crying.

Oh God. I backtrack a few paces. My heart is simultaneously bursting with joy and filled with dismay. Everything inside me wants to throw open the door, drag her inside, and claim her so *no one* else will ever have her.

No. I can't let her in. In my current state of mind, she'll be on her back and underneath me in ten seconds flat. *Oh no.* I'm enjoying that mental picture far too much.

I take a step back toward the door, my hand on the knob before I force myself to stop, grabbing handfuls of my own hair and clenching to the point of pain.

I can't. I can't.

She rings the bell again. "Culley—please let me in," she says, the sound of her sweet voice an absolute torment to my inflamed body and mind. "Are you really with her? What happened, Culley? Please open the door."

No one should ever come this close to the fires of hell. I'm hovering at the edge of an abyss, my hands shaking with the compulsion to open the door, my body an inferno of wretchedness.

Finally, I force words from my parched throat. My voice comes out stronger than I would have expected based on the shaky way I feel. "Go away, Laney. I'm busy. I'm... not alone."

On the other side of the port, she stands in stunned immobility for a moment. Then her hands come up to cover her face, and her shoulders begin to shake. My heart shrivels as she slowly turns and walks away.

Go to Brenna's place, I command her silently. I know my neighbor won't turn her away, even if she has to give up her own bed. And tomorrow, Laney will have her own place to move into.

She'll be fine, I tell myself. Me, on the other hand...

Pacing my living room like a caged tiger, I finally pick up my phone and text Brenna.

-Is she there?

The answer comes minutes later.

-She is. What the hell did you do?

-I'll talk to you in the morning. Take care of her.

There's no further communication from Brenna, and no sleep at all for me that night. The next morning, I call my neighbor.

"Hello?" Brenna answers.

"How bad was it?"

"Pretty bad apparently. She's gone."

My heart freezes. "Gone? What do you mean gone?"

"I mean she's not here. She got up and left sometime during the night. She took her purse and the clothes she was wearing. And Cupcake."

That last part is the one that scares me. "She didn't tell you where she was going?"

"No."

"Brenna..." My tone is a warning. If she's holding out on me, mistakenly believing she's doing Laney a favor by lying to me, I'll find out.

"I promise. I had no idea she even intended to go. I called her new apartment—they said she's not there. Where do you think she went?"

Considering it, I literally shudder. She could be anywhere. Knowing her, she spent the night out on the beach. Anything could have happened to her. "I don't know. But I know where she'll go today—the clinic."

"You really think so? She was pretty upset last night. I had the impression she was kind of done with the whole

L.A. scene. Whatever you said or did, it was a doozy."

My frozen heart gathers another layer of ice. My tone is tight and frantic. "Did she ever tell you where she's from? Think about it—any hints at all."

"No. She was always really tight-lipped about that. Sorry. What will you do?"

"Find her of course."

Chapter Nineteen
Assignment

Three weeks later

"Come dance with us," Deeanna says. The intoxicated pop star stretches her arms out to me, and she wiggles her fingers. Her glossy mouth forms a pretty pout. "Come on, Culley. You *used* to be fun."

I haven't had nearly enough to drink tonight to dance. I haven't had nearly enough to drink—period. That's how I spend most of my existence now. The only way I can get any kind of relief from the torment of my memories is to drown them in alcohol. I *really* need to go see Ava and let her wipe the whole mess of it clean.

Reluctantly I allow the singer to drag me out onto the floor, the swirling lights and pounding bass in L.A.'s hottest nightclub doing nothing to counteract the dead feeling inside me. It's my fourth night out this week. I'm tired. And bored. I wouldn't even be here if my absence wouldn't be noticed.

The girl undulates to the music, making obvious bedroom eyes at me. Her generous and barely covered "assets" bounce with the rhythm of the techno beat. All around us guys are craning their necks to look at her one-woman floor show, but none of it stirs even the least bit of interest in me.

I shout in order to be heard over the powerful sound system. "I think I'm gonna push off."

Her face contracts in a scowl. "Nooooo. You just got here. What's the matter? You got a girlfriend waiting at home or something?"

The innocent question slices through me like the sharpest blade. "No. I definitely do not have one of those."

One of her backup dancers shimmies up next to me. "Boyfriend?" he asks hopefully.

I give a rueful grin. "No. Not one of those either. I've got work."

"I call bullshit," the dancer says. "I know you don't have a shoot tonight. Stay here and party with us. Dee has some excellent S. It'll be a fun night. You can slam a few Red Bulls in the morning to get going."

"Tempting, mate. Tempting. But no. I'm afraid I can't do it. You all have some fun for me, okay?"

I head out to the parking lot, trying to shake off the putrid reaction I've been having lately every time I see people using S or hear them talking about it as if it's a good time. I actually feel compelled to talk them out of it. *Damn*

Laney. It never used to bother me. Now I can't help but think of her brother Joseph and the things she said about his loss. Somehow I've gone from wanting to eradicate S for her sake to actually caring about the whole sodding lot of the human race.

I've been unable so far to find much information that would help Ava and her Light Elven allies in their fight against the Scourge. So I go to work every day on some modeling gig or other, and I spend most evenings out, maintaining the appearance of continuing to work for my father.

It's hardly necessary anymore anyway. The roots of the epidemic have already been sunk so deep, the cases of S addiction are increasing almost on autopilot. Even if I were to stop pushing the drug entirely, the Scourge would continue to spread. Before long, it will even make its way to the small town where Laney lives, wherever that is.

Damn it—there she is again—always in my mind, waiting to take over and pull me into a depressive gloom at the slightest reminder.

I went to the clinic the morning after the charity gala looking for her. When I arrived, Shane stared daggers at me and said Laney had called him late the previous night, informing him that she would not return to her volunteer post there.

"I offered to hire her, to pay her for her work if money was the issue," he told me. "She said it was not that. It was a personal matter. She said she had to go home, that she couldn't stay in the city. She didn't have the heart for it. She was crying. I don't know what you did to her, man, but you did a real number on that girl."

He shook his head in disgust. "I'm not sure what she ever saw in you."

I didn't have the energy or the inclination to argue with him. "Me either, mate."

Before leaving, I used my Sway on him and each of the clinic workers, quizzing them about any information Laney might have shared regarding her hometown or even her last name. No one knew anything. Because she wasn't on the payroll, she'd never filled out any paperwork. I left the place no closer to finding her than I was when I arrived.

The hopeless, empty feeling hasn't dissipated since then. It's increased in fact. Any notion I had of time healing the gaping wound left by Laney's abrupt departure is now gone. It only grows larger every day.

Why didn't I open the damn door?

The sound of her voice, asking me to let her in, haunts my dreams. That is, when I can go to sleep at all. Most of my nights are spent tossing and turning, imagining the feel of her small body next to mine, burning with longing to touch her, to see her, to talk to her. I'd give up everything I have—eagerly—just for the chance to see her one more time.

Of course, if that actually were to happen it would change nothing. *Looking* is the extent of what I'd do with those precious moments. Over the course of the long, empty weeks since she's been gone, I've become convinced leaving was the best thing for her. Even if she were to knock on my door tonight and ask me to let her come back, I'd say no.

Maybe.

No, I would. I'd have to. She was wrong about me. There is no good inside. Though I'm no longer as interested in my father's approval, I still do his bidding. Even knowing what the human toll will be, I do it. It doesn't matter anymore. Nothing does.

I pull into the gated drive of Father's Bel Air mansion. The lavish home could be better described as a palace, featuring a lushly landscaped Italianate courtyard, elaborate ironwork, three pools, and a panoramic view of the city as well as a five bedroom "guest cottage." Inside the mansion itself, there are ten bedrooms and twelve baths, a gym, and enough gold leaf, marble, and chandeliers to put Versailles to shame. As far as I can tell, Father uses about a tenth of the place and appreciates none of it.

Leaving the keys in the car, I let myself in through the ornate iron and glasswork front door and head for his library office. I wasn't lying to the flirty back-up dancer. I really do have work to do tonight. Father summoned me by text to meet him here.

"Ah, Culley. Come in. Sit down." He's casually dressed in slacks and a cashmere sweater but still looks ready to host a cocktail party or pose for a spread in a lifestyle magazine.

I take a seat on the leather sofa flanking one wall of his office. He sits behind his desk.

"How was your evening, son? Find any fresh amusements?"

I know he's referring to girls. The answer is a resounding, "No." I have absolutely no interest in any of the girls who throw themselves at me during my nightly forays into the city's hot spots.

Though I'm at the age of bonding for Elves, and the drive to find a mate becomes increasingly insistent for our race at that time, my own libido seems to have gone on permanent hiatus. When Laney was around, all it took was a whiff of her sweet vanilla scent, or the sound of her voice, or one glance at her tiny bare feet and I was raring to go. Now? I could spend an entire night at the 4Play club in West L.A. and not feel a single stir.

"Yes, Father," I lie. "A few. L.A. is a wondrous city. I'll be sorry to leave it."

"Yes, it's been good to have you around. You have matured into a capable and reliable ally. But I know you'll enjoy living in Europe again. And it will be very advantageous to have you there, where you can influence the Court overseas. Speaking of which, plans for your wedding celebration are coming along nicely. Only a month to go in your enforced celibacy. No doubt you'll enjoy that perk even more."

"As you do?" I quip bitterly.

Though still married, my parents haven't lived together in years. Because they're Elven, neither of them can take another mate. Which means, for all practical purposes, my father is as celibate as I am, his everything-but dalliances with attractive human women notwithstanding.

There's no guarantee my own arranged marriage will be

any less miserable. But what does it really matter? I have no desire for any girl beside Laney anyway. I won't love anyone else—so it really makes no difference who I am forced to marry.

He gives me a grim smile. "Your mother and I have a powerful alliance—and an understanding. It works. We're both getting exactly what we want out of the arrangement."

"Did you ever love her?" I ask, suddenly curious.

He skewers me with a glare. "Have you heard a word I've said? Love serves no purpose. It's a silly human notion." He lets out a weary breath. "Letting you interact with them has been a necessary evil—I certainly hope their peculiar ideas and traditions haven't *infected* you. We have too much work to do to waste time pursuing pipe dreams and fairy tales."

"No Father," I say. "There is nothing in my life but the work."

The accuracy of the words hits me full force. Though my attitude toward humans has changed, my life has not. I am still living as I did before I ever met Laney—obeying my Father's commands, following his prescription for my life, putting all of *their* lives in danger. The only difference now is I actually feel lonely when I'm alone.

"Very good." He stands and walks around his desk, holding out a large manila envelope.

"What's this?"

"A list of our S factories with notations beside those that are new or set to come on line shortly. I'll need you to inspect them with Hakon, and get it done before your marriage takes place. It will require a bit of travel."

I get to my feet and take the offered treasure, trying to hide my excitement. "That's no problem. Anything you need."

This could be the break we've been looking for. With a complete inventory of the S production facilities, Ava and her allies might be able to concoct a scheme to shut them down or perhaps interfere with delivery of the drug. I leave Father's house with my mind spinning. I'll need to pay close attention at each plant I visit, making note of entrances and exits, operating hours, and delivery routes and schedules.

I can't say I'm "happy." I've blown my one chance at experiencing that emotion in this lifetime. But for the first time in weeks, my life feels like it might have a little purpose, some reason to go on. I cannot be with Laney. But there's a chance I could protect her and her friends and family from afar. Now I just have to figure out how to do it.

CHAPTER TWENTY
PERFECT WEAPON

Our first factory visit takes us to Denver. Father's private jet is at our disposal, so it takes Hakon and I only two and a half hours to reach the plant where we do a walk-through and interview the supervisor. The healer does his quality check of the product while I inspect the delivery vehicles and schedule information, making copies for my own later use.

Houston is our next stop, followed by Orlando. At each location, I gather what intel I can. I'm sure I'm missing something important, but without knowing exactly what the plan will be it's hard to know what to look for.

"I think that's all we can do for today," I say to Hakon. "Want to stay here tonight or go on to Charlotte and spend the night there?"

"Let's stay here, if you don't mind. I've always wanted to see Orlando. Ever been to the Magic Kingdom?"

I shake my head. "Nah. Mother rarely leaves Australia, and Father never had time when I visited him here in summers."

He looks at his watch. "Well, it's a little late for the parks, and I'm more than a little old for them, but maybe we could get a cab to Downtown Disney and have dinner, look around."

"Sure. Whatever. Sounds fine."

Though it's after nine when we arrive at the entertainment village, the parking lot is filled, and pedestrians pack the balmy well-lit walkways. Hakon and I stroll from restaurant to restaurant, laughing when we spot Planet Hollywood.

"If only they knew the place was filled with relics of Elven domination of the TV and film industry," he says.

"Well, I don't care where we eat—as long as I can get a beer and a burger—and soon."

"Agreed."

We select a cafe with sidewalk seating, having spent the entire day indoors. The food is fine, but the real attraction of the place is the people watching. Families of every size, shape, and race imaginable walk past, some smiling, some struggling with overtired toddlers who are beyond ready to call it a day.

Hakon watches a father and son go by, the little boy riding high on his dad's shoulders. The expression in his turquoise eyes could only be described as "wistful."

"Are you a married man?" I ask, wondering if he has a child of his own he might be missing.

His gaze darts to mine, his expression shuttering and becoming unreadable. "No, I... never married."

"Why not?" It's highly unusual among our people to stay single. The Elven race is perilously small in number, so members of both courts are strongly encouraged to marry early and start trying to produce offspring immediately. It takes most couples decades to conceive. Some never do.

"It wasn't in the cards for me," he says. "My duty to the Dark Court under Davis and now your father keeps me constantly busy. I don't get much time away from work. I would have been a poor husband. And I know my fathering leaves—would have left—a lot to be desired."

Trying to make light of his rather depressing explanation, he gives me a wide, dimpled smile. A zing of recognition shocks me. Who does he look like? Someone from my past—a school mate at Eton perhaps? Maybe one of the other male models I've worked with?

"Ah," I say. "Who needs home and family when you've got duty to keep you warm, right? No wonder my father loves you."

"Actually," he says. "I wouldn't recommend it. If I could go back and be your age again, I'd make very different choices."

My age...

That's when it hits me. When I picture Hakon at my age, he bears an undeniable resemblance to someone I've met recently.

Asher.

"*That* sounds like a good story," I prompt. "Care to

trade tales of lost loves and bad decisions?"

Hakon's eyes narrow speculatively. He's clearly wondering if he should trust me. Why would he? As far as he can see, I'm another one of Audun's loyal soldiers. We both know any disloyalty among the ranks is dealt with swiftly and severely. And hell, as far as I know, he's my father's biggest fan. But... there's something about him.

Maybe it's the circles under his eyes, or the dispirited way he goes about his job, or that melancholy look he gave to the father-and-son pair that makes me think he wouldn't be here if he had any choice about it. Just like me.

"I won't bore you with my life story," he says with a tight smile. "We're already exhausted as it is."

"And starved," I say. "Ah, right on time. Thank you love."

The waitress sets both our plates in front of us, warning us that they're hot. We both dig in. After a few minutes, Hakon comes up for air.

"So what do you think about the operation based on what you've seen so far?"

Is this a test? Is he now fishing to find out if *I'm* all-in on my father's scheme?

I give him a safe answer. "It all looks like it's proceeding according to plan, as far as I can tell. You're the expert, though. What do you think?"

"Oh, it'll work. I have no doubt of that. This latest incarnation of S is the most addictive substance I've ever seen—that the world has ever seen."

"What I don't get is... it's made of something that's

found readily in the Light Court. And yet, Altum's not full of S addicts. But Father warned our people to stay away from it. Why does it affect us—and the humans—but not the Light Elves?"

He takes another bite, chewing slowly before answering. "I have my theories."

"Such as?"

"Have you ever encountered pure iron?"

I have an immediate flashback to my painful attempt to cross the property line of the McCord's farm. "Yeah. Once, actually. It wasn't pleasant."

"Right. For centuries Dark Elves have avoided iron because it's poisonous to us. We don't have it in our homes, we steer clear of locations filled with iron, we make sure our children don't get hold of chewable vitamins containing iron. But at the most recent Assemblage I learned something from Wickthorne. The Light Elves have taken the opposite approach."

"What do you mean?"

"They purposely expose their children, starting in infancy, to small amounts of iron. They sometimes cook in iron skillets, wearing gloves of course, so trace amounts of the substance leach into the food."

"They've inoculated their population against iron poisoning."

"Yes," he says, growing more animated. "And I believe it goes further than that. I think the iron counteracts the active ingredient in S—the thing that makes it addictive. Earlier iterations of the drug contained much higher iron levels—that was the initial reason Audun cautioned members of the Dark Court not to use it. Some of the first chemists who were assigned to make it actually died. As we've perfected the formula, though, we've nearly eliminated the iron content. It's safer for our people to work with, *and* the addictiveness of the drug has increased exponentially."

"So now Dark Elves *could* become addicted to it."

"Yes, it would no longer poison them, but it *will* hook them if they're foolish enough to try it. And the humans… they truly have no chance."

"Sounds like you've created the perfect weapon."

His tone and expression flatten out into an unreadable blandness. "Yes. I have."

* * *

The next morning when Hakon and I meet in the lobby of our hotel, I take a risk and propose a change to our itinerary.

"I know we planned to fly from Charlotte to Memphis to Chicago today—what do you think about mixing it up and visiting the new Memphis plant last, spend the night there instead?"

He shrugs. "Sure. Why? No love for Chicago?"

"Oh it's not that—great city, Chicago. It's just that I've only briefly visited the South, and my last trip to Memphis consisted of only the airport and a quick drive-by. I thought I might take a day and explore, eat barbecue, listen to the blues." And pay a visit to my co-conspirators to share my new discoveries with them.

"Your father doesn't have an exact schedule for us as long as we get all the inspections done. So I suppose it should be fine. We even have a few days to burn if you want to take more than one."

Ah ha. He's all too willing to agree to this detour. Maybe he sees it as an opportunity to visit someone in the area that he doesn't see often? I give him another chance to own up to it.

"Have you spent much time in the region?"

Hakon shoots me a side glance, brimming with suspicion. "I've been there a few times. It seems nice enough, though I mostly just get in and out."

"Good then. Maybe you'll enjoy spending a little more time there yourself."

He gives a noncommittal nod as we climb into the taxi bound for the private air field. The day drags, partially because of my eagerness to get to Memphis, rent a car, and make the hour drive south to Altum tonight. And partially because as we fly over Georgia, and South Carolina, and later over Kentucky, Indiana, and Illinois, I can't keep from thinking of Laney. Is she down there somewhere, perhaps hearing my plane pass overhead?

I picture that pretty, stubborn chin of hers, tilting to the sky. Maybe she's enjoying a day at the park, or perhaps lying by the pool, feeling the spring sun soak into her skin. Maybe she's gotten a service dog, and they're out for a walk together.

Maybe she's thinking of me, too.

No. Don't go there. I shut down the highway of emotion running full and fierce from my brain to my heart. It's pointless to torture myself like this. I need to let go of the myriad mental images I have stored up of her. The best I can hope for is that the trip I take tonight to Altum will result in a cleaner and safer world for her and the children she'll have someday—with whatever guy is lucky enough to be chosen by her.

Aargh. No. Stop thinking about it.

I open the plane's mini-bar, grabbing the first small bottle I see, downing it in one go.

"You might want to tap the breaks on that," Hakon advises as I reach for another bottle. "We'll be touching down in Memphis in about half an hour. Unless you're planning to take a cab."

I lean back, leaving the other bottles where they are. "No. I'm going to rent a car. Maybe you should, too. Some pretty country around there."

We're so close to Deep River—surely he'll want to take the opportunity to visit Asher—*if* my suspicions are correct, that is. I'll follow his rental car, and if it heads for a certain small Mississippi town south of the Tennessee border, I'll have my answer.

He stares out the window at the ground far below. "No, I… I think I'll just stay on the plane. I didn't sleep well last night, and I have research to catch up on anyway."

"You sure? Seems like a shame to be in the area and not explore all the possibilities."

"Yeah, I'm sure." He turns to me with a sad smile. "At your age the world is still full of possibilities. Old men like me have already had ours… and used them up."

Chapter Twenty-one
Game Plan

Tromping through the steamy, sticky Mississippi woods, I wonder what the hell I'm doing here. Maybe I have a death wish? If the helicopter-sized mosquitos don't take me out, the guards at Altum probably will. I did stop at a gas station on the way and use a pay phone to call Ava to warn her I'd be coming. She assured me she'd go and smooth the way and prepare Lad and his bond-mate for my arrival.

The Light King really shouldn't worry. I only plan to stick around long enough to share what I've discovered about the S plants and the information about the iron content. Hopefully it'll be enough to help them—and to make up in some small way for the wrongs I did him and Ryann.

My "escorts" appear when I get within a half mile of the underground kingdom. One of the fierce-looking leather-clad men grabs the manila envelope from me and inspects it thoroughly as if the sheafs of paper inside might serve as some sort of assassination tools.

No, really, go right ahead, I say. I*t's not like I've got top-secret information for your king in there.*

If you do, you're a traitor, he replies. *If not, you're a liar.*

Either way, so flattering. The hospitality of the Light Court lives up to its sparkling reputation. What's next? A bed of nails? Truth serum? Lead on, then. I haven't got all day to be insulted in the woods.

Without even cracking a smile, the man grabs my arm and jerks me along with him and his still-silent companion. True to her word, Ava waits for me inside, at the bottom of the winding entrance tunnel. She looks beautiful, of course, and happier than I've ever seen her.

"Well, hello—"

"Culley!" She launches herself at me and throws her arms around my neck. "I knew you would come around. I knew you had it in you all along."

I stagger backward, partly from her unexpected strength, but mostly from shock. "Yes, it's er... good to see you, too." Peeling her from my chest, I glance to the side to see Asher. He looks more amused than perturbed, so I lift a hand in wary greeting. "Asher."

He really looks like he's striving to keep a straight face. "Culley. How was your trip?"

"Long. But enlightening." Now that I see him face to face again, I'm even more convinced he's related to Hakon. The dimples are the same, and the eyes contain the exact same rare shade of blue-green.

"Can't wait to hear all about it. Come on," he says, taking Ava's hand and gesturing for me to precede them. "Lad and Ryann are waiting in the palace. Does your father know you're here?"

I give him the don't-be-an-idiot look. "Of course not. Does *your* father know *you're* here?"

"Culley!" Ava shoots me an offended glare. "How mean."

"I'm not sure where my father is, actually," Asher responds in a measured tone. "I haven't seen him lately, though I'd like to. I have a lot I'd like to ask him."

I open my mouth to say something then think better of it and stay silent for the rest of the walk to the royal residence. I'm still not sure about Hakon. It's possible I'm making too much of the resemblance. After all, he did say he's never married or had children.

And part of me—an ugly part, admittedly—resents the idea that Hakon could be Asher's father. Hakon is a good man—a truly good man. And Asher's already won the girl away from me. If he ends up with a loving, kind father as well, while the best I can ever hope for is Audun Rune's conditional approval and a lifetime without Laney, well... let's just say I'm not there yet in my emotional growth. Co-conspirator? Yes. But a selfless do-gooder I am not.

Reaching the palace, we wind through hallways until we arrive in an office sort of room where Lad and Ryann are waiting. Both get to their feet, and Ryann gives me a friendly greeting. Lad regards me with a wary look, but his words are civil enough.

"Welcome Culley Rune. I understand it's your intention to help us by sharing some information?"

Though he's younger than I am, I sort of feel the need to approach Lad with reverence. He seems... well, kingly. Maybe it's the leadership glamour or the fact that I know now all he's been through and sacrificed for his people—and for the girl he loves.

"Yes. I've come to believe it's best for everyone if we stop the S Scourge," I explain. "I've been to the plants where it's being made, and I believe I've discovered something that could be a real breakthrough."

"How do we know you're not feeding us false information? We can't even trust what you say mind-to-mind as Ava has informed us your glamour allows you to lie that way."

My feet shift, restless, and I clear my throat. "Only to my father, actually. I think it's unconnected to my glamour, which as you know is related to appearance. But perhaps our shared DNA allows me some immunity to my father's glamour. I know when he's lying to me. And I am able to lie to him without his detecting it."

Lad looks around the room at his allies, no doubt seeking their input. He clearly has little faith in me, and how can I blame him?

"I'm reading his emotions, and there's no intent to deceive right now," Ryann says. "I think we can trust him."

Asher shrugs. "I'm not sure what other choice we have."

"I believe him," Ava says. She turns her attention back to me. "So then you *didn't* sabotage the tea company."

I shake my head. "No. It wasn't me. It had to have been another of Father's agents. I was... very angry with you when I said that."

"I understand." She nods and glances quickly over to Asher, no doubt remembering the emotional scene we all shared a few months ago.

Lad nods, decided. "Very well then. What have you learned?"

"For one thing, I've brought you all the layouts and delivery schedules from all the S production locations." There are wide eyes and looks of approval all around as I continue. "And—there may be a way to alter the drug to spoil its addictive properties."

"How?" Ryann asks.

"My father's healer, who's been supervising the medical research aspect of S production, told me the addictive properties of the drug increased as its iron content was reduced. If we can find a way to add iron back into the supply, maybe it'll cause the humans to start detoxing and then overcome their dependence on it. Maybe if we add enough iron, it'll stop being addictive altogether. And iron isn't something that will hurt humans."

"True. Good idea." Lad's face twists in concentration as he examines the contents of the folder I brought. "Of course, there is a large, highly addictive supply that's been manufactured already. But with these delivery routes and times you've brought us, perhaps we can ambush the delivery vehicles and remove that supply before it reaches the distributors. I can contact the Light Elven clans who are nearest each of the plants and tell them to start scouting out the routes for locations that pass through wooded areas, or at least unpopulated stretches of road where they can attack."

"That could work," I say. "You'd have to coordinate a simultaneous strike, so Audun would have no time to circle the wagons and set up security. He'll be furious, but a one-day strike that wipes out the existing supply will definitely not stop him. He'll order round the clock production to make up for the lost supply. That's when I'll add the iron boost to the production process."

Ava steps forward wearing a worried frown. "That sounds dangerous, Culley."

I let out a short laugh. "*This* is dangerous—just my being here and telling you this. But I'm through living my life in fear of my father—or standing idly by while he continues to hurt people."

Ava shoots Lad a look that says *See? I told you.*

"What about this healer?" Asher speaks up for the first time. "If he's involved in the production process, won't he detect what's going on and blow the whistle?"

I study him, noticing the shape of his nose. It's exactly like Hakon's. "Let me deal with him," I say. "It's possible he's not fully on board with Audun's plan. He seems somewhat sympathetic toward the human race."

Ryann nods. "That would make sense. I think it comes along with the profession. I remember Wickthorne taking care of me when I first arrived here, back when I was considered an enemy to the Light Court just because I was human."

"It'll be risky, but I may have to share my intentions with him," I say. "Either that or do something to take him out of commission if he finds out."

"I don't want you to hurt anyone," Lad says.

"I wasn't intending to hurt him. If I'm wrong and he is fully on board with Audun's scheme, I'll have to overcome him and I don't know… hide him away somewhere until we've succeeded. Maybe I'll bring him here."

Lad nods. "That would work. All right. I need some time to look this stuff over and consult with my soldiers. Then I'll set about contacting the other clans and secure their cooperation to take out the supply chain. Thank you Culley. I'll see you later. Ava, Asher—would you walk him out and show him his quarters for the night?"

As we exit the office I laugh and slide a glance over to my escorts. "I'll bet those 'quarters' come with a pair of guards. He still doesn't trust me completely, does he?"

Ava grins. "Not completely. You *did* knock him out with a copper bowl."

We walk together until we're outside the royal residence and on the path toward the family housing in Altum. Asher must have said something to Ava mind to mind because she says, "Okay sweetie, I'll see you up there."

Before he goes, Asher looks right at me, his distinctive eyes holding, not trust, but perhaps a bit of liking. "I'm not sure why you're doing this, but thanks man—for the sake of my mom and granddaddy and all the humans." He gives me a tight smile and steps away, walking toward the surface tunnel.

"So," Ava says as we resume our stroll. "Why *are* you doing this? It's her, isn't it?"

I don't look at her and don't answer, keeping my face forward and a tight grip on my heart, which is now thudding painfully. God, what a mess I am. Just the mention of her—not even her name—and I'm back in full-blown pining mode.

"Well, whatever your reason, I'm happy. You're doing the right thing by getting away from your father and helping the humans. And now… it's time to fix your personal life."

I snort a laugh. "I have no personal life."

"What about Laney?"

There it is, the white-hot lance of pain through my chest.

"She's gone, moved on. It's no big deal."

"It is a big deal. You cared for her. Brenna says you've been moping around like a kid who's been told he can never eat candy again. Why didn't you go after Laney when she left?"

I give her the kind of hateful glare reserved for use between siblings. "Since you and Brenna seem to share *everything,* I'm surprised you don't know already. I have no idea where she is. So even if I wanted to pursue her—which I don't—I wouldn't know where to begin. She's better off far away from me. I'm bad for her. One good deed doesn't suddenly make me a saint, you know."

"I see. So, if you *did* know where she was, you wouldn't go to her?"

My tone is decisive. "No."

"Okay then," she says, dropping the subject. "You know, we haven't had much of a chance to talk since you went back to L.A. I haven't really been able to tell you much about Asher."

"What a terrible shame," I deadpan. "There's nothing I'd love more than to hear all about your new sweetheart."

"You might be surprised. For instance, you might be interested to know... one of Asher's closest friends from Deep River High School died of an S overdose."

I stop walking and stare at her. "Are you really this mean... or just grossly insensitive? Why would I want to know that? You know I'm trying to make up for—"

"*His name*," she continues, ignoring my wounded tone and expression, "was Joseph. Great guy, apparently a talented actor. He had a younger sister... named Laney. And she's blind."

All the oxygen leaves my body at once. I stagger back, my eyes bulging so far from their sockets I fear they might actually leave my person. Ava wears a very pleased expression.

"She's... *here?*" I gasp. "Here. In Deep River, Mississippi."

Ava shakes her head up and down, her smile growing. "Asher can give you directions to her house if you want."

For a few moments I'm silent as thoughts and emotions whirl through me like a gritty red dust storm on the Outback. *She's here.* Within driving distance. Within *walking* distance. If I want to, I can see her—today. I am slammed with a longing so powerful it nearly knocks me to the earthen floor. The thought of seeing her beautiful smile again, smelling her enticing scent…

"No."

"No? But I thought you'd—"

"No. I don't want to see her. I don't want to know where she is."

"But Culley…"

"I said, 'no,' all right? And you can tell your little half-human boyfriend to mind his own business as well. 'True love' isn't for everyone, okay? I'm happier on my own. Now—if you'll kindly direct me to my room, I'm rather tired, and I'd like to be left alone."

CHAPTER TWENTY-TWO
SHADOW

I found her.

I spent the better part of the morning driving through town, making a loop from one end of Main Street to the other. I finally spotted her coming out of a diner called The Skillet holding the arm of some bloke with dark brown hair and biceps bigger than his brains. *Maybe he's some sort of guide.* A cousin? A friend? A new boyfriend?

I'm not sure, but it doesn't really matter. I'm only here because I want to make sure she's doing okay. I won't be speaking to her or even let her know I'm in town.

Last night I lay awake for hours, staring up at that damn sparkly ceiling in my quarters at Altum. A million imagined conversations ran through my mind, all of them beginning with, "I'm sorry."

But I won't be telling her that. I won't be telling her anything. The last thing she needs is to have me show up in her life again. She looks happy. She looks… well, stunning actually. I'd somehow forgotten how beautiful she really is.

The beefy guy walks her to his car—a Charger, and they leave together. I follow as they make the short trip up Main Street and pull into the library parking lot. The passenger door opens. Laney gets out—alone. She shuts the door and leans into the window, saying good-bye I suppose. I feel a low growl roll through my throat.

Really dude? You don't even open her door for her?

Laney steps back from the car, and it backs onto Main Street again, driving away. *Thank you, I believe I will.* I pull into the vacated spot and kill the engine, watching as Laney moves up the walkway toward the old Antebellum style house. I wait until she ascends the stairs and goes through the doors under the Deep River Public Library sign before getting out of my car.

The interior of the library is cool and dim compared to outdoors. I stop just inside the front doors and scan the area. A head pops up from behind a counter nearby.

"Hi. Can I help you?" the woman asks.

"Oh. No, I'm… actually yes. Could you direct me to the Braille section? I'm also interested in audiobooks. My… grandma lost her sight a few years back."

"Sure." The woman smiles at me. "Go straight back and you'll see the audiobooks in our multi-media section. And we have a limited Braille selection, but they're housed just past the reference section there on the right. Toward the back."

"Great. Thanks."

I move off toward the right, guessing that's where Laney has gone. The library is not busy. A few old men sit and peruse newspapers. A young mother holds the hand of a child, encouraging the toddler to push the call button for the elevator. The reference librarian looks up from her desk and smiles at me as I pass, but there doesn't seem to be anyone else in this section.

I take a left past reference, and there she is. My feet stop moving. I stop breathing. She's so close I could reach out and touch her. I don't.

Hearing me or perhaps sensing the presence of another person, Laney smiles and says, "Am I in your way?"

The pounding of my heart in my ears is so loud it nearly drowns out her voice. I don't answer her, don't move an inch. Her fingers stop moving across the raised bumps on the spines of the books in front of her, and she lifts her head, cocking an ear in my direction.

"Is somebody there?"

I don't dare answer, just ease back away from her as she takes a step in my direction and stretches out her hand. I want to grab it—grab it and hold on and pull her into my arms. Her voice is so sweet in my ears, the sight of her like a cascade of rain on parched earth.

Very slowly I take several steps backward and nearly run over the reference librarian who has apparently taken it upon herself to offer some customer service.

"Sir? Can I help you?" she says, darting a glance over at Laney and then back to me.

I give her a terse head shake and speed walk away, out of

the front doors and down the sidewalk to my car. Sliding inside, I inhale deeply of the hot air and shake my head at my own idiocy. *What am I doing? I'm a stalker now. Awesome.*

I start my car, vowing to drive away and leave her alone, but then it doesn't happen. Letting the engine idle, I sit watching the library doors. *Did she know it was me?* My heart resumes its ridiculous thumping at the thought of it. No. She couldn't know.

It could have been anyone standing there beside her. In fact, it would be extremely easy for someone with evil intentions to follow her, sneak up on her, catch her alone and vulnerable. I don't like thinking about it.

She probably feels safe here in her tiny Southern hometown, but if I can find her here, any other vile character could. The idea compels me to keep following her when she leaves the library.

Laney walks down the sidewalk. After she passes my car, I open the door and get out, trailing about thirty feet behind her. She goes into a small drugstore with an ancient looking clock mounted on a pole outside. I open the door and go inside myself, struck by the quaintness of the place.

It feels like stepping into a bygone era. The entire left side of the store is an old-fashioned soda fountain made of dark, carved wood with a mirrored back. A smiling teenage girl scoops ice cream for one of the kids sitting on the bar stools lining the front of the fountain's counter. A few small tables dot the checkerboard linoleum floor.

The other half of the store contains shelves of first aid

and personal care products as well as some gift items, and in the far rear a pharmacist and some assistants help customers. Laney's not one of them, so I start checking the aisles.

"Hey there," a friendly voice calls, making me think someone actually recognizes me. But then I turn and see it's just a store employee. "Can I help you find something in particular?"

"Uh, no thanks," I mutter and move quickly away from the helpful worker—who probably now assumes I'm here to buy gas relief medication or a treatment for some sort of fungus or head lice. Whatever. I need to find Laney.

Moving to the next aisle, I spot her. She's checking out with a small box of medication. Is she sick? A snatch of alarm seizes my heart. I want a closer look at that box, though of course, that still might not fill me in on what's going on with her. Elves don't use medication—the human kind anyway. Our healers work differently, using their glamour to counteract the maladies that occasionally affect our kind. They're more apt to be treating injuries than illness since it is possible for us to be injured or even killed in a violent way—or by a poisonous substance like iron.

Laney pays for her item and turns around, walking right past me down the aisle toward the front door of the drug store. I plaster myself against the shelf behind me so she doesn't brush up against me. And now I'm following her again.

Outside on the sidewalk, she pulls her phone from her pocket and brings it to her ear. "I'm finished," she says to the person on the other end of the connection. "Are you about done at the grocery?" There's a pause as she listens, and then she says, "Okay, I'll see you in a minute."

Laney feels her way to a bench outside the store and sits while I wonder who she was talking to. That guy from earlier? Does *he* grocery shop for her? She didn't say if she had another brother—I think she would have mentioned it. And now that I think about it, Ava didn't mention one either.

I walk quickly to my car, climbing in and backing onto Main Street, driving the short distance down to the drug store and parallel parking across the street from it. Laney seems to be listening to something on her phone as she waits to be picked up. I hit the button to lower my car window and strain to hear what it is. Ah—a song. *Oh my God, she's singing along.*

The sweet sound of her voice reaches down and wraps itself around my heart, tugging to pull it out of my chest and across the street to her. Why does this girl affect me so much? I hate it. But I also love the feeling of connection, of actually *caring* about something for a change. A car pulls into one of the diagonal parking spaces directly in front of Laney's bench, blocking my view of her. I start to open my car door, so I can get out and keep an eye on her, but she stands and goes to the front of the vehicle, making her way around to the passenger side and getting in.

As the car backs up again and drives away, I get a look at the driver. It's a middle-aged woman. Petite with short, light brown hair—has to be her mother. My heart leaps, and I throw my own car into gear, pulling a U-turn in the middle of Main Street to tail them.

They drive to nearly the end of the street where it turns into a county road. I try to stay a few cars back. I rented an inconspicuous car this time—a Jeep—but still, I don't want to push it. I'd be more worried if it was her father driving. Men tend to notice cars more than women do. Plus, I can see her mom's head turn to the side every few minutes—they're obviously in conversation.

Finally the last car between us makes a turn, so I slow my speed. Laney's mom turns right onto a side street, and I speed up a little, catching up. As I make the turn, I see the bumper of her car disappear over the hill at the top of the street. Applying a bit more pressure to the gas, I follow, crest the hill, and look around. Where did they go?

Then I see the car pulling into the garage of a house on the left side of the street. If the property didn't have a long driveway, I would have missed where she'd gone all together. I drive a ways down the street, turn onto another offshoot street, and park.

Great. Now what?

I wait for dark. Pulling my phone from my pocket, I check it for messages from Hakon or Father. Neither has called. Should I call Hakon? Ask him about Asher? Ask if he'd be willing to help me sabotage Audun's S operation? My thumb hovers over his contact info as I consider it. And then I turn off the phone and slide it back into my car's console. It's too risky.

To kill some time, I cruise back into town and park at

the Sonic drive-in restaurant. I am hungry, and I like the fact I don't have to get out and go in this place to order. Now that I've located Laney, I'd like to keep my profile here as low as possible. I push the button and order some fries and a shake with tiny candy bits in it. Might as well enjoy the local delicacies.

As I sit and wait for my food to be delivered, cars pull in and out of the place. Business really picks up as it gets close to dark and the teen population of the Sonic explodes. Guys and girls get out of their cars and sit on the hoods, chatting and laughing and flirting.

This is what Laney is used to. This is what she wants. Not some strange guy with megalomaniacal parents from literally the other side of the world who doesn't know anything about small town life, who's seen far too much of the filthy underbelly of the human experience and knows nothing about how to live among regular people, how to be a "boyfriend."

I get my food, pay the car hop, and go, driving back toward Laney's house and planning to eat while I stand watch. Now that it's dark and my car isn't quite so obvious, I park on Laney's street—not directly in front of her home but just shy of it in front of a wooded lot across the street. From here I have a clear view of the lighted windows. Every once in a while, someone walks past one, and my idiot heart springs to attention.

After about an hour, I see a car in the rearview mirror. It's the Dodge Charger Laney got into earlier today—the one belonging to the bicep drongo.

"Keep going mate," I mutter.

The car does not obey my command but pulls into Laney's driveway. Now we'll see who this fellow is. Instead of going in through the garage or opening the door and going inside, the guy walks up onto the front porch and rings the bell. *Damn it.*

A man—Laney's father I presume—opens the door, shakes the young guy's hand, and steps back to let him in. *Shit.* He's not a cousin or an unmentioned brother or just a friendly classmate giving her a lift. He's a boyfriend. Now I'm *really* not leaving.

The hours tick by as I wait for the git to leave. At around ten pm, the door opens again, and he comes out.

Finally.

I sit up straighter in my seat and watch as he turns back to Laney, who's standing in the doorway, framed by the interior lights. She looks tiny and adorable. They say a few words to each other, then the guy leans down and gives her a brief kiss.

My insides are instantly boiling. Who is he? How long has she known him? How serious is this thing between them? It can't be *that* big of a deal because she's only been back from California for three weeks. Three weeks and three days to be exact.

He walks to his car, gets in, and backs down the driveway, then spins the wheels and drives right past me. If hatred were visible like laser beams, I would have blasted him right off the road as he passed. At least he's gone. And the kiss didn't go on and on. It was maybe… five seconds. But who's counting?

Now the figures inside the house pass by the windows several times, and lights go out in some of the downstairs rooms while the ones upstairs pop on. Judging from the fact that two shadows are moving inside one bedroom, while the bedroom on the other side has only the faint glow of a television inside, I'm pretty sure which room is Laney's.

And what exactly are you planning to do with that information, creeper?

I'm not sure yet. For now, I sit and wait a while longer. When the light of her parents' bedroom goes out, I open my car door, step onto the street, and stretch. The night air is warm and still and smells of dusty asphalt and pine—a welcome contrast to the French fry smell that now inhabits my rental car's interior, probably permanently.

It feels good to move after sitting in one position for so long, so I take a few steps in one direction, turn, and walk back. A bit more walking would probably do me some good. Looking one way then the other, I cross the street and stand at the end of Laney's driveway, hidden from the house by a row of tall hedges that hug the mailbox.

It wouldn't hurt to go have one look at her. Just one more look before I regain control of my sanity and get back in my car and drive away, never to return to this little town she calls home. Keeping to the far right of the long drive, I walk along a row of pine trees that border the property. The low street lamp light doesn't reach over here, and the front porch lighting throws only enough of a glow to illuminate the front door and stairs. That's not where I'm headed.

Going to the side of the house where I believe Laney's

room is located, I stand near the foundation and look up. There are two possibilities here. The large front porch is covered by a roof that slants down directly under her window. The other option is a tall tree that stands on the side of the house, its large branches stretching near what appears to be another window to her room.

I'm nobody's idea of a Light Elven nature boy like Lad, but the simpler option, climbing onto the porch roof, is also the most likely to get me caught. It's on the front of the house, and if someone drives by, they could very well spot me in the moonlight. I hesitate, looking back and forth between my two choices. I've never done this Romeo shit before—I'm not sure which way to go. Why couldn't her bedroom have been on the back side of the house? On the first floor.

Finally, I settle on the tree tactic. Reaching above my head, I hook one hand then the other around the lowest branch and pull myself up until I can get a leg over it. I glance down at the designer pants and shirt I traveled in today. These won't be ready for their next close up. I'll probably have to leave them in whatever serves as a rubbish bin in Altum tonight.

Once that part is over, the rest is much easier. I make my way up, hand over hand, searching for stable footholds until I reach a sturdy branch level with her window. And there I stop—because I can see her.

She's sitting cross-legged on her bed, facing the TV screen, hugging a furry pillow in her lap. Beside her on the bed, stretched out in blissful comfort, is Cupcake. *Lucky little beast.* He's grown, and he certainly seems content with his lot in life. I would be too if I were the one stretched across Laney's bed, being petted and stroked—*oh wow.*

I've got to stop this train of thought before all the blood leaves my brain and I fall *out* of this friggin' tree.

Squinting to see better, I get a look at the TV screen. She's watching a movie I've never seen before, but I recognize the stars. The female lead is the daughter of a famous drummer—human, but pretty. The guy is Elven. An Englishman with a ready smile, he's the personification of tall, dark, and handsome. The volume isn't high, but I can hear bits and pieces of dialogue through the open window. The onscreen couple is arguing, and Laney is… oh god, she's crying.

My heart squeezes in my chest, and I move out farther on the branch, drawn to her. I want to hold her—or grab the remote and get rid of the movie that's making her sad. Why is she watching something like that?

I can't stand to see her unhappy, and then it occurs to me. Maybe she's been crying a lot since I've last seen her. Maybe she cries every night, movie or not. Maybe she wants to watch sad things because she *is* sad.

Over me? I'm shamed by the eager jump in my heart rhythm. I don't want her to be sad. But it also pleases me to think that she might be missing me the way I've been missing her.

When the scene ends, Laney picks up the remote and clicks off the TV. Now her room is completely dark. Is she going to bed? I suppose a lack of light doesn't necessarily mean she's sleeping. She doesn't need light to read or exercise or brush her teeth.

I'm not sure what to do now. I don't want to leave. Being even this close to her after spending the past few weeks apart, I feel calmer, more even. Maybe I'll spend the rest of my eternity as her shadow, living life, if not with her, at least near her. Of course, eventually someone will notice, and then the police will be called, and I'll be prosecuted as the Peeping Tom that I am.

What the hell is wrong with me?

I scramble down from the tree, intending to go back to my car, get in, and drive straight up to Memphis. Instead, I find myself standing beside her porch, staring up at her dark window. It's like there's a powerful magnetic force emanating from her room. I feel like if I lifted my arms and didn't fight it, I'd float up into the air and through that open window.

I won't wake her.

Climbing the porch railing and support beams, I vow that I'll only look at her a minute or two, maybe brush the softest kiss on her cheek, and *then* I'll go.

Getting onto the roof is much easier than climbing the tree was. In under a minute, I'm right outside her window screen, listening for any evidence of movement inside. Hearing none, I ease the screen up and carefully climb in. I don't know if Laney's father is the shotgun-wielding type, but it would serve me right to find myself on the wrong end of a rifle right about now. At least I'd be put out of my misery.

My heart is throbbing like a migraine in my chest as I get both feet on the floor and scan the room. No father. No rifle. There's no night light either, but there is enough moonlight coming through the window for my already adjusted eyes to see her. She's in bed, sound asleep, half covered by a thin quilt.

The floor is carpeted, so my feet make no sound as I glide across the room until I'm right next to the bed. Dropping to my knees, I gaze into her face. She's so beautiful it makes my eyes water. Her soft, even breathing is like a salve to my soul. My own breathing slows, my tense shoulders relax. My fingers ache to stroke her long, straight hair and caress her baby smooth cheek. But I can't. It would be wrong to touch her without her consent. Just *being* here is crime enough. I fold my fingers into my palm and squeeze them in a fist of frustration.

Laney makes a small noise, shifts in her sleep, and then wakes with a start, sitting halfway up. The movement brings her face inches from mine. I'm frozen in place, afraid to breathe, afraid even the resuming of my heartbeat will alert her to my presence and frighten her.

For long excruciating moments she stays frozen, too. Then she speaks. Her whisper is almost loud in the perfect silence of the room. "Who's there?"

She doesn't sound scared. Just certain. She knows she's not alone. I've got to get out of here. But how do I leave without terrifying her and causing her to scream and wake the whole house? Very slowly, Laney lifts a hand and reaches out, directly toward my face.

As her fingers close the distance between us, I ease backward, evading her without sound. If I don't start breathing soon, I'm going to pass out on her floor and the whole gig will be up.

Closing her fingers on empty air, Laney withdraws her hand, letting out a long breath. I take the opportunity to gather some long overdue oxygen myself.

She must hear me inhale because in one abrupt motion, Laney throws off the covers and sits up, turning so her tiny toes touch the floor beside her bed. If she stands and takes a single step forward, she'll trip over me.

"Culley?" She gasps. "Is that you?"

I don't respond. I don't move.

Only once before in my life have I ever felt such a mixture of terror and excitement and wonder. I was nine, visiting Kakadu National Park in Australia's Top End with my mum's servant Callum. We were hiking alongside the Yellow Water billabong, talking about how beautiful the day was and cataloguing all the turtles and bird species we'd seen so far. Suddenly, there was an enormous crocodile right in front of us. Either we'd stumbled across its resting spot, or it had stalked us in the lily pads along the water's edge.

I knew in that moment that it could be my last on this earth, but I didn't care. The experience of seeing that fascinating animal so close, so alive and beautiful and powerful and deadly—it would have been worth it.

This is like that ten times over. Hearing her say my name. Hearing that note of hope and even… *joy?* in her voice.

The enormity of my foolishness hits me all at once. I am not the only one this little walk on the creeper side could hurt. I should never have come here. If Laney thinks about me even a fraction as much as I think of her, then my nocturnal visit could re-open wounds for her that were apparently starting to heal based on what I saw with bicep boy today.

And she *needs* to get over me. Her feelings for me change nothing. I'm still bad for her. My world is still too dangerous, and even if it weren't, I'd only end up dragging her down to my level if we were together.

"I knew you'd come," she says. With a sob, she adds, "I miss you. I love you."

A fierce joy seizes me, inside and out. That's it. I have to go—noise or not. Shotgun or not. Scrambling to my feet, I cross the room to the window and duck out onto the porch roof. Before leaping to the ground, I glance back inside one more time to see Laney sobbing, stretching a hand out toward the window.

Chapter Twenty-three
Poetic Justice

"Why do you have to leave tonight?"

Ava follows me around my room in Altum as I gather my belongings and stuff them into my travel bag.

"I just do, okay?" I can't stay in Deep River another minute much less a whole night. If I don't get on the highway immediately, I'll wind up back at Laney's house, falling at her feet, and this time, confessing that I love and miss her, too. "My business here is done. I've given Lad all the information I have. You have my new number. Let me know when the Light Elves are ready to move on the supply lines. I'll be in contact if and when I determine that Hakon will help us."

"Where will you go now?"

"Back to Memphis. I'll... sleep on the plane or something, wait for Hakon to return."

"Culley, wait. I'm worried about you. You're not acting

like yourself. Stay one more night, get some sleep and a good meal in you before you take off again."

"Listen, I appreciate it. But you're not my sister, you're not my bond-mate—God knows how you passed up *that* tantalizing opportunity. Just... let me be. I need to get out of here. Tonight."

"You saw her."

I give her a death glare in answer and stuff the last of my things into the bag. Lifting it from the bed I turn to her. "Come here."

She takes a few steps until she's right in front of me.

"I'm fine, all right? I'll be fine. Now take care of yourself and give my regards to the Light King and his queen. We'll talk soon." I press a brief kiss to her forehead and leave the room.

I am *so* not fine.

I miss you. I love you. Laney's words repeat in my mind over and over as I drive ninety miles per hour on the highway to Memphis, my brain refusing to even dull the sweet sound of her voice. With every mile I put between us, the urge to pull a U-ey across the highway median and go back grows stronger.

Why did I go see her? Did I think it would make things better? Whereas before the pain of being separated from her was a steady smoldering burn, now it's a drought-fueled wildfire. I can hardly stand being inside my own body.

Reaching Memphis, I drive past the exit for the airport and head downtown, cruising past Beale Street and pulling into the parking lot of a club on the bluff overlooking the fast and wide Mississippi River. By now I've learned to recognize the clubs that offer cheap drinks and loud music, dark anonymity, and drunken oblivion.

Pushing through the doors of this one, I smile widely. Bingo. The house lights are low, the sound barely short of deafening. A shirtless DJ with blond dreads and full sleeve tattoos bounces at the far end of the room, and the dance floor writhes with zoned out club goers.

I walk directly to the bar, order two shots and down them both in quick succession. It's been hours since I've last eaten, and the alcohol hits my bloodstream quickly. But I can still hear her, see her, smell her sweet peach-vanilla fragrance. Throwing myself into the mass of bodies on the dance floor, I move among them, stopping and grinding with several girls who turn to me and give me predatory smiles.

Nothing. It does nothing for me except maybe make me feel more miserable. These girls aren't sweet like Laney. They don't have her innocent beauty. They hold no appeal for me at all. *Shit.* I am ruined for life. How am I supposed to go on living with this monstrous longing filling up every cell of my body?

"Hey, pretty boy." A guy bumps into me. "Want to score some S?"

I look down into his greasy face. This guy must be an independent operator. My father would never assign someone so unappealing to push his product.

"How much have you got?" I ask him.

He grins, showing me a poorly tended set of teeth and

motions for me to follow him. I do, curious to find out whether he's actually gotten his hands on some and how much of a personal markup he and his partner are applying.

The guy leads me to the back hallway where an equally shabby woman waits. She smiles widely at me, thrusting out a generous chest barely covered by a black tank top.

"Hey sugar. Looking for some fun tonight? I got S. If you want to go old school, I got some smack. Hell, for you, I'll even throw in a little free ride."

"Hey," the guy protests, but the woman only laughs, pretending she was joking, though I know she wasn't.

"Just the S will do. Where'd you get it?"

"A lady never tells her secrets. Don't worry. It's the real thing," she assures me with a wink.

"Fine. I'll take it. Three pills."

Her eyes widen. "Oh my, somebody's in for a good weekend."

Handing over my money, I scoop the pills from her palm and walk away, equal parts disgusted and frantic to get the drug into my system. Contrary to her assumption, I won't be spacing the pills out over several days. These are all for tonight. If I've ever needed an escape from my own scrambled thoughts and raging emotions, it's right now.

I've never tried any sort of illicit drug—S is the only one that reportedly even works on Elven people. I'm praying that it works tonight. If I don't do something quickly, I'll find myself flying back down the highway to Mississippi and proposing to Laney at sunrise.

I order a beer at the bar and swallow all three pills at

once. At first, I feel nothing but the rush of cool liquid down my throat.

Damn it. It doesn't work on Elves after all.

And then there's pain. A wall of it. A mountain of it.

I double over then fall to my knees. Molten agony coats my bones and pools in my organs. I've never felt such pain and sickness—wait—I have.

A memory floats over my fevered brain. A picture of that day I tried to cross the border of Asher's family farm and encountered the buried iron barrier. Only this is a thousand times worse because the source of the pain is not buried or even nearby, it's inside me. I can't get away from it.

Iron. The white trash couple must be selling an early version of S—maybe even some from the very first batch. Less addictive than recent batches, it contained high levels of iron.

I grimace against the internal torment and force out a groaning laugh. This is the death I deserve. It's really just a complicated form of suicide if you think about it. If I'd never stolen the raw saol residue from the processing room at Altum, S might not have ever existed.

The pain is lessening now, replaced by an all over numbness that's not exactly pleasant, though it's less excruciating. Through clouded eyes, I see a circle of concerned faces hovering above me. Someone screams something about 9-1-1 while someone else rips open my shirt. The freed buttons fly through the air in slow motion, spinning and changing colors as they reflect the DJ's lighting setup.

The music is still pounding, but instead of hearing auto-tuned vocals, Laney's sweet voice fills my ears. *I knew you'd come. I miss you. I love you, Culley.*

"I love you too," I answer, relieved to finally say it out loud. And I'm happy. Now she will be truly safe from me forever.

And then I see her beautiful face above me. All the others are gone. There's only Laney and her trembling smile and her shining eyes. For the first time ever they're clear and sharp and focused directly on me.

I see you, she says. *And you are beautiful.*

The lovely apparition begins to move away from me. I am desperate to follow. *Wait for me love,* I call out to her. *Wait for me. I'm coming.*

* * *

"Hurry. Get him outside. He's dying."

My body is being lifted and moved. The sounds and lights of the club fade, replaced by warm night air and the dizzying whirl of stars and smog overhead.

"Oh, I *knew* it," a worried female voice says. "What have you done, you big idiot?"

I know that voice. It's not Laney's. It's Ava.

A deep baritone responds to her. "He took something. I saw a lot of junkies when I was working as a volunteer firefighter. This one's bad, though. He might be OD'ing."

"Help him, Asher," Ava pleads.

Asher. That's who the deep voice belongs to. What's he

doing here? What are either of them doing here?

"I'm trying," he says. "But I'm not very good at this yet."

Good at what? Playing the hero and making me look like the schmuck? Oh, he's plenty good at that. Although, since I'm the one who's overdosed on iron-laced drugs, maybe I *am* a schmuck.

"Open the tailgate," Asher's voice instructs. "Okay good, now back up. I'm going to lay him down."

Lovely. I can't open my eyes to confirm it, but I do believe my former romantic rival has just carried me through the streets in his arms like a child. Like a schmuck. Like a—

"Asher! He's not breathing. Do something!"

All my muscles seize as a glowing heat fills my chest and belly. I feel like an egg in a microwave, boiling from the inside out. A loud cry rips from my throat, and then all the tension leaves my body at once, and the world goes blissfully cool and dark.

CHAPTER TWENTY-FOUR
DUAL IDENTITY

My eyelids open, heavy as iron themselves, but I manage to lift them and take in a hazy vision of colored lights. I'm still in the nightclub, though I guess they've turned off the music out of respect for the dead.

"He's waking up," a soft feminine voice says.

Trying harder, I force my eyes to open wider. Oh, not club lights—those are colored glowing stones.

"Is this… Alfheim?" I croak. It figures the afterlife would be just like Altum. An eternity in the Kingdom of Mud is about what I deserve after the life I've led.

Several giggles precede a carefully controlled response. "No, Culley. You're still alive. You're in Altum. You're okay, but you gave us a big scare last night."

Turning toward the voice, I blink several times. Ryann's face comes into focus. She smiles at me and glances over at Ava. Rolling my head to the side, I take in Lad and Asher's somber gazes.

"How do you feel?" Lad asks.

"I… I'm not sure. Okay I guess. Weak. A little nauseous. How did I get here?"

"Asher and I followed you to Memphis last night," Ava explains. "I was worried about you. And it's a good thing we weren't far behind, or you *would* be waking up in Alfheim today."

And in Laney's arms, I think bitterly. I much prefer the sweet end-of-life visions I experienced last night to a real life without her here on earth.

"*What* were you thinking?" Ava asks. "Why did you take S? You know better than anyone how bad it is."

"I was… having a bad night."

"Well, you could have died."

I sit up and look around, finally regaining my senses fully. "Why didn't I? I could feel it happening. My blood was poisoned with iron. I was walking toward the light, the whole bit."

"You can thank Asher for that," Ava said. "He healed you."

My head whips around to face the lanky black-haired boy who is now wearing an abashed expression. "How? Human medicine doesn't work on us."

"I know," Asher says, twisting his lips uncomfortably and nodding repeatedly. "Apparently that's my glamour. I'm a healer." He gives a weak laugh that tells me he was as shocked to learn this as I am. "I've been studying under Wickthorne since we figured it out. Last night was the first time I ever saved anyone, though."

"Well, you shouldn't have bothered," I growl. "Everyone would have been better off." What is the point? If I can't be with Laney, I don't want to be here at all.

"Culley!" Ryann and Ava exclaim in unison. Ava continues, "That is not true, and you know it. We need you. We'll never be able to end the S Scourge without your help. And what about Laney? Have you thought of what it would do to her if you died?"

"She'd get over it," I mutter.

Ava glances at the others crowded into the small bedroom. "Could you guys give us a minute please?"

With murmurs of assent, Asher, Lad, and Ryann move toward the door and leave the room.

I already know what Ava's going to say, and I don't want to hear it. I roll my eyes toward the ceiling and prepare to refute all her claims of how there's true love out there for me, if I'll only open my heart and reach for the stars and rainbows and all that shit.

Ava grabs my hand. "She *won't* get over it. Not if she loves you, and according to Brenna, she definitely does. No one is that hurt by someone unless they're very much in love. I know you weren't expecting it to happen this way, especially because Laney's human. But look at me and Asher. I thought he was fully human, and I fell in love with him. There was no getting over that. Now we're bond-mates."

My head jerks back. "You are?"

She blushes. "Yes. We're planning a wedding ceremony for June. And *you* have to be there—so I don't want to hear any more nonsense about taking yourself out of the picture for everyone's good. You have changed, Culley. The fact that you're here right now proves it."

I sit in silence for a few moments, letting her words sink in. A few weeks ago, I would have been enraged to learn that she and Asher had bonded. Now I feel... strangely free. And well, I'm actually happy for them. It's nice to see *someone* get their happily ever after. When you've been in love, you know how rare and wonderful a thing that is.

Maybe that means I *have* changed. But not enough to be worthy of Laney. I can never be. She's literally better off with anyone else, even that brainless gym rat I saw visiting her house. The best thing I can do for her is stay away.

And the best thing I can do to repay Asher for saving my worthless life is to tell him about his father. Now that I know about Asher's glamour, there is no more doubt in my mind he is Hakon's son.

I'm not sure why Hakon denied having a family. He's probably afraid—and rightly so—of the penalties my father would exact on any member of his Court for bonding with a human. What he would do to the human woman and her half-breed offspring is even worse.

"Could you call Asher back in here?" I ask Ava. "There's something I need to tell him."

She must have called him mind to mind because seconds later Asher enters the room, walking to my bedside and looking like a younger, thinner version of the man I've been traveling with.

"Are you feeling ill again?" he asks, his face filled with

concern. A born healer. No wonder he had a hero complex.

"No. You did a fine job bringing me back from the dead. I want to talk to you about something else. Your father."

He shrugs. "I wish I could help you. I don't know much about him."

I can't contain my grin. "But I do."

Asher practically falls into the chair beside the bed, gaping at me with open mouth and wide eyes.

"At least I'm ninety-nine percent sure he's your father. He has black hair and turquoise eyes, like yours. Sound familiar?"

Asher nods, apparently unable to answer verbally.

"I've actually spent a good deal of time with him lately. He's a healer, like you," I tell him. "He serves in the Dark Court."

Now Asher's hopeful expression clouds over. "The one you're traveling with? The one who's been so instrumental in setting up the S factories around the country?"

"Yes, but... no listen, before you jump to any conclusions, Hakon is practically a slave to my father. He has no choice about what he's doing, and for what it's worth, I don't think he likes it."

"Hakon?" he repeats. "My dad's name is "Hagen.""

"Both of those names have the same meaning. Maybe he gave you and your mother the less common version of the name?"

He frowns. "He doesn't want me to find him."

"If that's the case, it's only for your own protection. More likely, he doesn't want my father to find *you*. It would not go well for you and your mother *or* Hakon if Father knew about you. Believe me, you want nothing to do with him or the Dark Court."

"Well, I have no way of knowing if you're right. I can't contact my father. I only see him on the *rare* occasions he decides to drop in," he snarls.

"So you have not heard from him this weekend?"

"No, why would I have?"

"Well, he came with me—to Memphis. He's only about an hour away."

Chapter Twenty-five
Reunion

Asher grips the armrest as we pull through the gates of the private airfield, his fingertips digging into the soft leather of my expensive rental car.

"Don't worry about those gouges," I joke, nodding at his hand. "I sprang for the full liability coverage."

"Oh, sorry." He lifts both his hands, cracking his knuckles nervously. "It's... we have kind of a weird relationship. I only see him a couple times a year. It's always just for a day or even one meal. He'll hardly answer any questions about himself. I feel like I barely know him. I guess now I have some idea why."

"He was protecting you, mate. You and your mother."

I stop the car fifty yards from the private plane where Hakon waits for me and turn to Asher. "Listen, in case I'm wrong about Hakon—I think you should stay in the car and wait for my signal. If I get on board and discover he's not who I thought he was, I don't want him to see you or even know you're here. I'll text you "cancel," and you'll know to drive away. Take the car back to the rental office at the airport and have Ava come pick you up."

His forehead creases. "What about you? Won't that put you at risk to tell him you've been hanging out with humans and Light Elves?"

"Don't worry about me. I'm immortal, remember? I'm also one hell of a liar."

"I remember *that,*" he says with a grin. "Be careful."

"I will. Stay here. Don't let that hero complex make you do anything stupid," I warn. "Hey, what's your mum's name?"

"It's Jenna. Why?"

"No man can hide his reaction to the name of the woman he loves." *I should know.*

Leaving the car running, I walk across the tarmac and up the stairs of the Lear jet. Inside, Hakon lifts his head and gives me a weary greeting.

"Culley, I was wondering when you'd show up. You must have been enjoying your R and R."

"Yeah. I did. How about you? Go anywhere interesting? See anyone you know?" I don't want to come out and say it in case I *am* wrong about Hakon's relationship to Asher. If he's not his father, there's no reason to believe Hakon is anything other than loyal to Audun. I need to make him admit something.

His expression shutters, his tone turning wary. "What do you mean?"

"Well, funny story. I drove down to North Mississippi, met a lovely woman named Jenna."

Hakon's entire body tenses, his eyes filling with barely restrained violence. Aha. I knew it.

"Oh?" He's trying so hard to sound blasé.

"Yeah. She has a son called Asher. If I didn't know any better, I'd say he's Elven—at least partially. He looks remarkably like you."

Hakon sits frozen in one of the plane's swiveling bucket seats, which is angled toward the door. He doesn't say anything to confirm or deny, which of course is all the confirmation I need. I watch his eyes dart to the exit then come back to me. Poor guy. He probably thinks I'm spying for my father, and he's about to be executed for treason or something.

"Culley, I… I don't know what you're getting at," the gentle healer stammers.

"Relax, man. I'm on your side. Hell, I'm in love with a human girl myself, much good it does either of us."

He eyes me warily, clearly wanting to believe but not sure he should.

You can trust me, I tell him mind to mind.

How do I know that? he responds. I *know what your father's glamour is. You could have it, too.*

"But I don't. You can trust me… because your son does." I walk to the plane's door, open it, and motion to Asher, who immediately gets out of the car and starts my way. Turning back to Hakon, I say, "Asher is my friend…. isn't that right, mate?"

Asher steps through the plane's door with a wry smile. "'Friend' might be overstating it a bit, but yes, we're allies. Hi Dad."

He eyes Hakon with an insecure glance, his body language that of a child hoping he'll be allowed to join a group at the playground instead of being sent away or rejected.

Hakon immediately leaves his chair. "Asher. Son. I can't believe you're here. Are you sure it's safe to reveal your identity to Culley?" He flashes an apologetic glance my way.

"Yes. In fact, I knew the truth of his nature long before I knew yours. Or mine," he adds. "Why did you not tell me I'm half Elven? Why did Mom never tell me?"

Hakon shakes his head, tears filling his sea blue eyes. "I wanted to. So many times. I was afraid for you—for her. Even she doesn't know the whole truth. My world is dangerous. I have a very powerful—and merciless—master."

Again, he gives me the *I'm sorry* look.

"No, you're right," I say. "He's telling the truth about my father. But I'm not him." The certainty of it strikes me as the words leave my mouth. I don't hate the humans— not anymore anyway, now that I actually *know* some. And I don't blame Hakon for falling in love with a human. I'd be a major hypocrite if I did.

"Why did you leave us?" Asher asks in a bruised tone. "Why didn't you leave the Dark Court and live with us?"

Clearly this reunion isn't going to instantaneously heal old hurts. But at least they're together in one place, and they're talking. It's a start.

"I was afraid to," Hakon answers. "Audun was with me the first time I ever saw Jenna—when she was only a child. We were with a group, walking through your grandfather's lands, and she was playing in the yard. I was taken with the beauty and innocence of the child. I stopped to watch her, and Audun teased me about it. We resumed walking and came upon your grandfather clearing timberland at the back of the property. Mr. McCord actually got into an argument with Audun. I had to intervene, to suggest a gentleman's agreement before Audun did something drastic to the man. All I could think of was that little girl's face if she came upon her dead father. Of course at the time, I had no idea I'd fall in love with her ten years later when she became a woman."

He passes a hand over his face and lets out a long breath. "I'd actually forgotten all about her until the next Assemblage, when I traveled the ancient routes to Altum again. This time I was alone. I would never have ventured onto the farmer's land. I could tell he'd laid an iron barrier along the borderlines—smart man. But she was walking in the woods outside the border, digging up wild ferns to transplant into the flowerbeds near the house. She was the prettiest thing I'd ever seen with the sweetest smile. You've got her smile," he says to his son, who blushes deeply.

"We talked that day, and I went back every day during the Assemblage to see her. By the end of that two weeks, I'd fallen in love with her. I knew better—I *knew* better—but I couldn't seem to stop myself. We bonded. I thought that would be the end of it. I couldn't bring her back to the Dark Court, much as I wanted to. I knew what I'd done would mean I could never marry or have a child, but I told myself she'd get over me and move on. I didn't even know about you until the next Assemblage. You were nine by that time."

Asher nods. "When I was little and asked who my father was, Mom told me I didn't have one. She said the wood fairies made me. My granddaddy used to tell stories of the Fae folk. I didn't believe it, of course. I wanted a real father so badly. Kids teased me at school about being a bastard. Mom wouldn't even date anyone, much less marry someone so I'd have a stepfather. Granddaddy was amazing—he was always here for me. But still, he wasn't my *father*. You can imagine I was pretty angry when you showed up in my life all those years later claiming that role."

"Yes. I remember. You were a stubborn little boy. You were determined to hate me. But I think you also were curious about me."

"Of course I was. And then when I realized we looked alike—it was... well, it was big for me. Even though I only saw you a couple times a year, at least I knew you existed— I had a father out there *somewhere*. I started planning to move out of Deep River as soon as I was old enough and go on the road like you. I think maybe deep inside I harbored this fantasy of going on the road *with* you."

Hakon wears a warm gaze tinted with sadness. "You wouldn't have wanted to join me, son. I've had to do some pretty terrible things for my masters."

"Like the drugs?" Asher asks.

"Yes," Hakon admits, darting a glance over at me to check my reaction. He still doesn't trust me fully. "I will never outlive the guilt over all the lives I've taken."

Finally, I step forward, intruding on their father-son moment. "You weren't in it alone, old man. If you're looking to assign blame, most of it is mine. But we're going to make it right—if you're interested in helping."

His face brightens, his entire body straightening. "Yes. Yes, what do you have in mind?"

Asher and I fill him in about our tentative plan to destroy the existing S supply and sabotage the new batches by adding iron.

"Yes," he says, his voice gaining a note of excitement. "That could work. Plus, it'll have the added benefit of making the S factory workers too ill to come in. It won't take long for Audun to figure out what's happened, but hopefully by then the damage will be done."

"So you think it's worth trying?" I ask.

"I think it's worth dying for," he says.

While Asher and his father catch up, I go and speak with the captain about our flight plans. Hakon and I will need to get back to "work" soon so as not to alert Audun to our new co-conspirator status.

Emerging from the cockpit, I run into Asher. He's smiling.

"I want to thank you," he says. "And I take back what I said earlier. You *are* a friend—a good one."

He extends a hand, and I shake it, suddenly embarrassed. "It's nothing."

"No. It's *something*. This is major for me. I feel like my life is, like, all coming together at once. I finally know my father. And I know that he truly loved my mom and didn't just ditch her—and me—because he didn't care."

"That must be nice," I mutter.

"I finally know who I am," Asher continues. "And I'm learning to use my healing skills. I have an amazing fiancée who loves me. I owe most of it to *you.*"

"Well, I'm happy for you, mate." *Jealous as hell, but happy.* "I really am."

"Now we need to work on *your* happy reunion," Asher says. "With a certain pretty little human."

My heart squeezes painfully. "Nah. I've decided to let that go. It's for the best."

"Really?" Asher says. "'Cause I'm not so sure. Did she ever tell you about Brandon?"

The small hairs on the back of my neck stand up at the mention of her old boyfriend. "She did. He dumped her when she lost her sight, the dipstick."

Asher laughs at the Aussie term. "Yes, 'dipstick' fits him perfectly. She's back with him, you know."

"I didn't." Was that who I saw her in town with, the guy who didn't bother opening her car door for her? Was that who left her with a kiss on the front porch?

"Yeah. He told all the guys at school that she'd begged him to 'do her' when they were breaking up. If Joseph had been around, he would have pounded Brandon's ass for talking about his sister like that. I almost did it myself."

He lifts one brow and the corner of his mouth quirks with disgust. "When Laney came back to town from L.A., Brandon said he'd already screwed all the other girls at school, so he didn't mind taking her on as a pity—"

"Stop talking." I interrupt, pushing the words through my clenched teeth. "Where can I find this dead man?"

Asher gives me a wide smile, nodding in satisfaction. "You wanna drive or should I?"

CHAPTER TWENTY-SIX
NOT ENOUGH

After dropping my two passengers off at Altum, I drive into Deep River, intending to go straight to Laney's house. I convinced Asher it was the best plan of action. I'll speak to Laney first and give her the opportunity to dump that stupid bastard Brandon.

This time, I'm actually *hoping* he'll be there. Boy is he in for a surprise. I only hope she hasn't already given him the precious gift he has so little regard and respect for. My fingers grip the steering wheel tighter just thinking about it. No matter. Even if she has slept with him, she won't be doing it again after tonight. He doesn't realize it yet, but he's out of her life for good, one way or another. If I can't make her see reason, I'll ask Ava to remove all his memories of her—whatever it takes, he's gone.

There's no one at her house, or at least no one answers the door. I'm not quite sure of my next move. I suppose I could climb the porch again and use the window—assuming it's not nailed shut by now—and wait until she returns.

Deciding I don't have the necessary patience for that option, I get back into my car and drive through town. My pulse jumps when I spot a familiar Dodge Charger parked at the Sonic. Laney's future ex-boyfriend. She's probably with him. Slamming on the brakes, I back up on Main Street and take a left into the drive-in's entrance.

She's here.

I spot the back of her beautiful straight hair first, then my eyes drop to her hand, which is joined with that of a smug-faced boy in a pair of khakis and a polo shirt. Pulling my car into the first available slot, I park and get out. Now my heart joins the race, the beats gathering speed with every step closer I take to her and Brandon and the two couples they're chatting with.

Stopping in front of the group, I speak to get her attention. The others—especially the two other girls—are already staring at me.

"Laney."

"Culley?" Her voice is pitched high with surprise. "What are you doing here? How did you find me?"

"I need to speak with you. Would you mind taking a ride with me?"

She doesn't answer at first, probably too shocked by my sudden appearance to respond. Finally she says, "Okay," at the same time Brandon says, "I don't think so, buddy."

"I wasn't talking to you," I growl.

"Who is this, Laney?" Brandon demands.

"Um… he's someone I met in—"

"Culley Rune," I say, extending a hand along with a cocky grin certain to elicit fury. "You may have seen me on the cover of the latest GQ magazine. Or caught my Polo cologne ads on TV."

The girls in the group gasp and then face each other, giggling with excitement. "I knew it was him!" one of them says to the other.

"I don't care what kind of gay magazines you've been in," Brandon counters. "She's not going *anywhere* with you."

"Brandon." Laney reaches out to touch his beefy arm. "It's okay. Let me talk to him a minute. We'll stay right here."

His eyes narrow in fury, and his skin is the color of a ripe tomato, but he grinds his teeth together and says nothing.

Laney reaches out, waiting for me to take her hand. My own hand trembling, I usher her away toward the back of the restaurant's outdoor patio while Brandon and his group stare a crater through us both.

When we're out of earshot of the others, I stop walking. Laney immediately drops my hand, feeling for the warm brick of the Sonic's exterior wall beside her and leaning into it.

"Why are you here, Culley? What do you want?"

Her tone isn't exactly encouraging. She sounds suspicious and angry—which I understand completely.

"I want you to break up with that guy. I spoke to your

brother's friend Asher. He's told me about Brandon. How could you get back together with him after what he did to you?"

She throws her shoulders back, and her chest goes out. That little stubborn chin I love so much rises high in the air. "It's none of *your* business. Why would you even care?"

I exhale in a frustrated gust. "The guy's all wrong for you. It's obvious."

"Oh really? Well, who would be better for me then? Who's even going to *have* me?"

"What a stupid question. Anyone would be thrilled to have you."

"Anyone? You're wrong. I can think of someone right now who had his chance and turned it down in favor of just another blonde groupie."

"For your information, Nicole and I did not spend the night together. I left the gala and went home to bed. Alone. How did you know she was blonde?"

"Lucky guess," she snaps. "If you've come all the way from California to try to get me to break up with the only guy who's ever really wanted me, you're wasting your time. Brandon is *there* for me, and he's really sorry about the way things ended before. People make mistakes."

"He's not the upstanding, loyal, good guy you think he is. In fact, even *I* would do a better job of looking out for you than he will."

Laney goes very still. Her expression serious. "What are you saying?"

Now that my mouth has blurted it out, my mind is

scrambling to catch up. "Well... I've told you about my *true nature*. It comes with an... extended lifespan. Immortality actually. I think if you'll look at it logically you have to agree I'm the best person to look out for you and protect you for a lifetime."

"Because of logic," she says.

"Yes."

"And that's it."

"It makes perfect sense," I say, quite proud of my convincing tone of voice and confident delivery.

She stands silent, fists clenched for a solid minute. Then she turns and starts to walk off.

My hand darts out to wrap around her arm. "Wait. Where are you going?"

Laney whirls back around to face me. "Go home, Culley. Just... go."

"Be reasonable—"

"No. I don't want to be reasonable. I don't want to be protected and taken care of. I already have too many people who try to protect me and take care of me. That's what I ran away from. What I need is someone who *loves* me—not like a child, or a friend, or a charity case. I want to be loved passionately. And you don't *believe* in love."

I let out an exasperated laugh. "Oh, and I suppose you have passionate 'love' with that musclebound dimwit?"

She yanks her arm from my grasp. "Yes. Brandon *has* told me he loves me, which is more than I can say for some people. You can't even say the word with a straight face."

"Declarations of love mean nothing. Anyone can say

that. It's what people *do* that matters."

"And what about you? What did you do? You sent me away, you acted like you cared then immediately hooked up with another girl. You hurt me, Culley." She shakes her head. "How do I know you won't change your mind again or get bored and want some variety, like that girl at the gala?"

Emotion rises up inside me like an over-boiling saucepan. "You think I can't commit? Tell you what—get in my car with me right now," I challenge. "We'll go to a hotel room—or your room—or... a deserted spot at the end of the bypass if you prefer and seal this thing—*forever*. I get only one shot at bonding. I'll show you commitment that'll make your head spin."

I can see I've gotten through to her. Either that or she's imagining the logistics of bonding in the back of a rented Jeep. She stands for a minute more, warring emotions playing out across her face.

"It's not enough." A tear spills over her eyelid and streams down her face. Another matches it on the opposite side. Laney lifts both hands and swipes at her cheeks. "Why did you have to come find me? I was fine before you showed up here. I'm better off without you. Better off with someone I've known my whole life, someone I'm sure of, someone I can at least have some peace with."

I glance over at Brandon, who's staring a wide hole through me. "So, you'll give *him* another chance, but not me?"

"He can't hurt me the way you can," she says.

"I can give you more than he can," I spit out in desperation. "Travel. A posh place to live—with ocean breezes in every room if you want it. Cars, clothes, jewels. Name it. It's yours."

"Do you really think I want any of that? You *know* what I want. I want the real you. The money is not you. The good looks aren't you. I want what's inside." She reaches out and presses a tiny palm to my chest. "Your heart. But you can't give me that. Or you won't."

My fingers wrap around her wrist, trying to hold her there forever. "Laney," I force out through clenched teeth. This girl is killing me.

"I dreamed about you last night," she whispers. "I felt like you were right there with me in my room. I thought it was too good to be true." She waits a long beat. "Guess I was right."

Tearing her hand from mine, she whirls away and heads back toward her friends. Brandon rushes to her side, wrapping an arm around her shoulder and glaring back over his own shoulder at me.

Don't bother, buddy. Your loathing for me can't even come close to my own.

Chapter Twenty-seven
Something to Live For

I can't believe I'll never see her again. My mind literally won't accept it. I guess that will come eventually. After about fifty years or so.

At least I know she really is better off. She's right about me. I'll only hurt her. I've never been enough—for anyone. And whatever love she used to feel for me will no doubt be replaced by hatred soon, if it hasn't been already.

Back in Altum, Asher gives me a hopeful raised-eyebrow look when I walk into the saol water processing room. I shake my head. *Don't ask.*

He nods and bends back to the task he's working on with Hakon and Wickthorne.

My father's healer glances up. "Ah, Culley. Good news. Wickthorne has come up with a powdered iron solution that should be effective and inconspicuous to add to the new S batches during production. Now we just have to get it to the factories and start the process."

Asher speaks up. "Lad says he's heard back from some of the other leaders in the clans near the facilities. They can strike as early as next week."

"That is good news," I say, trying to muster some enthusiasm. I *do* want the plan to work, and I *will* play my part. If we succeed, life will go on as usual for the human race. I'm just not sure what to do with the rest of my life.

Asher gets up and walks over to me, holding out a small bottle.

"What's this?"

"Iron supplements—very low level. You should begin taking them as soon as possible. They'll help build your immunity to iron poisoning, but it could take some time. Until then, you and my father will have to wear gloves and be very careful around the new S batches."

I nod. "Thanks. You're becoming quite the healer. Planning to go to medical school?"

"I'm not sure. I'm interested in it, but I'd have to be careful using my healing glamour on humans."

"Why?"

Hakon answers for his son. "It's very powerful—capable of healing nearly anything. It would raise suspicion and perhaps expose our kind to public scrutiny if humans were suddenly healed from 'incurable' diseases. And there could be side effects for them. I'm not sure."

"I see." I turn and head for the door. "Well, I'll leave you geniuses to take care of this end of things. I'm going to— wait a minute." I whirl back around to face the healer trio, my heart nearly leaping out of my chest. "When you say your glamour can heal *anything*... does that include... blindness?"

Hakon and Wickthorne look at each other and shrug simultaneously. "I don't know. I've never encountered that one before," Hakon answers. "I suppose it's possible as long as the person wasn't *born* blind."

Not waiting to hear any more, I stride across the room and grab Hakon's arm along with Asher's. "Come on. I need a favor from you."

* * *

The three of us speed down the dark highway from Ryann's family land to Laney's house in town, blowing past the few other cars out on the road and grossly violating the MPH limitations spelled out on the county road signs.

It's not fast enough for me. My eagerness to reach Laney grows with each mile closer we get to Deep River. She has made her decision. But there *is* still something I can give her, and I can hardly wait. It's not what she's asked for from me, but I figure restoring her eyesight will be an unforgettable parting gift. At least I'll know whenever she watches a sunset or the waves rolling onto a sandy white beach, or her favorite movies, she won't be able to help but think of me.

"Do you think you'll move to Deep River when all this is over? To be with Laney? Or is it too uncomfortable to be so near the Light Court?" Asher asks.

I correct his wrong assumption. "Oh, I'm not going to be with Laney. I'll give her this gift and then leave her alone."

He twists at the waist and turns the whole top half of his body to face me in the car, staring me down as I drive. "You're kidding, right?"

"Not at all. I'm still wrong for her. She can do better than the likes of me."

I'm acutely aware of Hakon riding quietly in the back seat. He knows what I mean. He made a similar decision decades ago to protect the human girl he loved.

"She can do better?" Asher asks incredulously. "Tell me something—*who's* better? Who's going to love her more than you? Huh? Who'll do as good a job protecting her, providing for her? And who's to say she'll even move on? She might miss you and long for you her entire life. Did you ever consider maybe you're better suited than most humans to take care of her—because of your immortality? Will you stop loving her when she's old?"

I don't answer his question. I don't believe in everlasting love.

Do I?

I *am* breaking every speed limit ever created to get to a girl who's told me in no uncertain terms she wants nothing more to do with me. It doesn't matter what she says to me or what she might do. I want to help her anyway. I want to take care of her, to be with her, just to look at her one more time.

Will you stop loving her when she's old? Asher's words grip my heart like a vise. I *do* love Laney. And nothing will ever change that—not age, not time, not distance. But I can't get past the haunting memories of all the wrong I've done.

"I'm not good enough for her, mate. She's too fine and precious for me."

"Well, if that's true, then she's also too fine and precious to belong to some asshat like Brandon. Or to go through life alone—which is probably what's going to happen once he gets through using her and dumps her again. You think she's gonna bounce back from that easily?"

He grips my shoulder with a large hand. "I know you regret things you've done. Don't we all? But at least give her a chance to forgive you. Let *her* make the decision about whether you're good enough for her. As it stands right now, she thinks Brandon is the best she can hope for."

Finally Hakon breaks his silence. "Culley—I know what you're thinking. I have been there myself. But now I realize all the years I've spent apart from Jenna and Asher were a foolish waste of precious time. The time did not change anything, it didn't dull the pain of unfulfilled desire, didn't stop me from longing for her every single day. Forever is a long time to spend wanting something you'll never have. When all this is over and we've ended the S Scourge, I plan to go to her and beg her to forgive me for all the lost years. And there's another thing I have to say. I've been watching you. If I may be so bold, you *have* changed. I've seen it these past few weeks. I didn't know the reason before, or whether it was genuine or not, but I've seen a lot of good in you recently, a lot of reason to hope for the future of our people."

My hands grip the steering wheel until I imagine smoke coming from the leather cover. My heart is trapped in a similar vise. Hakon has longed for the girl he left behind all this time, remaining alone, loving her still.

Will she forgive him? Could Laney ever forgive *me* for the wrongs I've done to her family—to the whole human race? Maybe Hakon is right. Maybe I have changed. Is it enough to be worthy of Laney? No—but then, no one on this earth is.

Asher *is* correct about one thing—no one will ever love her as much as I do. And maybe… just maybe someday I *will* actually be worthy of her. It's something to shoot for. Something to *live* for. My foot presses harder on the gas pedal. The rest of my life is waiting for me at the end of this road.

We park down the street so the passing headlights won't draw attention to the car, get out, and walk to her dark, quiet house then up along the line of pine trees as I did last night.

"We're going to get shot," Asher warns. "Or eaten by some big ass guard dog."

"There's no guard dog," I reassure him in a whisper. "I… checked out the place last night."

When we reach the house, Hakon turns to me. "What now?"

"Now I climb," I say with a nod toward the covered porch. "That's her room, right up there. You two wait here until I explain to her what's going on."

Asher throws a sardonic glance over at me. "I *knew* you

wouldn't be able to resist going to see her last night."

"Just warm up that glamour, half-breed." I give him a good-natured shove, and he punches my shoulder in return. We smile at each other in the dark.

Hakon isn't nearly as amused. "I'm about a hundred years too old for this."

But he obeys my instructions and waits below with Asher as I climb to the porch roof and through Laney's window. As I near her bed, a floorboard creaks, and Laney wakes with a start.

"Who's there?" she demands.

"It's me," I say, sitting on the edge of the bed and placing a hand on her back to calm her. "Don't be afraid. We're not going to hurt you."

She sits up straight, the covers falling to her waist, revealing a pair of adorable ice cream cone covered pajamas. "We?"

"Your brother's friend Asher is with me," I explain. "Right outside. With his father—his *Elven* father."

Her jaw drops open.

"They're both healers," I explain.

Now that she's fully awake, Laney seems perturbed. "What are you doing in here, Culley? If my daddy finds you here, he'll kill you."

"Hmm... maybe I *should* go sway your parents first."

"What?" she asks, sounding alarmed.

"No, we'll deal with them if it becomes necessary. This shouldn't take long."

"What shouldn't take long? Culley, *what* is going on?

Tell me right this minute before I scream."

I take both her hands in mine. "I've thought of something I can give you—something that you *will* want from me."

She lets out an exasperated breath. "I've already told you that you don't have to *give* me anything. I love you because of who you are, not because of what you can do for me."

A shiver goes through me at her words.

"All I want from you is your honesty… and your love," she continues. "If you can't give me that, then please go and take whatever gift you've brought with you."

"I *will* be honest with you, about everything—the good and the bad. And if that doesn't send you screaming in the other direction… I want to be with you—always."

"Oh Culley." She rests her face against my chest. Her words are soft rushes of air against the exposed skin at my open collar. "Thank God. It absolutely devastated me to see you yesterday. I haven't been able to think of anything else for one minute. I was going to break things off with Brandon tomorrow because I knew I couldn't be with him when my heart was still so full of you."

My own heart threatens to soar right out of my body. Wrapping my arms around her shoulders, I pull her as tightly against me as I can without crushing her. She feels perfect. This moment is perfect. I'm so happy laughter spills out of me.

"Is something funny?"

"No. I was thinking… Brandon will never know how lucky he is. If you hadn't just said that, he was about to meet up with some very nasty Elven glamour."

She lifts her head and pulls back a little. "I didn't love him, you know. What I felt for him never even came close to how I feel for you." There's a long pause as we sit holding each other in the dark. "There's something you said yesterday that concerns me, though."

"What is that, love?"

"You can only bond with one person for eternity. And I'm not immortal like you are. Shouldn't you be with someone of your own kind?"

Taking her face between my palms I kiss her hard and quick. "Don't you understand silly girl? Eternity is worth nothing *without* you. You are worth any price. If you won't have me, I'll never bond with anyone. You're the only one who's ever seen the real me. And somehow you fell in love with me anyway. Besides, we *are* the same, remember? You told me that one time. You said our hearts are the same."

"I love you," she says and throws her arms around my neck, rising to her knees and kissing me with wild abandon.

I pull out of the kiss after a minute, laughing with joy but still struggling to make those three vital words come out of my mouth. I haven't said them to anyone since I was a young child. They've never brought me anything but pain and disappointment.

Staring down at her, I open my mouth, willing the declaration to come out. Instead, I say, "You are so beautiful. There is no one like you in the world—and I've seen a lot of it." I hesitate, drawing in a few steadying breaths. "There's something I have to tell you, and I hope your love for me can withstand it."

She wants honesty from me, and I have to give it to her. I have to tell her about my role in the S Scourge, about the possibility that *I* am the pusher who got her brother hooked on the drug. Even if it's the end of us, I can't keep deceiving her.

"Anything, Culley," she says. "I can forgive anything you've done. Tell me."

Before I can utter a word in response, her bedroom door flies open and hits the wall behind it.

I jump to my feet as Laney cringes back. I'm expecting her enraged dad or even the barrels of a loaded shotgun. What I see is a thousand times worse.

CHAPTER TWENTY-EIGHT
HIS PAST

"Father!"

Shock transfixes me. Audun Rune stands in the doorway, legs apart, hands out to the sides, looking like a maniacal pirate about to unleash a volley of cannon fire. Right behind him is Bjorn, his favorite bodyguard. The name means "bear" and the guy's as big as one—no secret why Father prefers him to all his other hired muscle.

"So *this* is what you've been up to," Father scoffs. He flicks the light switch and strides across the room to Laney's bedside, staring down at her as if she were a plate of spoiled food. "This is the reason you've betrayed your family and your people. A *human*. A defective one at that."

I rush him and throw a punch, but he ducks out of the way, smiling as if this is the most fun he's had in a long time. Bjorn grabs my arms and wrenches them painfully behind my back. The man's grip is like stone.

"Let me go, you big gargoyle," I demand, twisting and struggling to no avail.

"I spoke with the pilot and then flew to Memphis myself to find out once and for all why you've been so distracted and morose," Father says, strolling over to face me eye to eye. "And then I followed your car. You have not been honest with me, son. And *that*—well, that cannot be tolerated. I'm not sure how you managed to hide your immunity to my glamour from me for so long, but someone with so dangerous a power cannot be allowed in the Dark Court."

"That's fine," I spit at him. "I wasn't planning to stick around. Consider me gone."

"Ah ah ah—not so fast. It's too dangerous a power to be allowed in the *world*. Your mother will have my head if I kill you, but you cannot be permitted to roam freely any longer. Under my mansion is a set of underground rooms—with no door knobs. I think you'll find them a very comfortable place to spend eternity, if a tad dull."

Behind him, Laney slips from the bed and sneaks toward her bedroom door. I make a point of not watching her, praying she makes it out while Father is focused on me.

Of course Bjorn sees her. He grunts, "Behind you."

Audun whirls around and snags Laney's pajama top, dragging her back against him and sinking his nose into her hair. "And you, my sweet little bird with clipped wings..."

"Don't touch her," I roar, fighting against Bjorn's vise-like restraint. Fury throbs in my brain like a heartbeat.

Father shoves Laney onto her bed where she recoils

against the headboard, trembling. "You my dear will spend the rest of your pathetic sightless days in the fan pod of one—or many—of my friends in Europe. They do so enjoy variety, much like me—and my son."

Laney yells at him. "Culley is *nothing* like you. You're vile and evil. Culley is a good person."

Father's laugh fills the room, high and frightening and filled with malicious glee. "Oh, that's rich. A good person. You *are* blind, aren't you, little girl? In more ways than one. Did Culley not tell you about his past?"

"His past doesn't matter to me."

"Really? Then it doesn't matter to you that he was at the very inception of the S Scourge? Yes, I saw you that night at the gala—poor pathetic blind girl with the dead drug addict brother. Culley brought me the main ingredient for my pet project. S would never have existed without him."

Laney's face pales, and her breath hitches.

"Oh, I can see I've shocked you." His lip curls in perverse enjoyment. "Well, it might shock you further then to learn that my son, your wonderful knight in shining armor, is my most trusted and successful drug pusher. That's right. Every night over the last several months he's gone out to clubs and bars around the country—clubs in Los Angeles—and offered an irresistible sample to the people he encountered there. You stupid humans are only too willing to try anything that beautiful face has to offer. Of course, *you* wouldn't know anything about his glamour, would you? You see, Culley is the most attractive man anyone has ever seen—and I do mean *anyone*. Every man, woman, and child sees what they want to see when they look at him. It's quite wasted on you."

For an excruciating moment I wait to see how she'll react. And then it all crashes down—my hopes, my dreams, my future with Laney.

She turns toward me, her bottom lip trembling. "You killed my brother. It was you who got him hooked on S, wasn't it? Tell the truth—for once."

Oh God. The look on her face. A piece of my heart cracks off and falls to the floor.

"I... I don't know. It *could* have been me. I don't remember. I was going to tell you—I wanted to. I've changed, Laney. *You* changed me."

She struggles against Father's grasp on her wrists, furious at him, furious at me. "You'll never change. You told me the day you met me that you were a bad guy. I should have listened."

Now the rest of my heart crashes and burns. I never deserved her love, and now my past has driven a stake through it as I always knew it would.

Father's teeth gleam in the moonlit room. He's getting everything he wanted—as usual. Well, he may have succeeded in taking Laney's love away from me, but I'll die before I let him send her to a fan pod—or before I'll help him hurt any more humans. And I may very well die tonight. There's one thing I need her to know first.

Ignoring Father's presence I focus solely on her. "I know you can't forgive me for what happened to Joseph. I don't deserve forgiveness. But I want you to know I truly regret what I've done. I've been working to help Asher and my friends Ava and Lad and Ryann put an end to the S epidemic."

"You *what*?" Father roars, letting go of Laney's wrists.

In a blur of motion, Laney springs into action, lifting Cupcake from his spot beside her on the bed and tossing him at Bjorn.

"Get him, boy," she yells. "Culley! Run! Get out of here."

The cat lands on Bjorn's face and shoulders, claws out and screeching.

"What is that? Get it off," my captor yells, releasing me and reeling backward.

At the same time, Asher and Hakon come spilling through the bedroom window. Asher, not a small guy himself, rushes and tackles Bjorn. Hakon lunges after my father.

The commotion gives me an opening to get to Laney. My hands cup her face. "Are you all right, sweet? Did he hurt you?"

She nods rapidly. "I didn't mean those things I said—I was just trying to distract him. I know you're sorry. I know you've changed. I told you before—I could forgive you for *anything*. That is what I meant when I said I love you."

Before I can respond, Father breaks Hakon's hold and grabs Laney by the hair, yanking her off the bed and out of my frantic grasp.

Wrapping his forearm around her throat, he crushes her against him and spits venom at me. "Back off. You too, healer," he snarls. "You know it would take only a little more pressure to snap her neck or crush her trachea. I cannot believe you are a traitor, too—after all these years of faithful service."

"Slavery is more like it," Hakon says.

Turning to address me, Father says, "And *you*... you are just like your mother—so selfish, only thinking of her own needs and desires. You think you've won by working behind my back to end the S epidemic? It's too far gone now. Even if you did somehow manage to stop it, I'm always a step ahead of you. I have another plan—a hundred other plans to restore our people to their proper position as the rulers of earth."

I move toward him slowly, hands raised in front of me in a pleading gesture. He reminds me of a vicious, cornered animal. His eyes are wild and fever-bright.

"That's right—you're in charge. Please don't hurt her. Just let her go. This is between you and me. You already have great power, loyal subjects, all the money you could ever use. Let her go, and I'll be the son you've always wanted. I'll do anything you say. I'll marry the girl in Italy. I'll help you form alliances with the European leaders. You and I can move past this—I've learned nothing is beyond forgiveness. If Laney could forgive me for what I've done— how can I not forgive you? Let her go now, and we'll leave together."

He stares at me so long and so intently I think I've gotten through to him. Then he laughs. "My son the human lover. Maybe I *should* have tried this little morsel if her appeal is that powerful." He tightens his grip on Laney's neck, causing her face to deepen in color as she struggles for air. "You are a better liar than even I am, my son, but it's too late for all that. You have taken away something I care about. And now… I will take away what *you* care about."

Reaching into a pocket with his free hand, Father extracts a syringe. He thumbs off the cap and holds the needle to Laney's neck. "You, my little friend," he says against her ear. "…are about to become a world-class S addict."

"Don't," I yell.

"Audun, that's too much," Hakon says, his voice frantic. "It'll kill her."

"Even better," Father says and plunges the needle into Laney's neck.

CHAPTER TWENTY-NINE
WHEREVER YOU GO

Laney's scream of agony is the worst thing I've ever heard in my life. Terrified and enraged, I charge them, crashing into Father and knocking him backward, away from her. Hakon rushes forward and catches Laney as she falls.

Father is no larger than me, but he *is* stronger—he's more than three hundred years old, and for the Elven race, strength increases with age. The two of us roll across the bedroom floor, wrestling for dominance in this hand-to-hand battle.

He ends up on top, one knee on my chest and his hands around my throat. "I wish you'd never been born," he growls at me. "Then I could have had a chance at a son who is worthy of the Rune name."

My hands grip his arms, struggling to pull them away from my neck, but he is too powerful for me, and my strength is decreasing by the second as I run out of oxygen.

Finally my arms fall limp to the floor, unable to fight anymore. I don't want my father's baleful glare to be the last thing I ever see, so I roll my gaze to the side, looking for Laney.

She's lying on her bed, sprawled in an unnatural manner. Hakon is over her, his ear against her mouth, as if he's checking to see if she's breathing. *No. No, she can't die.* I make a desperate, delirious deal with the universe or with whatever powers are up there in Alfheim or otherwise. *Take my life, but spare her.* I would give up a thousand eternities as long as she can live in peace and safety.

"Father," Asher shouts. "Culley needs help."

Hakon whirls around and sees us, attempts to pull my father away from me. It's no use. He's a couple hundred years older than the healer, too. None of us stands a chance against him.

As my eyelids are closing, I see Hakon retreat and pull a small pouch from his medical bag. He shakes its contents into his palm. Coming up behind Father, he claps the hand over his nose and mouth and holds it there with all his strength.

Refusing to break his own brutal grip on my neck, Father doesn't move to stop him. Suddenly, the choke hold releases and Father gasps, falling backward and writhing on the floor. His face is swelling, growing darker, and his fingers scrabble at his own throat as his legs kick violently.

I sit up, still sucking vital oxygen into my lungs. "What's wrong with him?" I croak at Hakon.

"He's dying," the healer says in a sad, serious tone. "Of

iron poisoning. I filled my hand with the powdered iron meant for the new S batches. He inhaled it. It probably got into his mouth, too."

"You have to go and wash it off of yourself," Asher exclaims. "Now, Father, hurry. Culley—think you can help me with this guy?"

I glance up to see the bodyguard staring down at his dying master and still attempting to break free from Asher's hold. I get to my feet and go to assist him.

"Not bad, farm boy," I say to Asher before grabbing the guard's throat. "How would you like a nice big whiff of iron powder yourself, mate?"

The man's eyes go wide.

"No? Don't want to follow your master *that* far, huh? Well then, I suggest you leave immediately, and I wouldn't bother going back to the Dark Court. Nox will be running the show there from now on—with my full support. Your services are no longer needed."

Asher and I march the guy down the stairs and out the front door, right past Laney's parents who sit on the couch staring straight ahead at the dark TV screen as if catatonic.

"What did you do to them?" I demand, yanking the guy's arms painfully high behind his back.

"Nothing—they're just swayed," he says. "You can undo it."

"Lucky for you," I say. At the front door we let the guard go and watch as he runs across the yard to where Father's car is parked on the street. He gets in and drives away.

"Go help Laney," I say to Asher. "Please. I'll check on your father."

Asher runs up the stairs, taking them two at a time while I follow. Hakon is in a bathroom at the top of the stairs, leaning on the sink and letting water run over his hands. "I… I'm sorry. I'm afraid I may not be of any help to the girl. The iron in my system is repressing my glamour."

The healer has vomited and looks weak as a baby, but he's still conscious and thankfully not writhing around on the floor like my father is.

Was.

I enter the bedroom to find him still and quiet. Stepping over his body, I rush to join Asher at Laney's bedside. She's as motionless and silent as Father.

"Is she…?" I can't even say it.

Asher withdraws the two fingers he held against her pulse point. "She's alive," he says grimly. "But her pulse is weak, and I don't like her breathing."

"Where's the syringe? How much did he inject her with?"

I start searching the floor for the thing but Asher taps me on the shoulder. When I turn to look at him, he's holding the syringe. It's empty.

"He gave her the whole thing."

Hakon enters the room, looking gray and haggard, but on his feet. "That was liquefied S—something we've been experimenting with. Audun was planning to put it into the water supply as soon as he could secure a safe exclusive water source for Elven use. There was enough in that syringe to overdose a large human male, even an Elven one."

"Well *do* something," I order, more frightened than I've

ever been in my life. "Help her."

"I'm not sure if I can," Asher says. "This is different from healing you. You're Elven, and you didn't have nearly this much of the substance in your body. I don't know if I'm strong enough. I'm only a half-breed, as you love to point out."

I grip his shoulder. "I'm sorry brother. I should never have said it. Ava was right about you. You *are* a good guy, and now I know why—your father is twice the man mine ever was. As far as I'm concerned, you're full Elven. I believe in you. Do your best."

I sit on the bed beside Laney, holding her hand as Asher works. Cupcake is curled beside her head, staring at us all as if willing us to fix her.

Asher places a spread hand on Laney's stomach and one on her head. Closing his eyes, he drops his chin to his chest, his eyes squeezed shut. I've never watched a healer at work, so I'm not sure what to expect.

There's no glowing light or anything, but there is a sound. It's something like a hum or a vibration maybe. It starts out so low I'm not sure if I'm imagining it but then it grows louder until there is a very distinct noise in the room, evidence that it's working. Or at least that's what I hope.

Asher stays like that for at least a half hour, beads of sweat forming on his brow and his face contorting in concentration—or maybe in pain. Finally he lifts his hands and staggers back, looking exhausted.

I lean over Laney's face, eager to see her eyelids flutter open. "Did it work?"

There is no change in her appearance. She doesn't move.

"No." Asher lets out a long breath. "I'm sorry. I think she's in a coma. I can feel her life force in there, but it's like she's really far away, and I'm calling to her but she's out of earshot and can't hear me. Either she's too far gone—or I'm not strong enough."

He's got tears in his eyes as he shakes his head and repeats, "I'm sorry."

Hakon rises from a chair in the corner where he collapsed. "Let me try. We'll work together. Maybe our glamours in combination will be enough."

Asher nods, takes a fortifying breath, and steps back to the bedside. Hakon joins him. They each place their hands on her now, and I redouble my efforts to strike a deal with the universe, promising to be the greatest champion for the human race ever seen in the Elven Courts, Dark or Light. I vow to pay for the treatment of every S addict on the planet, to personally crusade against its use, shoot public service announcements, go on all the entertainment news shows I hate and warn against it—anything if she will wake up.

Again the humming noise fills the room. This time I can feel the vibrations of it in my chest. I watch in helpless silence as the healers work together to save the girl I love.

Hakon breaks his concentration for a moment. "It's not working," he says. "We're losing her. Culley—come help us."

I immediately put my hands on her—one on her cheek, the other over her heart. But I know it's hopeless. I feel as if the contents of my body are being sucked down into a deep whirlpool, spinning and sinking. I can't lose her. But there's nothing I can do to stop it.

"What can I do?" I choke. "I don't have healing glamour."

"But you love her," Asher says through gritted teeth, his voice strained with fatigue and effort. "If you're ever going to tell her, now's the time. It may be your last chance."

"Laney," I start and falter then begin again, speaking around a boulder in my throat. "Laney, sweet—I hope you can hear me. I don't want you to leave me. I need you too much. You're the only person who's ever truly cared for me. You've showed me that love is real and it's possible. I don't want it to end. I don't want you to leave this world. But if you must, know that I *will* find you in the next one. Because... because I love you. I've loved you from the very start, from the moment we met. And I will go on loving you no matter what. You once told me you could read hearts. Read mine now, love, and you'll know it's true."

I lift her limp, cool hand and press it to my wildly beating chest. "This heart is yours for eternity and will follow wherever you go."

There is no response. No flicker of life from her beautiful face. It's too late. She is gone.

I crush my lips to hers in a final kiss then reach across the bed to palm Hakon's discarded medicine pouch, drawing it close, feeling the weight of the iron powder inside, ready for the moment the two healers declare her dead.

Hakon sucks in a sharp breath. "I've got something. Do you feel it son?"

Asher smiles, never opening his eyes or removing his hands from her body. "I feel it."

"Culley, don't stop now, son," Hakon says. "Keep talking to her. She's moving toward you, toward your voice."

With a sound halfway between a laugh and a sob, I drop the bag of powdered death and take Laney's face between my palms, encouraging her to come back to me, telling her I am there for her and will never leave her side again.

"I love you," I say, kiss her mouth, then say it again. "I love you, I love you, I love you."

Laney's eyes open then close again. Open. Close. Asher and Hakon both let go and step back. I'm holding my breath, watching her chest rise and fall in a steady pattern. Finally her eyes open again and her hand lifts, fumbling for my face.

When her fingertips reach my wet cheeks and smiling mouth, she opens hers to speak. Her voice is rough, but the words are distinct. And distinctly amused.

"Boy—when you get started, you just don't stop, do you?"

The room fills with laughter and relief. Asher and his father embrace in a tight hug, but all my focus is on Laney.

"I *can't* stop saying it," I tell her. "I never will—as long as we both shall live."

Epilogue

"It's okay if it doesn't work, you know," Laney says.

She sits beside me in the kitchen of Asher's family farmhouse. As she's fully human, we couldn't take her to Altum for the Elven healing procedure. She doesn't seem nervous at all, but I'm a freaking wreck. What if it does work? What will she think when she sees me for the first time? Will it change things? Will she still want me?

It doesn't matter, I remind myself. This isn't about me—it's about her, making her life better, making her happy. As her betrothed, that's my new life mission.

"It'll work," I say. "I know it."

She squeezes my hand tighter. "But *if* it doesn't... it's okay. I already have everything I could want, even without my sight. And I already know you're beautiful—in *here*—where it counts." She taps my chest with a smile so sweet I wish we were alone in the room.

"You're the beautiful one," I murmur close to her ear. "I love you."

Asher clears his throat. "So then... should we get started? Culley... if you wouldn't mind stepping back?"

I immediately do, moving to lean against the kitchen wall, watching intently as Asher and Hakon step forward and place their hands on Laney's head, her face, over her nonfunctioning eyes.

Asher's grandfather, Mr. McCord is here, along with Ava, Lad, and Ryann, and Asher's mother Jenna. Her eyes are filled with wonder and pride as she watches her son and her love working as a team.

Hakon took a page from my book and threw himself at her mercy, seeking and finding forgiveness for his absence, confessing his true identity and the full explanation for why he had to stay away and asking if she'd still be interested in having him now that the threat of Audun's vengeance had been eliminated.

She was.

As for my father, I can't say that I miss him, but I *am* sorry things had to happen the way they did. I'd much rather he'd had a change of heart and found the kind of redemption and happiness I have.

He missed out on the best part of life—loving someone and being loved in return. Even his own wife, my mother Falene, doesn't seem too broken up about his death. Only I can see the mark she now wears as a widow. The rest of the world still sees her the way they want to—she is, after all, the source of my glamour gift.

It's a weird feeling being fatherless, though really, Audun Rune filled that role in name only for me. Many would agree the world is a better place without him. As for the Dark Court, Nox returned from abroad, announced that Audun was gone, and with him, his plans for Elven domination of the human race. So far, there have been few repercussions that I know of—at least in this country.

The Light Elves succeeded in hijacking the scheduled S deliveries and destroying the dangerous product, and the S factories were converted to produce new, iron-filled pills with lesser and lesser degrees of the drug's addictive substance. According to Shane, the stepping-down process seems to be working for S addicts, helping them come out of their addictions gradually instead of cutting off the supply cold-turkey, which might have been fatal to them. Within a few months, those factories will be shut down entirely and his clinic along with them.

The sunny kitchen fills with a now-familiar hum of energy, and my chest fills with bubbles of hope, making it hard to stay still. But leaving the room is impossible. I want to be the first thing Laney sees when she opens her eyes—if she sees anything at all.

After no longer than fifteen minutes, both men lift their hands and fall back, looking to each other, then the rest of us around the room.

"It's done," Hakon says. "Now let's see if it worked."

"Okay Laney," Asher encourages. "You can open them."

Ava stands beside me, bouncing on her tiptoes with excitement, and I grab her fingertips. She gives me a brilliant smile and squeezes so hard my fingers go numb.

Laney's eyelids lift slowly. Her pretty brown eyes shift from side to side then glance upward and down. Then she focuses on my face—she's focusing, I know she is—before her gaze goes to the other people standing around her in a group.

Her expression doesn't change as she spends time looking at each person, taking in the smiles, the ages, the different features.

It occurs to me there are three young guys in the room, all of us around the same age. She could look at Lad, Asher, and me, and have no idea which one of us healed her and which one is in love with her.

Finally she smiles, stands, and stretches out a hand to me. "Culley."

Overcome with emotion, I cross the room in two steps and take her into my arms. "Yes, yes sweet, it's me." Taking her face into my hands, I kiss her hard, and we both laugh and then cry.

Pulling back enough to see her face and let her see mine, I say, "How did you know it was me?"

She smiles through glistening tears. "I recognized you. When Audun overdosed me and I nearly died, you were there. You were *with* me. I heard you calling to me, and I started walking toward you. I *saw* you calling me back, telling me you loved me. You look *exactly* the same." She shakes her head. "Exactly."

"And… what do you think?"

She shrugs in an exaggerated way, lifting a sardonic

eyebrow and tilting her head to one side. "I guess you'll do."

I laugh and kiss her again, and then she's no longer mine alone. The others in the room come in for hugs and congratulations, all of us having witnessed a literal miracle. Lad and Ryann embrace her then each other, pulling back to stare into each other's eyes. I'm no longer baffled or nauseated by their intense connection—I understand it now. Love is real, and it's worth *everything*.

When the celebration dies down, Hakon draws Laney and me aside. "Can I speak with you two for a moment?"

We follow him to the relative privacy of the living room where he indicates we should sit on the couch opposite his chair. I don't like the serious look on his face. The nerves in my stomach wake with a start and begin a slow simmer.

"What's going on?"

"I want to talk to you about something. Remember I mentioned before that Elven healing glamour is not really meant for humans? That there may be side effects?"

We both nod, and now that simmering is becoming a rolling boil.

"I've seen it with my patients in the free clinic in Los Angeles, though none of those treatments were as drastic as what we did to save Laney's life or heal her today. I'm not certain, but I still thought I should warn you both…"

"Get to the point, man," I demand. "I'm dying here."

He smiles and places a reassuring hand on my shoulder and one on Laney's. "It's possible—very likely in fact—that what we did to save your life, and what we did here today, changed your body chemistry and cell structure. It's probably going to result in more than just restored eyesight."

"What do you mean? Is it going to give me cancer or something?" she asks.

He lets out a surprised laugh. "No, just the opposite. What I'm trying to say is that there's a very good chance you're going to have a greatly extended lifespan... perhaps even Elf-like immortality."

Both of us sit in stunned silence, processing his words.

"Now Laney," he continues. "I know this must come as quite a shock to you, but I want you to be prepared, to start thinking about it. An extended lifespan is going to bring a host of complications with it. If you fail to age at a normal rate, after a certain point there'll be a spotlight of suspicion on you, which could then put the anonymity of the Elven people at risk. Eventually, you'll have to say good-bye to all your family and friends and move far away from them or even fake your own death as the Dark Elven people do."

As Hakon continues to counsel Laney about all the possible "hassles" becoming immortal could lead to, my brain fills with a pyrotechnic display of astonishment, and hope, and joy.

Finally, she turns to me, her eyes shining with wonder and love. "Are you happy?"

"Happy? I'm overjoyed. This is the best day of my life."

Her nose wrinkles, and her mouth twists to the side with doubt. "But... there is one big potential problem."

"What is it, sweet?"

"Well, now you're going to have a heck of a time getting

out of singing Karaoke with me."

I laugh out loud. "Oh really? Well, the way I see it, there's no rush to finish that little bucket list of yours. I mean… why hurry? We've got forever."

THE END

AFTERWORD

Thank you for reading Hidden Desire! I really hope you enjoyed it. If you did, would you consider leaving a review at the retail site where you bought it? And if your fingers aren't too tired, at Goodreads, too? Reviews are so important for authors and help other readers find great books.

Never miss a new release from Amy Patrick by signing up for her newsletter at www.amypatrickbooks.com. You will only receive notifications when new titles are available and about special price promotions. You may also occasionally receive teasers, excerpts, and extras from upcoming books. Amy will never share your contact information with others.

And check out www.thehiddensaga.com for more goodies on the Hidden series and what's next in the Hidden world.

The Hidden Saga
Hidden Deep

Hidden Heart

Hidden Hope

The Sway, A Hidden Saga Companion Novella

Hidden Darkness

Hidden Danger

Hidden Desire

Hungry for more from the Hidden world? I'll have an exciting announcement in my newsletter soon! And if you haven't checked out The Sway yet, I think you'll enjoy this deeper look at Nox and Vancia's childhood connection and the inner workings of the Dark Court.

ABOUT THE AUTHOR

Amy Patrick grew up in Mississippi (with a few years in Texas thrown in for spicy flavor) and has lived in six states, including Rhode Island, where she now lives with her husband and two sons.

She's been a professional singer, a DJ, a voiceover artist, and always a storyteller, whether it was directing her younger siblings during hours of "pretend" or inventing characters and dialogue while hot-rollering her hair before middle school every day. For many years she was a writer of true crime, medical anomalies, and mayhem, working as a news anchor and health reporter for six different television stations. Then she retired to make up her own stories. Hers have a lot more kissing.

I love to hear from my readers. Feel free to contact me on Instagram, Twitter, and my Facebook page (where I hang out the most and respond to every comment.) And be sure to sign up for my newsletter and be the first to hear the latest news from the Hidden world as well as other new books I have in the works!

ACKNOWLEDGMENTS

I can't tell you how much I appreciate your love for this series and all the encouragement I get from my readers. Thank you for giving my books a chance to entertain you and touch your heart. I hope you will continue to love living in the Hidden world as much as I do!

Huge thanks go to my lovely editor Judy Roth for her wonderful work as always and to Cover Your Dreams for another brilliant cover.

I am forever grateful for my amazing critique partner, McCall, for her words of wisdom and huge heart. I'd be nowhere without my brilliant and hilarious Savvy Seven sisters, and I count so much on my Darling Dreamweavers and my Lucky 13 sisters for their support, good advice, virtual Prosecco, cupcakes, and cabana boys. #teamworddomination. I'm so proud of you all!

I'm blessed to be "doing life" with some amazing friends. Love to Bethany, Chelle, Margie, and the real housewives of Westmoreland Farm. Special thanks to Mary for the walks and talks and pots of tea.

To my first family for your unconditional love and the gift of roots and wings. And finally to the guys who make it all worthwhile—my husband and sons. And thank you to the rest of my friends and family for your support and for just making life good.

Made in the USA
San Bernardino, CA
28 November 2016